I0690725

VOLUME TWO

AIRSHIP 27 PRODUCTIONS

Pulp Mythology Volume Two

"The Lost Quest of Heracles" ©2021 Samantha Lienhard
"Grandmother's War" ©2021 Michael Panush
"Pecos Bill and the Sea Hag of he Gulf of Mexico" ©2021 Mel Odom

Published by Airship 27 Productions
www.airship27.com
www.airship27hangar.com

Interior illustrations ©2021 Gary Kato
Cover illustration © 2021 Ted Hammond

Editor: Ron Fortier
Associate Editor: Fred Adams Jr.
Marketing and Promotions Manager: Michael Vance
Production Designer: Rob Davis.

ISBN: 978-1-953589-05-7

Printed in the United States of America

10 9 8 7 6 5 4 3 2 1

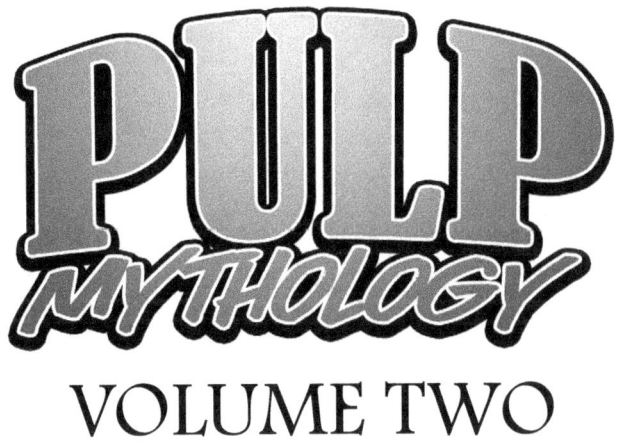

VOLUME TWO

The Lost Quest of Heracles

BY SAMANTHA LIENHARD

Shadows flitted across the gates of the Underworld. In the eerie light that guided the dead to their final rest, a warrior dodged to the side just as a massive beast snapped at his arms. Its second head lunged for him, but he leaped into the air, narrowly evading a strike from one massive paw as the third head tracked his progress.

Fighting Cerberus was not something most men would ever think to attempt. But not just any man attempted this battle—this was Heracles, hero of the gods.

Heracles hit the rocky ground and broke into a sprint. The monstrous hound bounded after him, all three pairs of eyes fixed on their target. At the last moment, he dodged again, and when Cerberus's momentum carried him past, jumped onto the beast's back.

Hands around the dog's neck, he struggled to subdue the first of the three heads by choking it into submission. It would have been much easier to use his sword or one of the other weapons he was proficient in, but he'd sworn to fight the great guardian of the Underworld barehanded.

After being put into service to King Eurystheus as atonement for his crimes, Heracles had performed eleven Labors for the king. He'd fought massive beasts, captured elusive creatures, and performed tasks that seemed impossible for one man to undertake.

Yet he returned from each one victorious.

"Capture Cerberus and bring him out of the Underworld," the king said. *"That will be your twelfth Labor."*

"And the final one?" Heracles asked.

"Of course—provided you succeed."

Eurystheus hated him, wanted him to fail. He must have thought that at last he'd given Heracles a challenge he couldn't overcome. Either he would fail and return emptyhanded, or he would be destroyed while trying. Even if a living man obtained passage to the Underworld and found a way to return safely, even if he fought the monstrous dog and captured it, he would still need to steal the beast from the Underworld, which its masters might not take kindly to.

Cerberus reared backward and threw Heracles to the ground. He rolled along the slope and leaped to his feet as the three-headed dog pounced. Heracles lifted the impervious skin from the Nemean Lion, one of the most precious trophies he'd won from his Labors, and deflected the blow.

What he wouldn't give for a proper shield in this fight. But he gritted his teeth and lunged forward again to clasp Cerberus's mighty jaws and punch the imposing muzzle. No weapons. No shields.

Heracles stood in the throne room of the Underworld and bowed.

He was no fool. Eurystheus intended him to either die in the attempt or bring the wrath of Hades and Persephone down on his head. Bad enough he already helped Theseus escape the Underworld; to take Cerberus by force would be a slight they couldn't overlook.

"What brings the son of Zeus here?" Hades asked from his throne. Beside him, Persephone sat silently.

"For my final Labor, King Eurystheus has demanded I capture Cerberus. I request your permission to take Cerberus to the king."

Hades laughed. "He certainly does not set you simple tasks, does he?"

"Indeed, he does not."

For a long moment, the god just looked at him, but then at last he nodded. "You may take Cerberus out of the Underworld—on one condition."

"I vow to return him to you once I've seen Eurystheus," Heracles said.

"Good," Hades said with a slight smirk, "but that is not my condition. No, my condition is this: you must capture Cerberus without the use of weapons or shields. Do this, and you can take him to the king."

No weapons or shields? Did he want to avoid undue harm to Cerberus? Did he believe it was impossible, a refusal while pretending to cooperate? Or maybe he just wanted to see if Heracles could do it.

Whatever the reason, Heracles had sworn to perform the Labors set to him by Eurystheus, and he had no desire to incur the wrath of another god. If barehanded combat against a three-headed dog was the price, so be it. He indicated his lion's-skin armor. "What of the skin I claimed from the Nemean Lion?"

"That is acceptable."

"Then I will fight Cerberus."

As Cerberus's head reeled backward from the blow, Heracles again leaped onto the dog's back and choked the middle head.

The massive beast stumbled as its second head went limp, and Heracles dropped down to nimbly dodge the final set of jaws. A creature as strong as Cerberus would recover quickly, so he needed to take out the third head while the other two remained dazed.

A dash to the side, a quick duck beneath snapping jaws, and then Heracles fell upon the final head with all the strength befitting the son of Zeus. Undeterred, Cerberus fought on and knocked him to the ground. The two wrestled in the Underworld until at last the dog shuddered and slumped. Exhausted, Heracles pushed the beast's bulk away and clambered to his feet.

The dog still breathed, but lay collapsed. Heracles had succeeded in his goal, although bringing Cerberus out of the Underworld would be another challenge.

"A job well done, cousin."

Startled by the soft voice, Heracles turned to face Persephone. She hadn't been there a moment ago, but he wondered if she had been watching the entire time.

"I used neither weapons nor shields," he said. "With my bare hands, I have subdued Cerberus. As per my agreement with Hades, I will now take him from the Underworld."

Persephone nodded. "My husband was pleased with your success. Here." She held out a great length of silver chain. "Use this to bind Cerberus. It will keep him compliant for the length of your journey."

"Thank you."

"It is no problem. We both wish you the best of luck with your remaining tasks."

"This should be my final one," Heracles said.

Should. Yet that was no guarantee.

At first, he had only been set Ten Labors, but Eurystheus found reasons to disqualify two of his victories and therefore increased the list. Would the king's hatred for Heracles ensure he would never be free? He might find any number of things to object to this time—the deal with Hades or the chain from Persephone, both perfectly within the requirements of the task yet which Eurystheus could claim invalidated his success.

Nevertheless, Heracles had made a vow. He had no choice but to take Cerberus back to the king.

Startled cries rang out as Heracles strode through the walled city of Tiryns with Cerberus in tow. The great dog had awoken on their way out of the Underworld, but Persephone's chain worked as promised. Cerberus followed Heracles as obediently as a puppy, all three heads looking around, jaws slavering as they passed meat-sellers in the marketplace.

No one made any attempt to stop Heracles from reaching the palace. He marched inside, Cerberus behind him, and threw open the throne room doors.

Gasps filled the room. From the throne itself, Eurystheus leaped to his feet, his face contorted with mingled shock and horror. He must not have expected Heracles to return successfully—or perhaps the sight of Cerberus was too much.

Well, if one claimed to want Cerberus brought to him, then one should be prepared to deal with the consequences.

Heracles stopped in front of the throne and bowed. "Your Majesty, I have completed the Twelfth Labor. I captured Cerberus, guardian of the Underworld, and have brought him to you."

Eurystheus sank down into his throne again, but remained tense. His lips twisted in distaste. "Indeed, you claim to have fulfilled my request."

"Claim?"

"You say you've captured Cerberus, but is that truly him? Why, he looks as tame as a pet. How could you get such a creature to obey you?" The king smirked, as if already planning the next impossible task he would command Heracles to perform.

Enough. Atonement was one thing, but it had been sheer cruelty to place Heracles in the service of a king who saw him as a rival, a king who had taken the throne once meant for him, a king favored by Hera. Eurystheus thought he could cast doubt on Cerberus's capture? Then Heracles would prove it.

He glanced at the silver lead in his hand. "If Your Majesty wishes, I will show you what Cerberus is capable of." He knelt and undid the length of chain from around the first of the three necks.

Immediately, Cerberus growled, his gaze fierce and wild once again. As the great dog snapped and struggled to free himself, the assembled courtiers gasped. One woman fainted.

Heracles reached for the second loop.

"Enough!" Eurystheus jumped up. "Bind that monster again!"

"But Your Majesty, how can you be sure it is really Cerberus? I wouldn't want you to think I tried to deceive you. Perhaps you should take a closer look, so no doubt remains." Heracles tugged Cerberus, still with one head free, toward the king.

"No!" Eurystheus lifted his hands and scrambled back behind his throne. "Stay away! Get that thing away from me!"

"You asked me to bring you Cerberus, Your Majesty. Now he is yours."

"Yes, you captured Cerberus and brought him to me, but I said nothing about keeping him. Take him away!"

"Then my final Labor is complete?" Heracles asked.

Beside him, Cerberus strained and snarled, as though he could sense the king's dislike.

"Yes, yes, by all the gods, yes! You've finished your service. I don't want to see you ever again. Just get that monster out of my palace!"

†††

Outside the palace, Heracles threw back his head and laughed. After twelve years of service, he was finally free. Since he was not bound to obey Eurystheus any longer, it was tempting to let Cerberus loose to wreak havoc, but while he'd enjoy getting revenge on the king, it would also endanger innocent people—and it wouldn't be fair to Hades and Persephone, since he'd promised to bring Cerberus back.

Heracles crouched to bind Cerberus and then led the great dog back toward the city gates.

Free at last. For so many years, he'd been trapped by the king's requests, seeking only atonement.

Atonement. With his service at an end, did that mean he'd found it?

The moment he emerged from the walls of Tiryns and reached the chariot waiting outside, Iolaus greeted him with an anxious smile. "Are you free?"

Heracles nudged Cerberus into the chariot, where there was just enough room for all three of them, and studied Iolaus. The boy, his nephew, charioteer, and companion, had never once faltered in devotion to him. Even knowing what he did. Even knowing it could happen again.

With the Twelve Labors completed, Heracles was free of King Eurystheus, but would he ever *truly* be free?

"My Labors are finished." He climbed into the chariot. "Now we need to return to the Underworld."

"Not necessarily," Iolaus said.

"What, you suggest we let Cerberus loose and hope he finds his own way back?"

Iolaus laughed. "Certainly not. While you were talking to the king, Adonis came by on his way to Olympus. He asked how you were faring with your Labors and was pleased when I told him you might be done."

Adonis? They had worked together in the past, but what did Aphrodite's lover have to do with Cerberus?

"Since he'll be leaving for the Underworld in two weeks, he said he'd be willing to take Cerberus back with him."

"Adonis is going to the Underworld?"

Iolaus blinked. "Don't you know about his arrangement?"

"I've been occupied for the past several years. What arrangement?"

"Adonis was raised by Persephone. While he prefers to spend most of his time with Aphrodite, Persephone insists upon having him with her some of the time. Therefore, he lives in the Underworld for one-third of the year."

A mortal man lived in the Underworld, not as a prisoner or a spirit, but as a guest who then returned to the world of the living for the remaining months? And he did this every year? It was a situation similar to Persephone's own, and yet Adonis was mortal…

"Heracles?" Iolaus asked.

An idea had occurred to Heracles when he first gained access to the Underworld, an idea that might well take him on a new journey, but one which would be worth it in the end. It strengthened when he found Theseus imprisoned and helped him escape, the rest of his life still ahead of him. This new revelation confirmed it.

People could leave the Underworld.

They could live in the Underworld.

Perhaps even the dead could leave and live again.

"Let's go see Adonis," he said.

Traveling from Tiryns, it took Heracles and Iolaus just under a week to reach Mount Olympus. Iolaus drove the chariot to the base of the mountain, and then Heracles disembarked.

"Stay here with Cerberus," he said.

After all, they couldn't leave the great dog unguarded, and the gods might dislike an uninvited mortal arriving at their home.

Or rather, he wasn't willing to let Hera see his nephew.

Jaw set, Heracles proceeded up Mount Olympus alone. Surely his precaution was unnecessary. Surely after his twelve years of service to Eurystheus, performing impossible task after impossible task, even the coldhearted goddess felt he had suffered enough. Hera's quarrel wasn't even with him, but with Zeus.

Yet he was the one she picked for her revenge, as though his mere existence offended her, and even though he doubted she would hurt Iolaus, he couldn't risk it.

Once he reached the top, Heracles headed straight for Aphrodite's abode, the most likely spot to find Adonis. It could be dangerous to walk in on the goddess of love unannounced, so he knocked.

"Who is it?" Aphrodite sounded as though she'd rather do anything than answer the door, despite the sultry note in her voice.

"Heracles. I'm looking for Adonis. My charioteer spoke to him near Tiryns, and I wished to see him. Is he there?"

"Oh, very well, come in."

The door swung open on its own and Heracles stepped inside. Aphrodite sat with Adonis on a chaise lounge, their fingers intertwined. Both were clothed, despite the scenarios Heracles had worried he might walk in on, but Aphrodite's near-transparent dress clung to her curves and Adonis's light garb covered even less.

The goddess and her lover were beautiful by any standards, with Adonis nearly as alluring as Aphrodite yet not lacking in strength any more than she lacked the inherent power of a goddess. Both were forces to be reckoned with, and when they sat together, it was as if their natures fueled one another. They made quite a pair.

Adonis met his gaze. "Are your Labors over?"

"When I returned with Cerberus in tow, the king was so frightened he immediately released me from his service."

"Hah! Nothing like a little fear to get people to change their minds."

"I'd started to worry he would find excuses to keep me in servitude forever, but now I'm finally free."

Aphrodite shook her head. "Free? Don't be a fool."

Heracles glanced at her. "What do you mean?"

With a languid stretch, she straightened on the lounge and shot him a look somewhere between contempt and pity. "There are two dangers in life you should always beware of incurring: a woman's jealousy and a god's hatred." She smirked. "Hatred born of a goddess's jealousy is something to be feared indeed. If you think you're 'free,' you need to remember how you ended up in this position."

Heracles folded his arms. "Hera has no reason to hurt me. I am not responsible for Zeus's actions." His protest echoed his own thoughts as he'd climbed Mount Olympus. "He's not even the father I grew up with. How can she continue to blame me?"

Aphrodite laughed. "You reason with logic. Hera reasons with emotion. The sight of you reminds her of Zeus's infidelity. She refuses to strike at him—she wants to keep him, not drive him away—so she takes out her wrath on his children instead."

He snorted. "Then I'll have to take greater care to make sure she doesn't see me."

Adonis clapped his hands together. "I suppose you won't want to linger in Olympus, then, so let's get down to business. From what Iolaus told me, I assume you'd like me to take Cerberus to the Underworld when I leave."

Aphrodite scowled, as though even the discussion of Adonis leaving irked her.

"No," Heracles said.

"No?"

"I know that is what you spoke of with my charioteer, but I came here for a different reason."

"What is that?"

"You are mortal, Adonis, yet you spend a third of the year in the Underworld. Is that only thanks to the grace of Persephone?"

Aphrodite's scowl deepened. "Does this line of questioning have a purpose?"

"Yes. I want to know if a man can enter the Underworld, stay there for a time, and return alive."

"Obviously," Adonis said. "You've done it yourself."

"Does that also mean that the dead can leave?"

That drew a sharp look from Aphrodite, her disgruntlement replaced by curiosity.

Adonis rose to his feet, eyes narrowed. "Heracles, what are you planning?"

Although he hadn't even spoken of his tenuous plan to Iolaus, Heracles drew a deep breath. "Ever since I set foot in the Underworld, it's been on my mind. Somewhere, the dead live on. If I could reach the Elysian Fields... I could see Megara and our children again, and perhaps bring them back."

His words hung heavy in the air.

Aphrodite bit her lip, but said nothing.

"This is dangerous," Adonis said. "Your wife and children are dead. The dead and the living are not meant to—"

"What if it was you?" Heracles waved his hand at the two of them. "You only need to live in the Underworld for a third of each year, and yet while you're here, you cherish the time you have together. If this time was taken from you, wouldn't you search for a way? If your stay in the Underworld was permanent, wouldn't you seek another solution?"

Adonis looked at Aphrodite and lowered his head. "Yes."

"Then you'll help me?"

"If I had the answers you needed," he said, "I'd give them to you."

"But you don't?"

"Our situations are different. I don't reside with the dead when I enter the Underworld, but with Persephone. Yes, that makes me a mortal living in the Underworld, but it's not the same as what you're after. I have no idea if the dead can leave the Underworld and survive."

Heracles rubbed his chin. Perhaps returning with Cerberus and simply making his request to Hades and Persephone would be best after all.

Aphrodite rose at last and stood in front of him, her gaze unreadable. "Do not take my earlier warning lightly, Heracles. Hera will not forget her grudge. She will watch you for any vulnerability, any weakness she can strike at, any way she can hurt you again. You think you've suffered enough, but it won't be enough for her. She wants to destroy you slowly, crushing you little by little until you can't take it anymore."

Heracles clenched his jaw.

"Knowing the danger," she said, "is this still something you want to do?"

Reuniting with his family, seeing them in the Underworld and learning they were well, asking their forgiveness and searching for a second chance—he'd find the closure his long years of so-called atonement could never bring.

He met Aphrodite's gaze and offered a short nod. "Yes."

"Then I suggest you seek out Orpheus."

"Orpheus?"

"He has experience in these matters."

In that case, it had to be done. Searching for Orpheus would complicate things, but whatever the challenge, Heracles would rise to meet it.

He would travel to the ends of the earth if necessary to see his family again.

✝✝✝

Heracles had met Orpheus once. They briefly journeyed together with Jason and the Argonauts, before Heracles was separated from the expedition. Although he went on to finish his Labors alone, he'd traveled with them long enough to know the stories about the musician were true— his songs and poetry were beyond compare. Music from Orpheus could bring peace to even the fiercest warrior spirit.

He never realized Orpheus had once walked this same path.

According to Aphrodite, Orpheus had returned home after his journey with the Argonauts, and he eventually fell in love with a woman named Eurydice. Eurydice disappeared on their wedding day, and when Orpheus found her, he was too late to save her life.

He then traveled into the Underworld in the hopes of being reunited with his bride, but came back to the mortal world alone. Although Aphrodite didn't know what prevented Eurydice's return, she still believed Orpheus would be the best one to give Heracles advice.

But what had become of the poet since then?

Heracles mulled over the problem as he descended Mount Olympus. The goddess said not even Apollo, to whom Orpheus had devoted himself, knew his whereabouts. Orpheus appeared to have gone into exile, isolating himself from men and gods alike.

Logic told Heracles he should abandon this quest and merely return Cerberus to the Underworld, or at least take his own chances without the poet's advice. He had always preferred *doing* to *thinking*, preferred combat to riddles—searching for Orpheus would try his patience.

However, he was not one to give up easily. Quitting would be like saying he couldn't succeed. He refused to accept that. Someone must know what had become of Orpheus.

At the base of the mountain, Cerberus had fallen asleep, all three heads resting on his paws, but Iolaus stood waiting faithfully with the chariot. "What news?"

"We need to find Orpheus," Heracles said.

"Orpheus?" Iolaus sounded puzzled. "I thought you went to ask Adonis to take Cerberus with him into the Underworld."

"No, I will return Cerberus to the Underworld myself."

"Then why are we here?"

"I needed to talk to Adonis. There's something else I must do in the Underworld, and now I know Orpheus might have the knowledge I need."

Iolaus nodded, if not understanding than at least accepting. "Where to?"

" HE TRAVELED INTO THE UNDERWORLD... "

Not an easy question at all. If Orpheus had isolated himself, would anyone know where he went? Who might the poet have confided in, if even Apollo couldn't find him?

Heracles thought back to his brief time with the Argonauts. The poet had been particularly fond of Calais, one of the two sons of the north wind. If they could find Calais, perhaps he could lead them to Orpheus.

Rumors about the Argonauts had spread ever since their return, including speculation about the sons of the north wind. Most was nonsense. Some even claimed *Heracles* had killed the brothers during their journey. The most popular story, however, said Calais and his brother had gone to help their brother-in-law Phineus by driving away the harpies that tormented him.

"Do you know where we might find Phineus?" he asked.

Iolaus looked perplexed by the question. "The one who aided the Argonauts?"

"Yes."

"As far as I know, he's still at his home where the Argonauts met him, trying to avoid the gods' attention in case they restore his punishment." Iolaus tilted his head. "Is that where we're going?"

Heracles hesitated. "This might be a long journey. If you'd rather I handled the rest on my own, I understand."

But his nephew only smiled. "You know I'm with you until the end."

"Thank you, Iolaus. Then yes, we should head for the house of Phineus."

He nudged Cerberus awake, and the massive dog stretched before joining them in the chariot. Iolaus didn't question his plans further, but merely sent the chariot into motion. Heracles clapped him on the shoulder. Such dependable allies were hard to find.

As they raced away from Mount Olympus, he thought about Phineus. The old man had been rescued from his terrible punishment, yet he lived in isolation, still fearing the gods.

Heracles glanced back at Olympus, and for a moment, he could have sworn someone was watching him.

✝✝✝

Reaching Phineus would be a challenge on its own. While there was an overland route to his house, it would take many more days than they had to spare if they wanted to return to the Underworld in a timely fashion.

But taking the sea route came with its own troubles.

Heracles added a few more gold coins to the pile he offered to the ship's captain. "It won't be dangerous. It's only the start of the path Jason took—before things got rough."

The man stared at the pile of gold.

His ship's schedule fit their needs perfectly. While its route didn't go to Phineus's house, it passed only a short distance away. Better yet, their return route would allow them to pick up Heracles once he finished, unless things went poorly. It was their best option.

Heracles added another coin.

"Well…" Gold was a powerful motivator. The captain rubbed his chin. "You're sure it won't be dangerous?"

"No more than any normal trip."

"Fine. We'll take you aboard. Then, as long as you don't spend too much time there, we'll stop for you on our way back."

"It's a deal." Heracles looked back toward where he'd left Iolaus and Cerberus and waved his hand for them to join him.

His nephew started forward, the three-headed dog obediently following.

The captain's eyes bulged. "What? No, no, definitely not. You didn't say anything about… about the guardian of the Underworld!"

"There's nothing to worry about," Heracles said. "I have permission for him to be here."

Technically. He and Hades hadn't specifically discussed taking Cerberus on a sea voyage, but nothing in their agreement prohibited it.

The captain shook his head. "We do not have room."

Heracles gritted his teeth. They couldn't just leave Cerberus sitting around somewhere. He'd have to back out of the deal and search for someone willing to take a three-headed dog as passenger, never mind how long it had taken to find even this ship. They'd traveled to the closest port, but they'd simply have to try another.

However, Iolaus lifted his hand. "I'll remain here with Cerberus."

"Are you sure?" Heracles asked.

"Yes. I'll see that no harm comes to him."

"Very well. I'll be back once I speak to Phineus." He looked at the captain. "Is that acceptable? You'll just be taking me as your passenger."

"Be ready to leave in one hour."

††††

Black clouds rolled in partway through their journey. Thunder rumbled as the wind picked up, and choppy waves tossed the ship from side to side.

"We were supposed to have fair seas for the entire voyage," one of the sailors said under his breath. "By the gods, where did this storm come from?"

They looked toward the sky as lightning flashed.

Unease prickled Heracles. By rights, he should have nothing to fear from a thunderstorm, his father being Zeus, but a terrible dread crept through him all the same.

Sudden impact sent the ship careening to the side. A massive wave tossed it into the air, and a dark shape parted the water beneath them—a massive fish that turned toward them again the moment they returned to the water.

From the other side, another impact sent the ship rocking.

"We're under attack!" the captain shouted. "All hands on deck!"

Two giant sea creatures, each as wide as the ship and nearly as long, circled them as the storm worsened. They assaulted the ship with single-minded determination, as though sinking the vessel was their only goal.

"You!" The captain pointed toward Heracles. "You said this would be a safe journey!"

"We've never had such trouble before," a sailor said, his gaze dark. "You must be the cause of this."

Another tremor shook the vessel. At this rate, the ship would capsize under the repeated strikes.

"He's brought down the wrath of the gods upon us!" another sailor shouted.

"He's cursed!"

The panicked crew would tear Heracles to shreds if they thought it would save their lives, and perhaps they were right. Perhaps he was to blame for this storm. Another glance at the frenzied monsters below made up his mind.

He ran to the side of the deck and leaped overboard.

Someone cried out, but it was too late for anyone to stop him. Cold water surged around him as he plunged into its depths. He swam for the surface, his strength enough to overcome the storm-tossed waters. His head broke through and he gasped for breath in time to see one of the monstrous fish swimming toward him. Despite its breadth, its sinuous body curled smoothly through the waves at incredible speeds. Trying to dodge it would only waste his strength.

Instead, he waited.

The creature rammed into him, and he wrapped his arms around it to hold it steady. It thrashed, forcing him backward into the waves again. But Heracles had fought many large monsters before—and he found himself glad for the restriction upon his fight with Cerberus, since it had given him practice not using weapons in such a battle. He released his grip as the monster opened its mouth to reveal rows of vicious, glistening teeth.

One powerful kick of his legs sent Heracles backwards out of its range, and he dove underwater.

While his adversary searched for him, he reversed course and propelled himself upward, surging into the giant fish from below. They sailed out of the water together and then crashed back upon it. Heracles wrestled the monster in the storm-tossed waters, waves crashing around them as thunder boomed and lightning flashed.

A staggering force slammed into his side. The second fish had given up its pursuit of the ship and joined the battle. Heracles kicked out against it, unwilling to relinquish his grip on his weakening adversary.

He grabbed a monster in each hand and squeezed them until they stopped moving.

The sudden memory made him pause, but he had no time to dwell on it. The second fish lunged for him again even while the first struggled. Sharp teeth sank into his shoulder. Again he planted his feet upon the monster's scales and forced it back, braced against the pain. He strained at the monster in his clutches. Surely it was almost dead.

Teeth bared, the second monster sped through the water with renewed vigor.

The crunch of snapping bones was music to Heracles's ears. He dropped the dying fish as its massive bulk went limp, then dove under the waves.

His second opponent followed. Heracles slowed until it drew nearer, gaze fixed on it to watch its movements. Once it was almost upon him, he dodged to the side and grabbed one of its massive fins. With barely a pause, he ripped it free. Blood stained the water crimson as he swam for the surface again.

But the monster was faster. He had time for only one gulp of breath before it slammed into him and drove him back under. It struck him again and again, each blow more powerful than the last.

Rather than resist, Heracles let the repeated strikes carry him backward, used the momentum to help him gain speed. Then he swam, not toward the creature, but away from it. Once he gained some distance, he turned to face his foe once more.

The massive fish charged. Again, Heracles waited. This time, he swam not to the side, but above it, and threw himself onto its back. It thrashed under his unexpected weight and flung itself backward as if to throw him off. He clutched it tightly, stealing a welcome breath of air when their struggles brought them to the surface.

They struck the water with a thunderous impact, and the monster dove deeper. It swam down and down, into still water, seeking to drown him if he didn't let go. Yet Heracles kept his grip and clawed at its scales in search of a weak spot.

Still deeper it swam. Even Heracles would need to breathe eventually.

Breath held despite his burning lungs, he twisted at the skull of the mighty sea monster. Yet his precarious perch made his grip less secure. No good. He needed a different tactic.

Heracles released it and reached for his sword.

The monster tossed him free, and he tumbled through the water. However, he'd drawn his sword, and as his adversary swam toward him for the finishing blow, he thrust his blade into the beast's eye.

Blood poured out around them. Bracing himself with his feet, he wrenched his sword free and swam upward. Powerful strokes carried him toward the surface, where he emerged into blessed air and filled his aching lungs.

Gasping, Heracles blinked in surprise at the blue sky. The storm must have cleared while he fought beneath the waves, as though it had never been there at all.

But it *had* existed… hadn't it?

Doubt gnawed at him—perhaps the entire battle had been another deception, a trick of his senses. But his shoulder burned from the fish's bite, and the ship was nowhere to be seen. They must have departed on their regular route, content to leave their "cursed" passenger behind.

That left him stranded.

Heracles turned slowly in the water. Not far away, waves crashed against the coast. His battle must have carried him closer to land—he only prayed it was near the shore he'd hoped to reach.

He sheathed his sword and began to swim.

It was a long time before Heracles reached the shore. He spent the night there and then resumed his travels, wondering with each step if he had doomed himself.

But at last, a lone house greeted him in the distance, and it matched the descriptions of Phineus's home. Thank the gods he'd reached his destination despite everything. Perhaps his luck wasn't so terrible after all.

He straightened his shoulders and walked to the door.

It opened, and Phineus stood before him, his sightless gaze fixed on him nevertheless. "Who are you? Why have you come?"

"My name is Heracles."

The blind seer flinched back. "Have the gods sent you?"

"Peace. The gods did not send me here." If anything, they had barred his progress. "I came only because I know you are the brother-in-law of Calais and Zetes, who once helped you. I hoped to ask Calais something."

Phineus shook his head. "The sons of the wind come and go as they please. From time to time, they visit me, so they will eventually return. If you wish to wait, I offer you my hospitality, meager though it might be."

Waiting was never Heracles's preferred option, unless he was assured of his goal in the end. Here, it might only waste time—and since he doubted the ship would return for him, he already had a long journey ahead to reunite with Iolaus and Cerberus.

"Or," Phineus said, apparently sensing his hesitation, "perhaps I can help you with whatever question you have for Calais."

"I'm searching for Orpheus. From the brief period of time when I knew them, I recall a friendship between him and Calais."

"Ah, Orpheus." The seer shook his head with a somber smile. "Such a sad story indeed."

"You mean because of Eurydice?" Heracles asked. "Or has an additional tragedy befallen him?"

"You remembered my brother-in-law's friendship with him, but you did not see enough to understand what was truly at work—not friendship alone, but unrequited love. Yes, Orpheus fell in love with Calais, and Calais did not feel the same."

His heart sank. "Then Calais won't know where he is?"

"The last time they spoke was at the Pangaion Hills. Orpheus had gone into exile there."

"Exile?"

"Out of grief, I believe. According to Calais, Orpheus made trips alone to Mount Pangaion and cut himself off from anyone who would attempt to console him. He wanted Calais to stay with him, but Calais refused. That was the last time they met. Orpheus might have left the Pangaion Hills since then, but that is where I recommend you begin your search."

"Thank you," Heracles said.

As he turned to leave, the seer reached out and clasped his shoulder. "One moment."

"What is it?"

"You are Heracles, the son of Zeus. The gods have touched you in many ways. I see tragedy in your future. Tragedy will haunt you and those connected to you. It will stalk your footsteps and follow you everywhere."

Heracles stiffened. He hadn't asked for a prophecy, especially not one like that. "Haven't I suffered enough?"

"Some would think so. Others would not."

He closed his eyes. "I've found a path that will help me escape this tragic future."

"Then I wish you the favor of the gods on the journey ahead."

Yet the old seer's prophecy rang through Heracles's mind as he left the house and stared out at the unforgiving ocean. Tragedy would haunt him. His knuckles whitened as he clenched his fists. The storm and monsters must have been sent by Hera, although how she managed it, he couldn't guess. Phineus's prediction echoed Aphrodite's warning that the goddess would not let him go so easily.

Still, he needed to take things one step at a time. Once he had his family back, then he could decide how to deal with Hera.

With a last regretful glance at the sea, Heracles turned north to take the overland route back to the port.

✝✝✝

Considering how poorly things had gone during the journey across the sea, Heracles expected to face danger at every turn. But while traveling was rough and he was forced to scavenge for supplies, nothing attacked him.

He traveled as quickly as possible, stopping only for brief rests and to hunt for food, which he cooked above a small campfire at night. All the while, he thought about Iolaus and Cerberus waiting for him and what his nephew might think when the ship returned with stories of sea monsters.

On his fifth day after leaving Phineus, the galloping of hooves up ahead made Heracles stiffen. He moved to the side of the path and rested his hand on his sword hilt.

But as the newcomer approached, Heracles drew sharp breath in amazement. He knew that chariot! Iolaus drove at its head and Cerberus rode behind him.

Heracles stepped into view and waved.

Iolaus tugged on the reins and brought the chariot to a halt. "It's good to see you," he said, relief evident in his voice.

"You as well," Heracles said, "but what are you doing here?"

"When the ship returned to port without you, the captain claimed you died along the way. I knew if you'd survived, you'd most likely need to take the overland route back, so I set out to find you."

With a laugh, Heracles embraced his nephew and joined him in the chariot. "You've saved us several days of travel—" He cut off abruptly. In his surprise, he'd missed the long gash across Iolaus's cheekbone. "You're wounded!"

Iolaus reached up to the cut and shook his head. "We ran into some trouble, but it was nothing I couldn't handle."

Despite the note of pride in his voice, unease prickled Heracles. "What sort of trouble?"

"Everything!" Iolaus laughed. "Bandits, animals, you name it—this route must be cursed. No wonder Phineus doesn't get visitors often."

Heracles rubbed his chin. The land route was long and arduous, but for his charioteer to have faced such obstacles, that spoke of something else at work.

Something darker.

"Did you speak with him?" Iolaus asked.

"Yes." No point in worrying too much about why their journey had been more dangerous than his. They were together again, after all. Heracles dragged his attention back to the matter at hand. "We might find Orpheus at the Pangaion Hills. If he's no longer there, we should at least find a sign of where he's gone."

"And we're taking Cerberus?"

"Yes. Having Cerberus by my side when I return to the Underworld might help."

Chances were good that regardless of what Orpheus suggested, Heracles would need to petition Hades and Persephone to let him see his family. It was in his best interests to be on their good side. Bringing Cerberus back to them and then asking for a favor sounded ideal.

As long as they weren't annoyed about him keeping Cerberus for so much time, of course.

"When you return to the..." Iolaus shook his head. "What exactly are you trying to do? After all I went through to get here, I feel I should at least know the reason."

Fair enough. Heracles sighed. "I want to see my wife and children."

"But they're—"

"Orpheus made a failed attempt to retrieve his bride from the Underworld. He should have information that can help me."

"A *failed* attempt and you want his advice?"

Heracles set his jaw. "We're going to the Pangaion Hills."

"I'm just not sure—"

"To the Pangaion Hills."

Iolaus let out a long sigh, but he didn't press the issue.

†††

It was another week of traveling, but soon their destination came into view. A chill crept into the air as they entered the mountainous region of the Pangaion Hills. Fog descended upon the mountains. It hadn't been a long journey, but in that short time, the weather had completely changed. Heracles tensed and reached for his sword.

Iolaus reined in the horses to slow the chariot's progress. They could only see a few feet ahead through the fog. Cerberus lifted one head and whined.

A strange creature emerged from the mist, its form massive and bestial. A chimera? No, it lacked the disparate nature inherent to chimeras. Its powerful wings, hooked tail, and hard-edged hooves all looked natural, like the creature was meant to have those parts. In all his years of adventuring, Heracles had never seen anything quite like it.

This was something new.

The creature turned toward them and roared, baring its teeth. Heracles and Iolaus drew their swords.

Another emerged from the fog, followed by a third. The trio of monsters stared at the chariot. They stood poised as if to spring, but none made any attempt to come closer. Not predators, then, but...

"They're guarding the mountains," Heracles said softly.

Iolaus glanced at him. "Are we going to fight them?"

"We must, if it's the only way to reach Orpheus."

Two of the beasts sprang forward without warning, as if the name was a signal. Heracles leaped from the chariot and turned to see Iolaus rolling out of the way. The closest of the mountain's guardians lunged for Heracles, and he slashed at it with his sword only for his blade to be parried by a massive hoof. Still he pressed forward.

To his side, Iolaus was holding his own, although he seemed to lack the strength to overcome his adversary. No matter. Heracles would help him once he finished his own foe.

But what of the third?

A shadow fell over him. Heracles spun around just as the remaining beast swooped down from above. Its wings had carried it high into the sky, and it dove toward him with all the force and fury born from such momentum. Heracles slashed at its legs, but it only veered past and swept its tail into him instead. The tail struck him with more force than he expected and knocked him off-balance.

Flight gave it the advantage. Heracles would have to leap toward it on its next approach and take out its wings—but even as he regained his footing, his first opponent charged him.

This time his sword thrust struck true, but the bleeding gash in the creature's side barely fazed it. Heracles retreated to stand back-to-back with Iolaus. If they could take out one of the guardians, this would become much easier, yet if they lowered their guard, the others would strike.

Fighting like this wouldn't be enough.

He sheathed his sword and crouched. As the one in the air dove toward them, he leaped and caught it by its wings. It reared backward with a roar. If he could cripple its ability to fly, the odds would swing in their favor. But he had to move swiftly. Iolaus could only distract the other two for so long.

The wings were powerful, but a sharp twist should be enough to break them. Heracles tightened his grip.

A hideous bellow rose up all around them, as if from the very stones. More of the creatures emerged from the fog, two on one side and two more on the other. They advanced toward Iolaus. Abandoning his efforts, Heracles leaped down to defend his nephew. He hit the ground with a harsh impact that sent a jolt through his legs, but he drew his sword again. This was bad. Two against three, they could manage, but two against seven...

Wait—they were not two, but *three*.

"Unbind Cerberus!" he shouted.

"...HE SLASHED AT IT WITH HIS SWORD..."

Iolaus looked at him like he'd lost his mind.

"Do it!" Heracles steeled himself to fend them off alone to buy Iolaus time.

The younger man didn't question him, but raced to the chariot. He fumbled with the silver chain while Heracles battled the mountain's guardians, then pulled it free. With a growl, the three-headed dog shook as if to rid himself of the lingering touch of the chain, then bounded past Iolaus.

Heracles looked at the massive hound and tried to meet the gazes of all three heads. "Well, Cerberus, looks like we need to work together. I promise to take you home, but I need a little help first."

By the gods, he hoped the beast understood.

Then the mountain's guardians were upon them.

Heracles fought off the closest two, but as a third lunged for him, a massive paw knocked it out of the way. Cerberus growled and dashed forward to harry them further. Iolaus's opponents turned away from him to face this new foe. One made the mistake of attacking, and the three-headed dog pounced upon it like it was a toy.

They had balance again. As long as Iolaus held his own, Heracles and Cerberus would be able to take out the rest.

Suddenly, an eerie note pierced the fog. A somber melody filled the air around them. Heracles tensed, prepared for whatever new danger it might herald. Yet something about the music sounded familiar... He looked toward the mountain peak. Somewhere up there, Opheus was playing his lyre.

The creatures lifted their heads as well. All seven of them, wounded or not, shuffled backward into the fog. For a moment, nothing happened. It was like the Pangaion Hills had been frozen in time. Then the fog cleared, and the mountain's guardians were gone.

Cerberus sniffed at the air, then settled back on his haunches with a yawn. One paw lifted to scratch at his ear.

Heracles blinked around in surprise and sheathed his sword. If it was good enough for Cerberus, it was good enough for him. The guardians had left.

"What was that?" Iolaus asked.

"I think we're being allowed passage."

"Those monsters are still lurking around somewhere."

Heracles considered that for a moment. It didn't seem like a trap, but it wasn't wise to take chances. He glanced at Cerberus, who seemed perfectly content to sit with them. "Let's leave Cerberus unbound, just in case we need him."

Then he started up the slope.

✝✝✝

High in the mountains, a man in a hooded cloak walked alone. His posture was stooped, but his head lifted as Heracles, Iolaus, and Cerberus crested the cliff. "Go away! Leave me in peace."

Despite his anger, the man's voice still contained hints of the melodious tones once used to soothe flaming tempers and entertain the crew of a deadly voyage. He was indeed Orpheus.

Heracles raised his hands in a gesture of peace and stepped forward. "We mean you no harm. It is I, Heracles. We traveled together once, on our journey with the Argonauts."

Orpheus met his gaze, eyes narrowed. Shadowed by the hood, his face was largely unchanged yet creased with lines from sorrow and stress. "My adventuring days are over. Whatever this is about, I cannot help you." He turned away.

"Wait!" Heracles reached out. "Orpheus, you are the only person I know of who has done what I hope to do. I need your counsel. Aphrodite herself suggested I consult you."

"I want nothing to do with the gods or their heroes," Orpheus said. "All I want is to be left in peace for the remainder of my days."

"We won't cause any trouble."

He let out a bitter laugh. "A son of Zeus arrives at my home with the three-headed guard dog of the Underworld and begins to fight my guardians, yet I should not expect trouble?"

Heracles bowed his head. "We only wanted to climb the mountain. When your guardians attacked, we had no choice but to—"

"Save your excuses. It matters not to me. What is it you seek, passage into the Underworld? Ask elsewhere; there are many who can help you."

"I've already been to the Underworld," Heracles said.

"Then why do you need me?"

"I need to speak with someone who is dead."

"I cannot help you."

"You went into the Underworld after Eurydice! Aphrodite told me!"

Orpheus rounded on them. The sudden motion tossed his hood back, and he glared at Heracles. "Have I not suffered enough without the gods sending you to tear open old wounds? I've forsaken love and turned away from the cruelty of the gods. Please, Heracles, leave me be. I only called off the guardians because I knew you would destroy them if the battle continued. They protect these mountains because I want to be left alone. Don't make me speak about what happened in the Underworld."

The poet's lament made Heracles's own sorrow rear up all the stronger. Seeing Megara and their children again was not just something he wanted to do, but something he *needed* to do.

"We came a long way to see you," Heracles said. "We fought monsters and risked our lives. We're tired from our journey. If you don't want to talk to us, can't you at least offer us respite?"

It was clear the poet didn't want to, but he let out a long sigh, his personal desires undoubtedly at war with his sense of hospitality.

At last, he nodded.

†††

Orpheus helped them secure the chariot in the lower regions of the hills where he assured them it would be safe, then led them even higher into the mountains, up increasingly narrow paths until they reached a cave entrance partly-concealed by the rocks around it.

Cerberus was too large to enter the cave, but settled down outside the entrance without complaint once Heracles and Iolaus followed Orpheus inside.

Clothes and skins had been set out on the ground, and a fire pit sat in the middle, but the cave was otherwise barren. Strange lodgings for a poet. Yet Heracles kept his thoughts to himself. Clearly Orpheus's failure to bring Eurydice back from the Underworld, or perhaps her loss itself, had struck him hard. Phineus hadn't exaggerated when he called it exile.

Orpheus started a fire and sat down alongside it. Heracles and Iolaus joined him. For a while, no one spoke.

At last, the poet said quietly, "How did you find me?"

Heracles hesitated. "We heard rumors that you had been seen in the Pangaion Hills. Since it was our only lead, we decided to come here and hope you hadn't merely been passing through."

Iolaus gave him a sharp look, but Heracles ignored it. After what happened between Orpheus and Calais, saying they'd gone to Phineus for answers would only make matters worse.

"Rumors?" Orpheus asked. "I hope this doesn't lead to more visitors."

"Most won't be as determined as we were."

He snorted. "Good. My hospitality only goes so far these days." He waved his hand around at the cave. "I don't have much to offer you. I take what I need to survive, nothing more. Sometimes I question doing even that."

"We can hunt once we're out of the mountains."

"Good," Orpheus said.

Keeping Cerberus fed as their journey stretched on might prove difficult, however. Surely he'd want more meat than they'd been able to provide so far. Heracles glanced at the massive dog, who lay with one head near the entrance to see inside. He seemed content enough for the moment.

Heracles returned his gaze to the poet. "Do you still sing?"

"Yes. Poetry and music are the only things I have left that bring me joy."

Iolaus tilted his head and spoke up at last. "Can we hear something?"

Silence followed his question. It stretched on so long, Heracles was about to change the subject, when the poet suddenly rose and walked to the other side of the cave. From within a small bundle, he pulled out a lyre and then rejoined them.

Eyes closed, he began to play.

The notes rose steadily, their melody somber. It was a dirge or lament, and soon Orpheus joined the sound of the lyre with words. His voice low and sonorous, he sang of lost love and injustice ignored by the gods. Yet despite the song's sorrow, it contained beauty. The beauty of happiness fallen out of reach forever.

Heracles knew such happiness once, before Hera took her revenge. Yes, he could see why Orpheus felt bitter toward the gods who left terrible deeds go unpunished while the innocent suffered for them.

Outside, Cerberus let out three howls in unison with the song. Heracles bowed his head. He and Orpheus were far from the only ones to lose people they loved, and few people had the opportunities he sought. Yet he couldn't go on without trying.

When Orpheus finished, the final notes hung in the air between them. He put down his lyre. Iolaus wiped his eyes and looked away.

"Please," Heracles said softly in the silence that followed, "tell me what happened when you went to the Underworld."

"Why?"

"My wife and children are dead. I long for a chance to be with them."

"You know I failed," Orpheus said. "You think you can do what I could not?"

"I want to know what happened to you so I know what to expect."

He let out a long sigh. "I would spare you that pain."

Heracles remained silent. He couldn't give up, not if there was even a small chance.

"Even without my guidance, you'd just continue on your own, wouldn't you?"

"Yes."

"Very well," Orpheus said. "Even though I will never be reunited with my beloved in life, perhaps you will be able to find peace."

"Thank you."

The poet stared into the fire, his gaze shadowed. He took a deep breath and then let it out. "What Aphrodite told you is true. When I lost Eurydice, I felt I could not go on without her. I traveled into the Underworld and played my song of sorrow for Hades and Persephone. My grief softened their hearts, and they agreed to hear my request."

Of course Orpheus's music could move even the gods. After hearing him play, Heracles understood.

"They gave me permission to bring Eurydice back to the land of the living with me."

His heart leaped, but his stomach clenched. It hadn't worked, so something must have gone wrong.

"There was one condition: I could not look at her until we returned to the light. Hades instructed me to lead her out of the Underworld, and once we emerged into the mortal world, she would live again and I could look upon her. I believed I was strong enough, and so I set out with Eurydice following me." Orpheus ran his fingers through his hair. "I was so close… So close to being with her again…"

Iolaus looked down at the ground, as if embarrassed to hear such a personal story.

Heracles waited, dreading the conclusion even as he longed to hear it.

"As I walked," Orpheus said, "I detected no sign of her behind me. No speech, no footsteps, not even the sound of her breathing. She was still dead, after all."

Then the shades of the dead made no sound as they moved. Heracles had never considered that.

"I became paranoid. What if Hades had tricked me? The longer that terrible silence stretched on, the more convinced I became that I walked alone and that once I left the Underworld, I would not be able to return. The exit lay in front of me. I had only a few more steps to take… and my nerve broke. I turned around to see if I had been deceived or if Eurydice had truly followed me."

"Was she there?" Iolaus asked, his voice soft.

"Yes," Orpheus whispered. "She looked so sad… She looked into my eyes and faded away right in front of me. I'd failed. Hades had only set a single condition, that I not look back until we reached the light, and I failed. I lost my only chance to be with Eurydice again in life. Now, all I can do is pray for death to reunite us."

Silence followed his story.

Then Heracles took a deep breath. "So if I can convince Hades to make the same deal with me, all I need to do is trust him to keep his end of the bargain."

"It sounds simple, doesn't it?" Orpheus gave him a sad smile, his regret apparent. Wistfulness filled his voice. "It isn't easy once you're there."

"I have nothing to lose," Heracles said. "This is my only chance. If I emerge from the Underworld and they haven't followed me, I'll be in the same position as if I didn't go at all. It's worth the risk. I will not look back."

"Perhaps you truly can do it, then."

Yes, he would go to the Underworld and meet any conditions set before him. Whether it was a test of strength or nerve or trust, he wouldn't falter. His family would be together again.

"Is that why you have Cerberus?" Orpheus asked.

At the cave entrance, the dog's ears pricked up.

"For me," the poet said, "my music convinced them to give me a chance. Are you going to bargain with their guard dog?"

Heracles shook his head. "I parted on good terms with Hades and Persephone. They gave me permission to take Cerberus away. When I bring him back safely, I think they'll view me favorably enough to grant my request."

"I wish you well. May you find the happiness I lost."

"Thank you, and thank you for your hospitality as well." He rose and nodded to Iolaus. "We will trouble you no longer, Orpheus. It's time we were on our way."

Iolaus scrambled to his feet. "Yes, thank you."

"Be careful," Orpheus said. "Even if you escape the snare I fell into, you might learn the Fates have a dark path planned for you."

"I will handle it."

"Farewell, Heracles."

As Heracles and Iolaus left the cave and led Cerberus back down the mountain paths toward the chariot, another soft lament rose from the cave behind them. Orpheus's heart-wrenching music followed them all the way out of the Pangaion Hills.

From the Pangaion Hills, they traveled across the countryside for three more weeks to the cape where Heracles had descended to the Underworld before. Gods willing, the same entrance would allow him and Cerberus passage again.

The sun shone brightly overheard as they stood looking out at the ocean, in sharp contrast to the darkness he would soon enter.

They'd faced so many dangers since his decision to make this request of Hades. Heracles stared into the water and thought about everything that had happened, from the disastrous ship voyage to their battle against Orpheus's guardians.

With a deep breath, he turned toward the narrow path that led to the Underworld. "Remain here and wait for me."

Iolaus nodded, and then held something out. "You'll want to take this."

It was the silver chain Persephone had given Heracles to bind Cerberus with. Heracles had almost forgotten about it. Cerberus padded up alongside them and barked at a distant bird. After their fight in the Pangaion Hills, they'd never put the chain back on him, but he'd traveled to the cape without complaint. The massive dog must have come to consider them allies, or at least not enemies.

Heracles turned to Cerberus, who regarded him calmly. He patted each of the three heads and slung the chain over his shoulder. There would be no need to bind Cerberus for the remainder of their journey. Instead, he beckoned for him to follow. "It's time to go home."

As if he understood, Cerberus bounded to his side with another bark. Together, they made their way down the narrow path. The imposing cave entrance at the bottom served as a gate to the Underworld. Cerberus sniffed the air, then took the lead. Heracles followed him into the cave.

While still intimidating, the dark path was not quite as threatening as the first time he entered. Then, it had been completely unknown. He caught up to Cerberus, and they walked side by side into the land of the dead.

The air grew cooler around them. The cave's natural walls gave way to gray stone. At first glance, it could still be mistaken for a cave, except that it was lit from within by an eerie green light. Strange shadows danced along the walls.

Rushing water broke the silence, but Heracles and Cerberus didn't go near the river. Instead, they crossed a narrow, rocky path to the gates where Cerberus normally stood guard, onward through a shadowed hall toward the throne room. Although Cerberus's ears pricked up when they passed the gates, he padded along without pause.

Heracles opened the doors to the throne room.

With Cerberus by his side, he stepped up to the thrones of Hades and Persephone and held out the silver chain. "I have completed my Labor and returned with Cerberus."

Persephone took the chain and looked with curiosity at the unbound guard dog.

"I suppose I shouldn't be surprised," Hades said, his voice dry. "Of course you would demonstrate your skill by leaving Cerberus unchained."

Heracles laughed. "No boasting intended. We ran into danger along the way and unchained Cerberus so he could help us. We never got around to redoing the chain, and he didn't give us any trouble." He turned toward the dog. "Thank you for your assistance, friend."

Cerberus regarded him for a moment longer and whined, then turned and bounded deeper into the Underworld.

Persephone smiled. "He likes you. That's unusual."

"We did spend a fair amount of time together. I've grown fond of him, too."

"Thank you for bringing him back," she said. "Many people would find it a great boon to keep a creature such as Cerberus by their side, especially with the ability to bind him."

"This is his home. He belongs here. The only boon I needed from Cerberus was the proof that I had completed my final Labor."

Hades raised his eyebrows. "Have you been freed from the king's demands, then?"

"When Eurystheus saw Cerberus in all his glory, he practically commanded me to stop serving him."

"Would that my fellow gods let you go so easily."

Heracles gritted his teeth, his good humor gone. Did everyone he met need to hint that Hera would continue to cause him trouble? He'd completed the tasks set for his atonement, and there was only one last thing he wanted. He took a deep breath. "Your Majesties, in addition to returning Cerberus to you, I came here to request a favor."

The god of the dead barely reacted. Perhaps he heard this sort of thing often. "What favor?"

"My wife Megara and our three children have been in the Underworld ever since their deaths twelve years ago. I wish to see them again and, if possible, bring them back with me to the land of the living."

"Heracles—"

"Please," he said. "All these years, I've atoned for my sins. Please let me see them again. We were separated unjustly."

"Is that not how death separates most people?"

That argument, he couldn't refute. Orpheus and Eurydice hadn't been separated by any sense of justice, and they were far from the only ones to be forced apart by tragedy. What made Heracles so special, that he should demand such a thing?

Yet he'd done things no other mortal could. He'd gone into the Underworld and returned with Cerberus. He'd completed his Labors.

Up above, Iolaus waited for him. For *them*. His family could be united again, and then... and then... go off somewhere alone, like Phineus, like Orpheus, somewhere isolated from the gods so they could finally live together in peace.

"You've suffered so much," Persephone said softly.

Heracles met her gaze. Did she regard him with sympathy? Could she warm Hades's cold heart?

The goddess turned and looked at her husband. "Let us speak for a moment in private."

Hades nodded, and the two of them retired, leaving Heracles alone in the throne room of the god of the dead. What a strange place to be, but then, he'd lived a strange life. Perhaps the same was true for anyone connected to the gods, whether by blood or by circumstance. Soon Adonis would be arriving for his stay in the Underworld, after all.

Heracles thought back to the strange sensation when he left Olympus after meeting with him. Who had watched him and Iolaus depart? Was it Aphrodite and Adonis, observing his progress and wishing him well? Was it Zeus, hoping to catch a glimpse of his son? Or was it Hera, thinking upon her revenge?

The door opened again and pulled Heracles from his uneasy pondering. Hades and Persephone returned to their thrones.

"I have decided," Hades said, "to offer you a deal."

" I HAVE DECIDED TO OFFER YOU A DEAL. "

Good. It would likely be similar to what Orpheus faced. Heracles would remain strong and keep Orpheus's tragedy in mind. Whatever challenge Hades posed, he would overcome it if it meant even the slightest chance of being reunited with his family.

"Following their deaths, your wife and children were rewarded with a place in the Elysian Fields. You must travel there yourself. After you have met with them, it will be your choice as to whether you want to remain with them, take them with you, or depart alone."

He frowned. "That's it?"

"That's it," Hades said.

No conditions, no catch, no rules he had to obey? Did the god believe Heracles would change his mind once he got to the Elysian Fields? Perhaps upon seeing their happiness there, he wouldn't want to take them back to the cruelty of the world? Yet he'd also been given the option to remain. One way or another, they would be reunited forever.

How could this possibly be the deal Hades offered? Even if Persephone had spoken on his behalf, there had to be something more to it.

"How will I get there?" he asked. "I didn't think it was possible for the living to enter the Elysian Fields."

Hades raised his hand, and a door appeared on the wall behind his throne where before there had been only a smooth wall. "We must go there from time to time. Since you are the son of Zeus, the pathway will open for you."

Cautious, Heracles approached the door. It opened onto darkness, yet from the other end of the vast tunnel, a gentle breeze brought the soft scent of flowers. Elysium. The Elysian Fields.

He paused at the threshold. "I can walk through this hall to reach the Elysian Fields, where I will meet Megara and our children, and then I can decide to either bring them back through this doorway and then into the mortal world, or remain there with them?"

"That is correct," Hades said. "Or the third option, leaving the Underworld alone."

"If I bring them with me, we will be free to leave the Underworld together? They will be restored to life and truly live again?"

Hades seemed almost amused by his questioning. "Yes."

Strange. It sounded too good to be true. Heracles looked into the darkness. There must be something significant about the method of passage. "What is this hall?"

It was Persephone who answered. "It is a hall of memories. As you walk toward Elysium, you will re-live prominent memories from your life. It only troubles the living, so do not worry about it hurting your family if you choose to take them with you."

A hall of memories? Something in her voice caught his attention. She was the one who had suggested this, he was certain of it. Was this the test? Make him re-live his memories to see if he changed his mind?

Memories. They haunted him anyway. Persephone's hall would have no power over him.

Heracles stepped through the doorway.

Heracles and his brother were asleep, not even a year old. A sudden sound woke him from his slumber, and he blinked around in confusion at the dark room. It wasn't their mother, it wasn't their nurse, it wasn't any of the people who brought them toys...

At the center of the room, two massive blue-scaled snakes uncoiled and slithered toward them. Vicious fangs glinted as they opened their jaws wide.

Beside him, Iphicles woke up and started crying. He tried to crawl away, but the snakes were faster. They lunged forward to strike.

Heracles darted in front of him. Whatever these things were, they were making his brother cry. That meant they were bad. He grabbed the attacking snakes, one in each hand, and pulled them away from Iphicles. They struggled and tried to bite, but he squeezed tighter to make them stop.

At last, they stopped moving.

The creatures had become little more than ropes in his hands, limp and harmless, but Iphicles was still bawling.

Heracles waved the snakes in the air to show Iphicles they weren't scary anymore. He played with them like toys until his brother finally laughed.

When their nurse entered the room and saw him playing with the dead snakes, she screamed. She took the snakes away from him, and everyone in the house seemed upset, but Heracles had protected his brother, so it all worked out quite well.

"Heracles," his mother said, "would you come here for a moment? We need to speak with you."

Heracles left his work and entered the room where his parents sat waiting for him. Strangely, Iphicles wasn't present and they made no move to call him. This conversation must be about him alone.

He sat down and waited for what was to come.

His parents exchanged glances, and then his father cleared his throat. "Heracles, I've raised you as my son. I consider you my son, and I love you as though you truly are. However, I am not actually your father."

Baffled, Heracles couldn't even respond. What would make his father say such a thing?

"Iphicles is your half-brother, despite being your twin. It's rare, but it happens, especially when the gods are involved."

The gods?

"Your real father is Zeus."

He stared at his parents—or rather, his mother and her husband, if what they said was true. His actual father was *Zeus*? He was the son of a god, and not just any but the king of the gods himself?

His father—no, Amphitryon—met his gaze, his face creased with concern. "We're telling you this now because you're in danger."

"Do you remember the serpents that attempted to kill you and Iphicles?" his mother asked. "You were very young at the time."

Heracles managed a nod. The incident seemed so strange when he looked back on it, an infant killing two monsters, but at the time it had felt normal. Maybe his heritage explained how he did that, why he always was capable of feats beyond others his age.

"Those creatures were sent by Hera to kill you."

"To kill me? Why would the queen of the gods want to kill me?"

They exchanged glances again. After a short period of silence, his mother said, "Hera is a jealous goddess, as well as the goddess of marriage, so she hates her husband's... affairs. You are the target of her hatred. She will try to destroy you."

A chill crept across his skin. This explained many of the incidents that happened to him as a child. For a while, he and Iphicles assumed he simply had bad luck or a habit of finding trouble. It was more than that after all. Because he was Zeus's illegitimate son, Hera wanted him dead.

"We renamed you Heracles," his mother said, "in her honor. But it wasn't enough to appease her. Sometimes I wonder if she took it as a further insult."

Heracles sighed. Well, he'd hoped for an exciting life and dreamed of glory. Surely he would get that, with a goddess out for his blood. Nevertheless, his mother's next words made his stomach twist with dread.

"We want you to be prepared, because Hera will never let you live in peace."

†††

Heracles sat by the fire, resting after a long day. He enjoyed his life of glory, but there were times when he wanted something different. Yes, it would be nice to live quietly like this with his family.

Yet the world was dangerous. It needed heroes to protect the innocent.

One day, his sons would join him. They were growing up to be fine young men, all three of them, Therimachus, Creontiades, and Deicoon. He wasn't sure if they would all be warriors, but whatever path they chose, Heracles would help them in any way he could.

As he relaxed, the back of his neck prickled. Heracles rose and turned toward the door.

Shouts came from the other side, distant and muffled. He moved as if in a daze, hand on his sword. Something was wrong. Then adrenaline surged through him. Megara! The children! He had to find them and protect them.

Heracles burst into the outer room and came face-to-face with a soldier. He didn't recognize the style of armor, but the soldier ran at him with a cry. Heracles grabbed him. No mortal could stand up to the strength of the son of Zeus. He snapped the man's neck and tossed his broken body against the wall.

Someone yelled. He turned and saw two more soldiers. What were they doing in his house? Where was his family?

Fear crept through him. This was another attack. Hera couldn't let him live in peace, and so she'd sent these men to attack his wife and children. Or perhaps to take them away.

He lunged forward and grabbed one of the remaining soldiers. "Where are they?"

"Who?"

"Don't play games with me!" He slammed the man against the wall. "Tell me where they are!"

The third soldier tackled him from the side. Heracles turned toward him with a bellow of rage. No one would hurt his family and get away with it. He'd defeated countless foes stronger than these. Hera must be losing her touch, to send such weak soldiers after him. The others couldn't have gotten far.

Heracles dispatched the two soldiers with ease and then raced out of the house. His gaze fell upon a woman standing in the yard.

The goddess Hera.

He lunged for her. "Where are they?"

"What are you doing?" she shouted.

She'd caused him so much pain and suffering, but this time she'd gone too far. He grabbed her. "Tell me where they are! If you don't, I'll—"

"Who?" She twisted ineffectually in an attempt to free herself. "I don't know what you're talking about! Have you gone mad?"

To be taunted by the author of his miseries on top of everything else was too much for him to bear. His blood boiled. Let the wrath of the gods be on him, but Hera would never trouble his family again.

He snapped the goddess's neck and let her body fall to the ground.

Then he hurried to the edge of the yard. There must be footprints or some other sign of the soldiers' passage. He'd go to the ends of the Earth to find his family if necessary. Yet there was nothing, not a single clue to point him in the right direction.

Laughter rang out above him.

Heracles jerked his head up. Nothing. Yet a wave of dizziness swept through him. The laughter had sounded like Hera, but that was impossible. He rubbed his face to clear the sudden haze over his thoughts. Exhausted as though from a huge undertaking, he turned around.

Megara's body lay in the grass.

With a cry, he ran to her. He dropped into a crouch and lifted her into his arms, but it was too late. Her neck had been broken. Just like...

No.

It couldn't be.

Cold dread seized him, and he raced into the house. Where he'd felled the enemy soldiers, three bodies lay on the floor: Therimachus, Creontiades, and Deicoon.

With the evidence in front of him, he could see what had truly happened in the battle. Therimachus had run to greet his father, but Heracles struck him down. Creontiades cried out in shock, and Heracles attacked him next. Deicoon fought bravely to try to save his brother, only for both of them to be killed.

All three boys, murdered by their father, then joined by their mother when he left the house.

Heracles sank to his knees. His family lay dead by his own hand. He didn't have to question why. Only one person hated him enough to do this. Hera had inflicted him with madness to make him see them as enemies.

But even if blame lay with her, he was the one who had killed them.

✝✝✝

Aphrodite laughed as Heracles explained his situation. "There are two dangers in life you should always beware of incurring: a woman's jealousy and a god's hatred." She smirked. "Hatred born of a goddess's jealousy is something to be feared indeed. If you think you're 'free,' you need to remember how you ended up in this position."

He was free of Eurystheus, but perhaps not of Hera.

✝✝✝

"He's cursed!" the sailors shouted, as the unexpected storm tossed their ship into the waves and sea monsters surged forward to attack.

✝✝✝

"The gods have touched you in many ways," Phineus said. "I see tragedy in your future. Tragedy will haunt you and those connected to you. It will stalk your footsteps and follow you everywhere."

"Haven't I suffered enough?" Heracles asked.

"Some would think so. Others would not."

✝✝✝

"Be careful," Orpheus said. "Even if you escape the snare I fell into, you might learn the Fates have a dark path planned for you."

His mournful music haunted Heracles and Iolaus as they walked back to their chariot.

✝✝✝

Heracles stumbled forward into sunlight. Disoriented, he blinked. Was this another memory? No, he'd never been here before. Green grass extended as far as he could see, fields and meadows filled with flowers. The sun shone from a clear blue sky, and a gentle breeze ruffled his hair. It was like all the world's beauty had been gathered into a single place.

The Elysian Fields, the final resting place for those who lived truly good lives.

He took a single step. The terrible memories that had bombarded him only moments ago felt like they belonged to another time. Here, only peace and happiness existed.

All he had to do was find his family. He would bring them back into the mortal world so they could live their lives together as they should have... or he would stay in this peace with them. They would never be separated again.

Motion caught his eye, and he drew a sharp breath.

A woman walked toward him across the grass. Twelve years had passed since that terrible day, but Heracles would recognize Megara anywhere. She was as beautiful as the day they met, the day her father offered him her hand as thanks for his defense of Thebes.

Behind her, three smaller figures followed. Therimachus, Creontiades, and Deicoon. Pride in his little future heroes rose up in Heracles just as it had when they were alive.

The memory of four bodies lying on the ground made him flinch. What would they say to him? He'd found atonement as far as the gods were concerned, but as for his family...

Megara stopped in front of him. "Heracles."

He dropped to his knees. On that day, he should have known something was wrong even through his madness, should have realized those soldiers didn't act like enemies. "My love, I'm sorry... I'm so sorry... Can you ever forgive me?"

She took his hands and pulled him to his feet. "What you did was not your fault."

"But I'm still the one who..." Heracles shook his head. "Please, forgive me."

"I forgave you long ago."

He looked past her to the children. "My sons... I was always so proud of you. Even when you had to fight me, you were so brave."

They ran to him, and as Heracles stood in the grass of the Elysian Fields surrounded by his family, it was as if no time had passed at all. He held them close and shut his eyes.

"You're alive," Megara said suddenly, her voice filled with surprise. "You're here, yet you aren't dead."

"Hades granted me permission to come."

"To visit us?" she asked.

"I came to—" But even as he began to speak the words he'd held in his heart for so long, he hesitated.

The memories from his journey through the door flashed through his mind again. Hera, in her jealousy, had stalked him ever since his birth. She wanted nothing more than to make him suffer, and she continued to watch. Aphrodite and the others were correct. His tragic path had not ended just because he completed his Labors. If he brought Megara and their children back to the mortal world, it would only be a matter of time before Hera found a new way to torment them.

He couldn't bring them back only for them to suffer.

"Heracles?" Megara asked.

Persephone hadn't made him walk through the hall of memories to *hurt* him, but because their clarity would make him remember what was at stake. It was not a challenge, but a warning. Bringing his family out of the Underworld would end in pain.

"I came to stay with you," he said instead. "Hades and Persephone will allow it. I can stay here in the Elysian Fields with you forever if I choose to do so."

"Are you done with your life as a hero?"

He almost laughed. Years ago, as a young man, he thought the life of a great hero who performed glorious deeds was what he truly wanted. That was before he'd known those brief quiet times with his family. If he could have them back and stay with them in the Elysian Fields, he would give up his glory in a heartbeat.

"You've helped so many people." Megara looked into his eyes and smiled. "I don't know what would have become of Thebes if you weren't there for us."

Those days were over. Let someone else take on the mantle of hero for a while. The gods turned a blind eye to injustice and only intervened when it served their own petty desires. No one on Olympus had stopped Hera, not even Zeus.

How could he return to a world where such cruelty went unpunished? Even if the gods condoned Hera's desire for revenge against Zeus's children, they should have at least ensured she restricted her revenge to him alone.

She'd gone after Megara and the boys not because of anything they did, but only because…

Because Heracles cared about them.

Despite the warm sunlight, his blood ran cold.

"Is something wrong?" Megara asked.

Hera targeted the people close to him, the people he cared about.

"Heracles? What is it?"

"She wouldn't," he said under his breath, more to himself than to Megara. "If I stay here, she won't have any reason to hurt me anymore."

"Heracles?" Megara looked at him with concern.

Terror flooded him. His life included more than just Megara and their children. If Hera persisted in her revenge even with him in the Underworld…

"This route must be cursed," Iolaus said. *"No wonder Phineus doesn't get visitors often."*

The old seer had predicted tragedy both for Heracles… and for those connected to him.

"Persephone!" Heracles stepped away from his family and raised his voice. "Persephone, I must speak with you!"

The doorway to the hall of memories rippled, and the queen of the dead emerged into the Elysian Fields. His sons greeted her with happy cries, and it warmed his heart to see she was loved by her subjects.

But he had no time to dwell on it. "You can see events in the mortal world, can't you?"

"I can," she said. "If you remain here, however, that will not be knowledge for you to have."

"There's only one thing I need to know." He took a deep breath. "My nephew and charioteer, Iolaus. Is he all right? Will you send word to him that I've decided to remain behind?"

Even if Iolaus wasn't in danger, Heracles hated to think of him waiting and waiting only for Heracles never to return.

Persephone closed her eyes for a moment. Then she gave him a sad smile.

His heart leaped into his throat. "What are you looking at me like that for?"

"You may be able to speak to him yourself soon enough."

"What?"

"At this moment, Iolaus fights a band of warriors. They are normally honorable men, but their minds have been poisoned by a strange madness.

Blind to the nature of their foe, they see Iolaus as a dangerous enemy."

Heracles clenched his fists. "Hera is responsible for this, isn't she?"

"That, I cannot say."

"Help him!"

"We do not interfere in mortal lives."

His shoulders slumped. "Did you know this would happen?"

Persephone met his gaze. "No. I knew you needed to relive your memories, to be reminded of the tragedies you've faced, but I didn't know your nephew would be in danger."

He should have given Iolaus instructions to leave once a certain amount of time passed... but Hera might have stalked him anyway, knowing he was one of the last remaining people Heracles loved.

"If it's any consolation," Persephone said, "your charioteer has lived a good life. He will be admitted into the Elysian Fields." She turned to leave.

"Wait!"

She stopped.

Heracles shook his head. "He's going to die because of me. I can't—I can't allow that. That's not what a hero would do. I'm not the sort of man who can stand by and let him die!"

Persephone pointed toward the door. "The option to leave still remains, but once you make this choice, you will never be able to change your mind. You can't dwell among both the living and the dead."

Heracles looked at Megara, who had listened to the entire exchange in solemn silence. He looked at Therimachus, Creontiades, and Deicoon, with whom he'd had so little time. He thought about Iolaus and everyone in the mortal world who needed the help of a hero.

He could do so many good things if he chose life.

Megara reached out and clasped his hands. "We'll see you again when it's your time to join us, Heracles."

"I don't want to leave you," he whispered.

"There are people who need you now. We'll be waiting."

He embraced her, then crouched and embraced each of his three sons in turn. He clung to them, hating this goodbye even as he thanked the gods for letting him see his family one last time. At last he straightened and took a deep breath. "One day, I'll return to you."

Then he sprinted for the door.

✝✝✝

Heracles burst into the land of the living and veered toward the distant sounds of combat without breaking stride. Soon the battle came into view, his faithful charioteer fighting off a band of armed men.

With a roar, Heracles leaped into the fray and slammed one warrior away from Iolaus, then spun around to knock another back with his shield.

"Heracles?" Iolaus sounded shocked. "Where are—"

"Later." He drew his sword. "We have a battle to finish."

Back to back, they fought their enemies. As the maddened warriors fell, a sense of peace came over Heracles. His days would still be filled with conflict and hardship, and he undoubtedly had a dark path ahead, but this was the life of a hero. Someday, death would take him and he would be reunited with his family in the Underworld, but that time hadn't come yet.

Until then, he would fight.

THE END

Travels With Heracles

When people talk about Heracles, they often forget how tragic his story is. They talk about his strength, Labors, and quests—and overlook the part where Hera inflicted him with madness and he killed his own family.

It's easy to focus on the adventures of Heracles, but the tragic side is a key part of that Greek mythology feel.

Having written one pulp fiction story already, I had already decided I wanted to try my hand at pulp mythology. I always enjoyed reading Greek mythology, and last year I had it on my mind even more than usual after my marathon through a certain Greek mythology-inspired video game series.

With all of that in mind, I decided to write a story about Heracles that would set him on a new adventure without ignoring the tragedy in his past.

From there, all of the pieces started to fall together. I wanted to include the death of his family, so what if he was searching for a way to reunite with them? I needed to send him on a journey, so what if he went to get advice from Orpheus? There had to be a spark for his quest, so what if the story began in the Underworld during his fight with Cerberus? Piece by piece, these elements set up several mini-adventures along the way of the larger story.

I spent a lot of time reading myths, looking at maps, and trying to figure out the path Heracles would take, but it all worked out quite well in the end.

At first I considered having Heracles travel alone, but I changed my mind and added his nephew and charioteer, Iolaus. Now, when you start looking into mythology, one thing quickly becomes clear: there are a lot of different versions of these stories. For example, one version of Heracles's madness has him only kill his sons, while Megara survives and ends up marrying Iolaus. Sometimes Iolaus is Heracles's lover in addition to being his nephew. I had to pick and choose which myths I wanted to adapt, and those are two versions I decided wouldn't be right for this story.

So I had Heracles and Iolaus—and then I realized Cerberus could accompany them. I've always had a soft spot for the Underworld characters, and sending Cerberus on the journey was an opportunity I couldn't ignore. Not only did it give Heracles a clear reason to return to the Underworld, but having the three-headed dog eventually become his ally was one of my favorite parts to write.

After all this, I finally had a completed story. Two beta readers (who both approvingly referred to Cerberus as a giant puppy) helped me fix it up from there, and I thank them for their help. Then it was time to think of a title.

Fortunately, I knew exactly what I wanted to call it: "The Thirteenth Labor of Heracles"!

...until I looked that up to see if it had already been used and learned it was the unofficial name given to the myth where Heracles is challenged to have sex with 50 women in one night. Oh. Well then. Referencing that even indirectly would be a *bit* out of place in this story of Heracles trying to reunite with his first wife and their children.

With some help from friends, therefore, I finally decided on "The Lost Quest of Heracles."

As I mentioned earlier, I love mythology, and writing about Heracles was a lot of fun. I wouldn't mind returning to the world of pulp mythology again—with another adventure worthy of these mighty heroes.

†††

SAMANTHA LIENHARD—has been writing for most of her life, especially in the fantasy and horror genres. She graduated from Mansfield University with a B.A. in English and a minor in Creative Writing, and then from Seton Hill University with an M.F.A. in Writing Popular Fiction. When she isn't writing, she can usually be found playing video games. Her publications include a comedy novella called *The Zombie Mishap*, a Lovecraftian horror novella called *The Book at Dernier*, a Lovecraftian horror novelette called *It Came Back*, the pulp fiction story "The Domino Lady Takes the Case," and several short horror stories. She also writes for video games and has worked on the scripts for several indie titles, including *Ascendant Hearts*, *The Trials of Olympus III*, *Two Till Midnight*, and *Eternal Radiance*.

Information about all of her work can be found at her website: http://www.samanthalienhard.com

Grandmother's War

BY MICHAEL PANUSH

It is my duty to keep Grandmother's house clean. I wipe the floors with lye and pick up the bones of unfortunate travelers from under her table, saving them for her broth. Once that is done, I scrub the counters of her kitchen, picking up scraps of strange herbs that will make a man sleep forever or always tell the truth, Grandmother uses these to brew her tea. Then comes the parlor. I use a duster made with raven feathers to clean the silken cushions on which she reclines during the day, and pick up the flakes fallen from mummified dead creatures that dangle from the ceiling. When that is finally done, my bones ache and my little scraggly beard is filthy. If a flake of dried skin looked good, I might chew on it.

Because my job is not yet done.

"Dmitry!" Grandmother yells when sees me being slow. "You have grown lazy. What good is a lazy domovoi, eh? I tell you—a lazy domovoi is good for soup. You don't want to be soup, get moving." She'll flash her fangs, which shine ivory bright in a sea of wrinkles below a nose like a sea cucumber. "My yard—is it to be fit only for the hogs to dwell? Is my house to squat in filth, like a hog in the mire? Well?"

"No, Grandmother." I curl myself up and clasp my hands.

The Baba Yaga will then grab something nearby. Perhaps a bowl still sloshing with sauce, or a puppet she had been crafting with sad, glass eyes that followed you around the room. She'll hurl that at me. "Then move your bones, slack-jaws!"

"Yes, Grandmother!" And I'll dash to the door.

Would she turn me into soup? Perhaps. But more likely, there will be no milk in my bowl or black bread on my plate. So outside I must go, with a pail and bucket of water. To polish the skulls.

They stand on the fence posts surrounding Baba Yaga's house. Each skull has fire in its eyes, glowing brighter as the sky darkens. They stare into the ancient forest surrounding the house, their gaze lost amongst boughs like pillars where the cold mist clings. Sometimes, their jaws open and close, snapping hungrily as I work the rag and the water over ancient, cracked bones. They speak to me too, whispering for mercy or cursing me or just wondering how they came to stand sentinel forever, outside Baba Yaga's chicken-legged house. But I never answer. I just wet the rag, drag it over the bone, and move on.

A domovoi always has more chores to do.

That's what I was doing, washing the skulls, when the *muzhiks* came.

My feet clasped the fence post, and I curled up over my work, the rag clutched in both hands, going up and down the skull like a mother cat's tongue as it cleaned the kittens. The trees outside the grove rustled and I smelled them— the heavy scent of dirt and loam, the musk of unwashed farm animals. About a dozen peasants, coming out of the trees and entering the clearing where the house presently rested. The hot, sour stench of fear—that clung to them too.

They wore their finest garments. White cloth, embroidered with delicate flowers, and greatcoats trimmed with fox or wolf fur. The kind of clothing they would wear to festivals once a year, when the work of a serf ended for the span of a day, or when they went to petition the lord for something.

Now, perhaps they were going to see the Grandmother.

They clustered together at the edge of the fence post, in the gaze of the skulls. Mist pooling around their mouths. Unsure of what to do, and huddled together like sheep when the wolf is close.

I scrambled down from the skull and drew myself to my full height— about the size of the ten-year-old girl, her hair in intricate blonde braids, who had accompanied them. Though my pointed ears made me a little taller than her.

"Do you wish to see her?" I asked.

The leader of these peasants, a barrel-chested man with a beard like a bramble bush, held his cloth cap in his huge, knotted hands. "Please, domovoi." He managed. "We have come from the nearby village. We beg to see her—to ask a boon of the Baba Yaga."

This was most unusual. Usually, Grandmother's guests were desperate runaways. Orphans, cast out by cruel stepmothers to starve in the wood. They wandered to her chicken-legged house and she would bring them in, and maybe greet them with kindness—or maybe boil their bones in her soup. But this? A whole party of *muzhiks*, resembling a herd of harried deer?

"Oh." I bowed my head. "Well. I'll fetch her, then."

But the door to the hut opened first. Grandmother knew. She always knew.

The knees of the great chicken-legs bent down, the claws digging into the gray earth for better purchase as a little ramp—like a ship's gangplank—crashed down. Then Baba Yaga emerged. Waddling her way down the ramp with a twinkle in her eye. The sunlight shone on the gold worked into her dress and jerkin, the jeweled rings set in the wrinkled and gnarled fingers that ended in claws. Those, and her sharp teeth, told the world that she was more than a babushka. She walked down, slow as a rising sun, making a show of bowing and curtseying to her guests, giving them a wave with both hands. The chicken legs extended behind her, the house going tall and covering her in shadow.

Grandmother liked drama.

"Yes?" She rested her hand on a skull. Its lower jaw opened and closed. "You have come to seek an audience with the Baba Yaga. Now, you have it. What is it you want, little man?" Even though the bearded peasant towered over her.

He looked to the other *muzhiks* for support. "We need your help."

"My help, little one?" She puckered her lips, brimming over with false sincerity. "Why do you ask me for help?" Next to her, the skull tried to say something. Baba Yaga slammed its jaw shut, silencing it. "Is it the crops? They do not grow. Or maybe there are too many wolves. They eat your sheep and goats. Is that it?"

"No, grandmother." The peasant closed his eyes, shaking and terrified. "It is—it is—" His face had gone the color of a bruise—he could hardly manage the words.

"Out with it, you slack-tongued oaf, or I'll skin you right here!"

"The Knights!" A peasant woman, her reddish hair in a single braid, shouted the answer.

"Knights? Like the bogatyrs?" She licked her thin, bloodless lips. "They've tried to collect my head now and then. A hag's head would be a fine trophy for a knight errant. I use their armor as washbowls and their swords to clean my toenails." She patted the skull. "And their heads…"

"No, grandmother," the bearded *muzhik* explained. "Not those knights. New knights, from the west. Germans—Prussians." He shuddered. "Teutonic Knights."

Teutonic Knights? I knew there were lands west of here. A great many lands. But they might as well be on the surface of the moon. A domovoi's place was in the home. But if those Teutonic Knights had come here? That might mean trouble.

"Prussians?" Baba Yaga cupped her chin in thought. "I've seen Germans before. Wearing stinking furs and farting loudly."

"Not like these," the *muzhik* shuddered. "They ride from the West, with hatred in their heart and strong iron blades in their hands. They say that we are not Christians—and in truth, some amongst us still worship the old gods and the old ways. Perun with his lightning, and the spirits in the trees. But these Teutonic Knights believe that all of us are damned, and their Pope has commanded them to deliver us from the devil—with fire and sword." He sighed. "They have declared against us a crusade."

"Is that it?" Baba Yaga asked.

"Their leader, their Grand Master—Grand Master Gustav Von Greisbach. As cruel as he is strong. His men surround the village. They charge in, clad in iron, and crush the defenses, and then—and then…" He trailed off. We could imagine what these murderers would do.

I shuddered. A domovoi keeps the house safe. Anything that destroys that safety was too terrible to contemplate.

Baba Yaga listened carefully. "You have warriors. Do they not have swords? Russia has seen invaders in the past. I remember when the Northmen came here, and now their children and their children's children live amongst us. And there are the Magyars, and the Huns, and the Tartars, and so many more. Let Russia deal with her enemies."

"We have gone to the boyars for help. They argue and feud with each other. And these Teutonic Knights—they make war differently than the others. They fight like they are clockwork machines. They do not raid—they charge in and stay, and burn whole villages to the ground. Butchering everyone or herding them away as slaves. They are clad in armor, and tear their way through our ranks. Already, the lands of the Poles have fallen—we are next." He clasped his hands. "I beg you, Baba Yaga—we need your help. You are the greatest sorceress in the woods. You could—could turn them to frogs perhaps. If you could just save us from the Teutons—"

"Perhaps you could lick the crust from my toes, if you so wanted to flatter me." Baba Yaga sneered and folded her spindly, bony arms. "All right, you've asked your question. Here is my answer: no."

"No?" The peasants stared at each other. The bearded fellow bowed his head. "Why?"

"Because you have abandoned me." Baba Yaga's eyes, half-hidden in a sea of wrinkles, burned like embers still alive amongst a pile of ashes. "In the old days, you would leave offerings in the woods. A bowl of dumplings, still warm. Fresh-cut flowers. A little glass of vodka. You would remember and keep me in your hearts. Now?" She spat on the ground. "Feh! You have your churches and your new God. You've forgotten the old ways."

The peasants stared at each other, saying nothing.

"Now these other Christians, who consider themselves different than you, ride across the land, burning and destroy, and you come to me for help? Bah!" She waved a clawed hand at the assemblage. "Go to your churches and your ikons, your painted saints and stained glass. Ask them for help. See where that gets you."

The little girl had been standing near an elder peasant, listening to everything. Just like I was. She peered out and noticed me, before reaching into the pocket of her scarlet embroidered jacket. Perhaps she found me cute. A bedraggled stray pup, lost in the rain. She produced a small wheel of white cheese, wrapped in a handkerchief. Perhaps a snack that she could enjoy later.

Except now, she held it out for me.

A domovoi has but one desire—to get morsels of food. We soak up spilled milk with dirty rags. Pick up spilled crumbs. Catch sneaky mice and wring their necks. All we ask in return is a little bowl of milk, a spare crust of bread. The leftovers. Those morsels sustain us.

But this child was offering me cheese, not because I had cleaned, but out of pure kindness.

I crept out from under the fence and extended my scrawny hand. She set the cheese in my palm.

"Please, little man." She whispered the words, her eye cast nervously at Baba Yaga, who still fulminated with all the rage of an abandoned god at the *muzhiks*. "Take it. You are so skinny. This will help you."

I held the cheese close with both hands. "Thank you." I tucked the cheese into the leather pouch held around my neck by a cord and crept back to the fence.

"Dmitry!" Baba Yaga glared down at me. "Will you grow roots? Are you to be a tree? You have work to do. Go!" Her sharp tongue made me dart back from the fence. Anything to avoid Grandmother's displeasure. I scrambled back over the dirt—but paused and looked back. Baba Yaga now faced the muzhiks a final time. "Why are you still here? Leave an old woman alone."

"Grandmother—" The peasant woman cried.

"Go. The knights can butcher you and the wolves can play with your bones for all I care." She raised her hand. "Must I say it again?"

They departed—clustered together and heading back through the trees. The peasant girl went last. She paused at the back and glanced at me—and raised her hand in a parting wave. I returned the kind gesture.

She had been as scared as any of them. And why wouldn't they be? The people of Russia suffered. From their lords, from rampaging invaders, and, recently, from these cruel knights of the West. It was the way of things. But now, they had perhaps been abandoned by Baba Yaga herself. And that was a true tragedy.

I glanced up at Baba Yaga as she watched the party of peasants depart. "Grandmother, may I ask of you a question?"

"You just have, haven't you?" she demanded. "Out with it, Dmitry!"

I clutched my hands. "If these Teutonic Knights kill them all, who will be left to leave you offerings? To fill their children's hearts with tales of the Baba Yaga?"

She lunged down, grabbed my beard with an iron grip, and tugged me hard. I sprawled onto the ground. "What do you care? And what do I care for them? They've already forgotten me. Go back to your chores, Dmitry. Leave me to my work." She left me lying in the dirt and went back to the house. Once more, the gangplank settled down with a rattle. Baba Yaga stormed her way inside, leaving me alone in the cold yard.

My chores awaited.

Always, after the fence post, were the chicken legs themselves. I took the rag from my belt, crawled over to those giant legs, and went to work—carefully polishing the nails. After that, I'd use my teeth to trim them. Biting down on the hard chitin of the nail, the taste bitter and the sharpness slicing my tongue, and I would chew the edges until they were smooth. Sometimes, the chicken legs would rest peacefully and let me do my job.

Today was not such a time.

I raised the rag to clean. "Easy there—easy—" Making soothing and clucking noise with my tongue. Such as would soothe a chicken.

But the legs were not soothed. They lashed out and the kick sent me into the air. The world rushed around me, the skulls watching with their glowing eyes, until I crashed back into the earth and rolled over—once, and then twice. I came to a rest, whimpering, and sat up. The leg had returned to the earth.

They matched Baba Yaga's moods. Grandmother controlled them— they walked where she wanted them to walk—and when she was agitated, the legs were agitated. So the visit with the peasants had not left her completely uncaring. The talk of their destruction at the hands of the Teutonic Knights bothered her greatly.

She still had a heart, though small and hidden away, like a seed in the very middle of an apple. She still cared.

I sat up and patted my chest. The legs had gone still again, begging me to come close. Probably so they could give me another kick.

"That's the way you want it, huh? Then let your nails be dirty. See if I care."

I settled down on my bony rump and glared at the legs. Then I reached into the pouch and drew out the cheese. My dirty nails pressed into the white flesh of it, digging deep, and I shoved it almost whole into my mouth. A smooth taste, the rich creaminess of it mingled with just enough spice to add bite. I devoured that cheese, plucked the crumbs from by beard, and devoured those too.

The girl who had given it to me. What would become of her? What if the Teutonic Knights fell upon her village this very evening? Or tomorrow? Perhaps she'd receive a merciful end. A sword's swing cutting her down in an instant. Or maybe it would be worse.

And what of all the other innocents, who would suffer under the lash of the Teutonic Knights?

I couldn't stay here and do nothing. Unlike Grandmother, I had never been worshipped with garlands of flowers or prayers told to the trees. A crust of bread. A bowl of milk. That was all a domovoi needed. And the girl had given me a full wheel of cheese.

I had to help.

The left chicken leg tapped on the ground. Impatient. It wanted its nails clean.

"May you grow gray with waiting!" I threw a clod of dirt at it and went into the woods.

The forest surrounding Grandmother's house is a strange place. The trees stretched up to form a ceiling of branches and only thin shafts of sunlight make it through, so that the forest floor is lost in shadow. The wind stirs the trees, and it sounds like they are talking quietly to each other. There are words in the songs of the birds, the howling of wolves, and the growling of bears—to say nothing of the conversations you overhear if you listen carefully to the chatter of squirrels.

Try to find your way from one end to the other and you are certain to be lost. Centuries later, they'll find your skeletons tangled in the roots of a great tree. But if you go in and wander, aimlessly strolling along the twisted paths and ancient groves, then you are sure to find what you're looking for.

This is just what I did, for I am a very smart domovoi.

For perhaps an hour, or maybe two, I wandered. Up above, the sky darkened, and the sun faded away. Silver moonlight crept down, and made the boughs and branches as white as the cheese I had just devoured. I didn't eat a fruit from any branch or a pluck an acorn to gnaw on. This was the Old Forest, and you didn't take of its bounty without leaving an offering for the Leshy.

That's how I found him—getting lost and wandering. I turned a corner around some giant oak and found a clearing, a moonlit glen, where the Old Forest Leshy did his work. He sat on a moss-covered stone wearing a coat of leaves, as big as three bears stacked on top of each other and twice as hairy. His hand stretched out, his stubby fingers—each covered in skin like ridged, knobby bark—twirling in the air.

Below him, delicate tendrils of a sapling stretching out of the earth and reached to the sky.

I was not the only audience. All around the Old Forest Leshy, squirrels played. They danced along the branches. Scrambled up his tangled beard of leaves to scamper over his shoulders and the shaggy crown of his head, and played about his feet. More squirrels than I could count. A squirrel army.

It might be the army that would save Russia.

He looked over his shoulder and acknowledged me a snort. "Master Domovoi." His words like the rustle of the wind through the branches. The Old Forest Leshy offered his hand, the palm open. Big enough for me to stand on. "A long way from your kitchens and bathhouses."

"Bathhouse's are serviced by banniks," I explained. "Completely different creature."

"All right." He had thick eyebrows of moss, and a pair of antlers flanking his head. "What do you want, Dmitry?"

"Have you heard of what has befallen our country?" I waved my hand to the distance, indicating the countryside. "These invaders from the West. These Teutonic Knights."

The Leshy snorted and forest mist drifted from his wrinkled nostrils. "Yes. I have heard. I see them through the eyes of deer and fox and rabbit. Iron men. They carve their way through the heart of Russia, slaughtering all in their path." He waved to the distant trees. "In fact, a camp of them is not far from here. Some of my squirrels have spotted them." He tapped the side of his head. "I think even their leader is with them."

I remembered what the muzhiks had mentioned. "Grand Master Gustav."

"Yes. That is his name."

So, the invading camp was so close. Like an infestation of rats, always perched near the pantry. If there were rats in Grandmother's house, trying to steal our supplies, I would lie in wait close to the hole. When the mouse emerged, my hands would lash out and do the rest. Perhaps this was an opportunity to see these Teutons—and show them a taste of the magic of my homeland?

To send them scurrying west, back to their castles, and leave us in peace.

"I need an army," I said.

"I have squirrels."

"They'll do." I hopped off the Old Forest Leshy's hand and landed nimbly on all-fours. "I'll take a pack of them. Bring them to the camp of the Teutonic Knights and set them loose. When this Grandmaster Gustav sees his men bedeviled by squirrels, he will know that the Gods of this land are against him." I laughed at the thought—it came out high-pitched, like a creaking hinge. "Then they'll run."

More mist from the Leshy's nostril. "You're certain?"

"They are just men. You are the woods. What chance do they have?"

He liked that. The forest always approved of flattery.

The Old Forest Leshy came to his feet and called to the squirrels—speaking in their language. He chattered and clicked, making a squeaking noise before clapping his hands. Instantly, every squirrel in that clearing froze. They went still, apart from the quivering of their noses and whiskers. Their bushy tails prodded the air, their little claws clasped. An army, hearkening to the voice of its commander.

He spoke again, and they sprang up. The squirrels darted onto the trunks of the trees, speeding around them and going to the upper branches. They moved as one.

The Leshy pointed to some direction of the clearing. "That is where you must go. Lead them to battle, Dmitry—and tell me what becomes of it." His directions would be accurate. The Leshy alone could wander these woods without getting lost. If he asked me to go a certain way, it would certainly lead to wherever he wanted me to go.

That's what happened when you got directions from the Lord of the Forest.

"Thank you." I bowed my head. "There will be victory. We'll have our free Russia once more."

"Maybe." He scratched the bark-skin of his mossy face. "Farewell, house spirit."

"Farewell, forest spirit."

I leapt up, grabbing a branch, and pulling myself up. My arms ached as I pulled myself along the branch, the rough edges scraping my thighs,

"THAT IS WHERE YOU MUST GO."

before dropping down and plopping on the forest floor. I took off after the squirrels. Not an easy task. They moved like sets of furry lightning through the woods. Leaping from branch to branch, swirling around the boles of trees, balancing perfectly as they ran over narrow boughs. The most I ran was when I had to prepare the Baba Yaga's meals in the kitchen, and would scurry from the jar bearing her favorite beetles to the stove where fat taken from ravens sizzled and burned.

So, they reached their destination faster than I did. My lean legs slowed as the forest thinned, revealing a wide meadow near the banks of fast-flowing stream. That's where the Teutonic Knights had made their camp, stretched out on brilliant grass studded with winter flowers in a city of starkly black and white tents.

I slowed and sought cover. There, a fallen log half-covered in moss. I scrambled behind it and hid there. The squirrels gathered around me. They gathered thickly on the branches, their tails flicking back as they stared out and watched the invaders.

So did I. The Teutonic Knights had arrayed their camp with all the order and geometry of the woven designs on a fine rug. A stockade of sharpened stakes surrounded the camp, and many-turreted tents waited within. All had monochrome coloration, apart from the brilliant flags and banners to various great houses, companies, and lords that fluttered slightly in the breeze. Campfires rested at regular sections, where the men-at-arms leaned on their pikes and halberds and huddled in their white cloaks.

The Knights themselves? Where were they? I scanned the camp, and then I found them. Strolling about in the clear, cold air. Testing the swing of their swords, morningstars, and battleaxes before the mouths of their tents. They wore armor and chainmail, enough to catch the sun and make them gleam. Surcotes and capes as well, all emblazoned with the bold black cross of their order. And their helmets—as fantastic as something that Grandmother would keep in her cupboards. Great milk pails with an array of horns, fins, plumes, and spikes.

So there they were. These men of iron who made war on my home.

Well, we would see how long they lasted when the woods made war on them.

I faced the squirrels, fixing my gaze on a particularly plump gray specimen. "Go. Terrorize them." I pointed and gave him the command.

The squirrel leapt down from the branch and charged out. His fellows followed him. Not obeying my command, but what the Old Forest Leshy had told them to do. I perched on the log and watched the great swarm streaming for the camp.

A moment later, they struck.

They reached one of the sentries first, a lean man with a pointed helmet, and he froze and could barely lower his pike before they swarmed over him. Then they raced past and struck the encampment itself, and the battle was joined.

The squirrels leapt onto the faces and chests of the Teutons, and scratched with their little claws and bit with their little teeth. I leaned out from the log, trying to watch it all. Squirrels crawled their way up pants legs and into sleeves, clawing and squeaking with all their might. They piled their way into tents, ripping at the fabric and gnawing at the strings.

I clapped my hands and yet out another joyous squeak. "Yes! Yes!"

The invaders tried to fight back. Their broadswords hacked down and their pikes stabbed. Little squirrel bodies were cut apart or skewered. Bushy tails flew. I could make out the carnage from my perch. Furred flesh spilled on the grass.

But the bulky armor rendered the knights slow, and the squirrels were fast. Some fell to the blades, but more scampered out of the woods to replace them. They scrambled their way up the armored legs of knights, clambering up breastplates and under hauberks. Gnawing on gambesons to get at the flesh inside. One big knight, a towering man of iron, lost his balance and fell hard, his sword clattering to the ground next to him.

"Gustav!" He called out, bellowing the name of the Grand Master. "Gustav! Aid us!"

Gustav—Grandmaster Gustav Von Greisbach. The lord of these iron men.

Well, let him come and vanish under the squirrel tide. If he perished, maybe the others would lose heart and flee.

The tent flap opened and a knight emerged. Gustav. He had every bit of hair shaved from his head, so it seemed like the head of a huge infant projected up from a suit of dark armor. He wore no surcote, only a cape with the black cross against white. A sword rested on his belt. He walked out, his sabatons crunching on the grass—one falling hard and stomping a squirrel into the earth—and surveyed the carnage.

What would he do? This fearsome warlord who so frightened the *muzhiks*?

Then he reached into his cape and drew out a pouch. He dug into it. Gustav moved calmly, as if he was seeking some spice to add to a dish, and not in the middle of a heated battle between man and squirrel. Then, he drew a feather out of the pouch.

A brilliant red feather, as long as a forefinger. It coursed with light. The orange of a flickering flame, with strands of red running up and down the stalk. It seemed amazing that Gustav could hold the fire in his hands and not be burned. But that was the magic of the feather and the marvelous creature who wore thousands more like it.

"The Firebird." I whispered the word.

How had Gustav gotten the Firebird? Or did he only have a feather? It was a treasure of the Motherland. Baba Yaga had sought it for years and now, here was the Firebird's feather, in the hands of a German invader.

Gustav held the feather to his lips like a child with an orb of dandelion seeds, and blew. Pure flame shot out. Even from where I stood, the heat washed over me and sweat emerged on my limbs.

The fire rushed over the swarm of squirrels. It caught them, the flames catching onto their fur and tails. The squirrels raced away, fire clinging to their bodies. It burned them too fast for them to spread it. Some managed a few steps before they dropped and writhed, their squeaks fading away as they burned. The flame incinerated other squirrels where they stood, leaving nothing but charred skeletons.

"No..." I clasped the side of my head. The Teutonic Knights, wiping away the squirrels of Russia's woods—with the Firebird's feather. It was impossible. But those squirrels still burned, Gustav walked slowly and blowing a few more gusts of fire into their ranks.

Their squeaking vanished a few moments later, replaced only by silence and the flickering of little flames.

These Teutonic Knights—I had underestimated them. They were more than marauders, charging in and destroying everything in a blind fury. The *muzhiks* had spoken truth. They were like machines. Systematic and calculating, with the right strategy and tactics to stop even the forest's attack.

I had to get back. To tell Grandmother about this. She would know what to do.

I leapt down from the log and started back. Then a harsh voice called out in German. They repeated it in a rough Slavic tongue. "What's this? You there—stop!" I'd been spotted. I jumped down, just as a crossbow twanged.

No choice. I threw myself down and the bolt hummed over me and thudded into a tree. I rolled over—ready to run again. Only to see a pointed pike leveled at my face. The pikeman, his face covered with a moustache and beard, loomed over me. If I moved at all, he'd skewer me. His hand lashed out, fixed around my ankle, and he dragged me back through to the meadow.

Dirt rubbed against my beard and my skin. My arms flailed. My teeth chattered. What would become of me now? I glimpsed the faces of the Teutonic Knights, some shaking their heads and others staring in amazement. They spoke in harsh German.

Then a shove put me at the feet of Grandmaster Gustav. I looked into his pitiless face. Up close, scars stood out boldly. He asked a question in German to the pikeman, who answered. Then he knelt beside me, the joints in his armor clicking. "What are you, little one?" He stroked his chin with a gauntlet as he spoke. "Forgive me. The language of Slavs comes not naturally to my tongue. But the customs of the people interest me greatly. So, I ask again—what are you?"

There was no point in lying. Not about this at least. "A domovoi. A house spirit. Dmitry is my name."

"A house spirit." He cracked a sudden smile. "A slave for the slaves." He repeated it in German and a laugh went through the ranks of the knights. "And whose house do you serve, domovoi?"

That, I shouldn't tell him. "You'll see. You'll see soon enough."

"It doesn't matter. I can oversee your interrogation later, at my leisure." He grabbed my wrist with his iron fingers and pulled me to my feet. "For now, you'll go in a cage. We'll take you to Grauheim, my new castle on the borders. Then you will join us for the feast and then we'll talk." He shrugged. "And then I'll feed you to the fire. And the same to everyone else in your savage land."

They dragged me away. A cage awaited—suitable for carrying one of Gustav's hunting hounds. It was a little big for me. They locked me inside, set me on a wagon, and I rumbled off.

Grandmother would know where I was. She knew all. But would she come for me? Callous and cruel as she was, I just didn't know. I'd told myself that she had a heart, but now? I wondered if that was true and if I'd go into the fire after all.

Darkness, for a long time. Mingled with the hum and rumble of wagon wheels against cold earth, and the whickers of horses and muttering of men. Sometime during that journey, I must have fallen asleep, for the creaking of a barbican opening stirred to me wakefulness. Jostling my cage. Then, strong arms hauled me out, placed a leash and collar around my neck, and dragged me into a courtyard surrounded by castle walls, and a grand feast.

This must be Grauheim—Grandmaster Gustav's castle. It certainly looked imposing. A mountain of tan stone, shining in the setting sun. Tables had been laid out in the courtyard, heaving under the weight of roasted pork, platters of capons drizzled in a honeyed sauce, steaming sausage, and stein upon stein of ale and beer. The knights feasted, gnawing at the food, sloshing their steins and spilling over their beards and chins, and servants hastened about with trenchers to aid in the feasting. Some of the knights started a rollicking drinking song and the others joined in, swaying back and forth and hoisting their frothing goblets as they drank and guzzled. All I could think of was the mess they would make.

A great bonfire in the corner of the courtyard provided warmth, and cast dancing faces of the leering, drinking knights. Something burned in the fire. Food for the feast, perhaps?

The man-at-arms, a lean fellow with a down-swept moustache, dragged me through this wild scene on my leash, and brought me to the head of the table where Grandmaster Gustav himself sat. He patted the bench next to him. What was I to do? Sit on the floor like a sullen dog? I scrambled up and sat next to him.

He pushed a plate in front of me. Warm bread and cheese and scraps of roast pork. "Go on." He spoke in my language. "You need your strength. Eat."

I stuffed my mouth and let the juices run down my chin and into my scraggly beard.

Gustav laughed at that. "Hungry, *ja*? You are always hungry, you Slavs. God has starved you. That is why he wants us to win." He raised a stein to his lips. "Look at what God has given to the Teutons, to Germans, and Prussians. All the food we can eat, so we grow big and strong." He dabbed his mouth with a napkin. "I know, I know. The order's dictates demand small meals. Drinking only on special occasions. But we have had a string of victories. What is that but a special occasion? I say we feast!" He hoisted up the stein, to cheers from his men.

I paused in my eating. Another smell from the bonfire. Something else, roasting.

"What's that?" I stared at Dmitry. "That smell?"

"Oh. Yes." Gustav pointed to the fire. "Think about it. You people consort with pagan gods. Even when you call yourselves Christians, it is false. The Holy Father in Rome says otherwise. And what waits for heretics and heathens but the fires and Hell?" He stood, his armor clanking, and motioned to the bonfire in the corner. "So why not give the sinners some hellfire before I give them to the devil?"

That's when I peered into the fire and noticed them. A half dozen poles, set amongst the flames. On each of them, a human burned. Flame coursed along the shapes, roasting them down to the bone, and the smell of burning flesh drifted over the feasting. A few still twitched and shook, but the fire had done its work before I arrived.

Some of the burned bodies seemed terribly small.

I covered my mouth with my hands and shivered. The singing and feasting next to charred corpses—the merriment so close to death—made the cruel scene even worse.

The roast pork lost its flavor. A heaviness rose in my chest, and I pushed the plate aside. It is the job of a house spirit to serve humans, to help them, and receive offerings in return. To see people burned alive—that struck like an icicle into my heart.

"Who—who were they?" I asked.

"It doesn't matter." Gustav shrugged. "Peasants. Pagans. We capture many in our raids. Some we'll use as slaves to build more castles or till our fields. But the Slavs with heart—the ones who cannot be made to obey— we burn as a warning to the others." He shrugged. "God made the Slav to serve. The sooner he learns his place, the better."

"You are a monster." I clicked my teeth. "Clothe yourself in iron, surround yourself with pious words. It changes nothing."

"How strange, to be called a monster by a little troll like you." He gave me an indulgent smile. "And you know, I asked some of my other prisoners about you, and about the local gods of this place. The devils that these heathens worship. And you are quite the conundrum, Dmitry. You're a house spirit. A domovoi. You said so yourself. But the squirrels you attacked us with—the ones I roasted." He grinned a little at that. "Those come from the Leshy. The Lord of the Woods. A friend of yours, perhaps. But not your master."

"Mistress." I glared up at him. "And she'll come for me."

"Oh?" He folded his arms. "Who is she?"

"The Grandmother of all these lands. You feel her in the leaves of the trees in the forest and the bite of cold. She is Russia. She shall come for me."

"Good." He bobbed his head. "I'll feed her to the fire as well." He sprang up, grabbing the chain from my neck and pulled it hard. I fell off the bench, away from the food—and now, I did long for one last bite. "Brethren!" He called to his men, speaking in German. They ceased their raucous singing. Then he switched back to Russian. "I speak in the language of these lands, because I want this one's mistress—this Grandmother—to hear." He tugged hard at the leash. The collar bit into my throat and up I went, going to my tiptoes to avoid choking. "You want this one to live? You want to save your servant? Then make your appearance. Otherwise he goes into the fire. Or into the bellies of my hounds."

Silence.

He looked down at me. "Perhaps she's not coming." He repeated it in German. His knights guffawed, slapping each other's backs and reaching for more beer. But Gustav didn't laugh. I got the feeling he rarely did.

The fire behind us guttered and rushed. It swept up, before settling down. It had to chill those knights as well. Gustav spun around, dropping me to the earth. His hand went to his sword. The laughter vanished from the other knights. They sprang to their feet, many drawing their weapons. Others hastened for the crossbows set in a rack by the castle wall, and swung them to face the skies.

Wind blew hard from the east. The tablecloths and banners fluttered madly. My heart surged. She was coming to save me.

"Grandmother's here!" I shouted.

A strange shape floated down from the sky, dipping low to reach the castle walls. A giant conveyance, bowl shaped and constructed of ancient, carved stone. Baba Yaga perched in the bowl, wind stirring her hair, her sharp teeth shining in the moonlight as she swooped down like some giant falcon. A long pestle, constructed of the same stone, rested in her other hands, and she jabbed that down and stirred the air, steering herself into the courtyard.

She flew over the tables, sending trenchers flying and steins of beer sloshing onto the laps of the knights, then reversed course and spun past the bonfire. Finally, she came to a halt right in front of Grandmaster Gustav—and me.

Silence, amongst the knights. Gustav opened his mouth to speak, but I darted in front of him and reached for her. "Grandmother! You've come for me!"

She glanced at me and sniffed. "Eh? You? No, I didn't come here for you." Her crow's squawk of a voice full of impatience.

"What?" She didn't come to save me. My heart chilled. "But Baba Yaga, if you didn't come to save me, why are you—"

"Shut up, Dmitry." She silenced me with a wave of her hand. Then she clutched the rim of her mortar with a clawed hand and looked at Gustav. "Let the grown-ups talk."

"Baba Yaga." Gustav had drawn his sword, but didn't put it near me. Instead, he let it dangle down. More a prop than a danger. "I've heard about you. The captives we've interrogated are full of stories about the Grandmother in the woods. Tell me, do you really have a chicken-leg house?"

"Oh yes." Baba Yaga gave him an almost sweet smile—a child braggat.

"Fascinating. Truly, the devil has no shortage of wonders he can conjure." Gustav stroked his chin. "And the way you are formed—claws and sharp teeth on an old woman's body—it is such a strange mixture of the normal and the bizarre. I will study you carefully when I take you apart." He nodded toward the crossbowmen. "Because, for all your magic, you forgot about mortal steel. Do you have any reason why I shouldn't give the order and fill you with crossbow bolts?"

She stirred a long, thin finger, a ladle stirring soup. "I'll make the wind blow and turn the bolts back." Wind stirred. Was it her doing? Or not? "Each man who sends a bolt whistling toward me will have it land in his own neck. They'll choke to death on their own blood." Wind made the banners dance and shifted under the tablecloth. She faced the crossbowmen and repeated the words in German, giving them a grin and a cackle.

The crossbowmen shifted. Some lowering their weapons and staring at each other.

Fear—that was how Baba Yaga fought.

Gustav called out to them, perhaps trying to reassure his soldiers. He glared back at her. "Do not try and frighten me, devil. I am a holy warrior, blessed by—"

"'*Do not try and frighten me, devil!*'" Baba Yaga spat his words back at him, in a whining, mocking voice. "'*I am a holy warrior!*' Please. I've heard it all a thousand times. From evil step-mothers and cruel lords to bogatyr knights errant intent on slaying me. Their skulls sit on my fence posts. Maybe yours will end there too." She leaned closer and a tongue like a worm snaked over her lips. "But you are more interesting. You have something I want. The Firebird."

So that was. Grandmother didn't care about me—or she said she didn't, at least. She wanted the Firebird. That creature held immense power. If Baba Yaga had that, she would be the greatest spirit in Russia. Akin to the Gods.

"Aye—I have it. I keep it in my castle." Gustav pointed his sword at her. "It is a creature of immense power. If I had to tell you what I went through to get it, the warriors and monsters I had to slay—well, we'd be here until Christmas. But why would I ever give it to you?"

The Baba Yaga tapped her claws against her cheek in thought. "I could just take it. Kill all of you, have Dmitry clean your bones for my soup, and then put the Firebird in a cage in my chicken-leg house. It would be easy."

Would it? Baba Yaga claimed to have great power, but she had been bested before. Clever children occasionally outwitted her—sometimes, I would give them help—and she'd lost fights with giants and dragons before. Could she last against these many knights? Against a castle? I doubted it. She was bluffing.

Gustav seemed to know it to. "But you're not doing that. Otherwise, we wouldn't be talking."

"What a smart little man you are!" She clicked her teeth. "No, I much prefer to make it interesting. Tell me, Grandmaster Gustav—are you a betting man? Do you enjoy a wager? The roll of the dice?"

"Not particularly."

"Oh—too bad. Well, I have a wager for you. The greatest game of all. A duel." She flashed her hands. "You against me, tomorrow—at dawn. If I win, I'll go back to my chicken-leg house with the Firebird."

Wagering for the Firebird? Baba Yaga wanted it dearly. That was clear. With the Firebird's power, she could have everything. She'd cook the bogatyrs in their armor before they even reached her home. In fact, I feared what she would do. She was so dangerous without the Firebird. With an endless source of that power, what would become of Russia?

Gustav rested his sword in the earth. "What if you lose, Baba Yaga? What do I get?"

"Russia."

By all the Gods! She'd wager away the entire country with this monster in iron for the Firebird.

"Say that again," Gustav said.

"You will have Russia. From the steppes to the forests to the cities. Free to do with what you wish. You'll wipe away the weak boyars and butcher the peasants, or enslave them. If I even survive your victory, you have my word that I'll not stop you." She gave him a brilliant grin. "You'll have your conquest, Grand Master. And all you have to do is beat me in single combat."

He smiled a little at that, making his scars twitch.

"You really think I'd agree to it? The devil never plays fair. He cheats.

You'd have some secret up your sleeve."

"Oh, I fully intend to," Baba Yaga said. "But you can as well. We'll not do any of this 'honorable duel' nonsense. This will be a wizard's duel, in the old style. I'll bring as much as I can to the battle and you can as well. Stuff your sleeves with secrets and may the best witch win."

"And I suppose you'll want me to come alone?"

"No—quite the contrary. Bring your entire army. Summon your mighty host." She made a circle with her long, clawed fingers. "Surround me. In return, I ask only that you let me choose where the battle will be held. And since you'll bring your army with you, that advantage shall matter little. Do you understand?"

Grandmaster Gustav looked at his knights. They bristled with weaponry, just waiting for his command to fall upon Baba Yaga. "Where?"

"Dragon Peak. A day from here." She patted her conveyance. "As the mortar flies."

"Hmmm." Gustav examined his sword, giving it a test swing. "I'll bring blessed steel. I'll cut you apart."

"You'll try."

He spun his blade about a final time, clasped the pommel with its black cross worked into the metal, and returned it to its scabbard. "Then I agree. You've challenged my honor and I'll match that challenge. It is the duty of a knight."

"Wonderful!" Baba Yaga clapped her hands together. Then her eyes fell on me. "Oh, and maybe you can give me Dmitry back. I'll need to sweep up the house now and again."

"What? Oh, certainly." He dropped the leash. "Dawn, then. Dragon Peak."

"Until then, O holy knight." She clasped her hands in mock prayer, before swooping down and extending her pestle. "Come on, Dmitry. Up you go."

Even being back in Grandmother's embrace was better than the Teutonic Knights. I scrambled up the length of the pestle and settled into her vehicle. Then I looked back at Grandmaster Gustav. "My mistress will defeat you. I promised that she would, and she will. You only have to wait."

"She's a Slav. A Slav devil, but a Slav nonetheless." He shrugged. "God made them to lose." Then he glanced at Baba Yaga. "I won't shake your hand, Baba Yaga."

"I'd sooner eat your fingers." She gave him a wave. "Tomorrow."

"Tomorrow." He gave her a courteous bow. "Farewell."

"YOU REALLY THINK I'D AGREE TO IT?"

Baba Yaga jabbed her pestle into the air and the mortar rose rapidly. We zoomed over the parapets and castle walls, passing the fire where the dead prisoners burned. Baba Yaga glanced down from the rim of her flying mortar and looked down at their charred remains, visible now as the fire—starved of human fuel—began to fade. Was that a twitch of her lips? A glimmer of sadness in her eyes? Did grandmother care about that torture and death?

I pointed down. "Innocent people. Peasants mostly. Captured by Grandmaster Gustav and put to the torch."

"Shame." She looked away. "A waste of people. They could have played a part in one of my schemes. Or even ended up jarred in my pantry or in one of my stews. But to burn them up—it is just a waste."

"That's the Grandmaster's way," I said. "Grandmother, how are you going to defeat him? He does have an army, after all."

She sucked her teeth. "You have served me all your life, little Dmitry. You know my ways, better than anyone. Has Baba Yaga ever picked a fight that she could not win?"

It was true. More often than not, Grandmother got her way. Even when fate turned against her, she found some way to get a little of what she wanted. "But, Grandmother, Gustav and the Teutonic Knights will gather an army together. And you saw what he can wield? Swords, maces, crossbows. All the armor of man, blessed by their priests. What we do we have?"

"Foolish domovoi!" She slapped my head, nearly knocking me out of the mortar. "What do we have? We have Russia. And Russia will not let us lose."

"But you bargained all of Russia—"

"Enough of your blathering." She gripped the pestle tight. "Hang on."

She dug it down like an oar, and we gained in speed. We zoomed through the air, the wind rushing around us and making my beard dance. I struggled to hold on. The Baba Yaga had a plan—she always had a plan. That's what I told myself as we zoomed along to some unknown destination before a duel with the masters of knights.

♰♰♰

The rush of air ended and the mortar descended from the sky, into a clearing in the Old Forest—where I had been that very morning. The Old

Forest Leshy wouldn't get lost in the forest, and neither would Baba Yaga. She knew just where to go. There was the same fallen log, covered with moss, and the same leaves scattered about the earth. The Leshy himself still sat at the log, just where I had left him. The trees seemed more like to move than he. Baba Yaga descended on the mortar and I perched on the rim to watch.

The Old Forest Leshy was keening. Making a sobbing, wailing sound and shaking his great antlered head. Muddy stream water burst from his eyes and ran down his face. Grass and flowers grew where it hit the earth. He thrashed a hand down, scouring the soil. Where it landed, saplings pierced the soil and jabbed up toward the heaven. The sound was a terrible one. Like a wild beast stuck in a trap—right before it decides to gnaw off its leg.

All around him, spread out like warriors on their biers, sat the bodies of squirrels. At least a hundred of them, a sea of burnt fur and roasted flesh in the clearing. These were the squirrels that I had led to battle against the Teutonic Knights—and they had all been wiped away. For the Leshy, they were like children.

And he had lost them all.

No wonder he wept.

I clasped my hands, the guilt curdling in my gut. "Master Leshy." I leapt down from the mortar and settled on the ground, and then hurried to the log. "My apologies. A thousand apologies." A whine left my lips as well. "I should have known the Teutons would be ready. This is my doing—"

"No, domovoi. I agreed. I sent them. They followed my command. What do you control, but the soap and water to wash a dirty countertop?" He sighed deeply, the wind of it stirring the branches. "These squirrels. That one, used to gorge himself on acorns. He was as swollen as a bear sleeping for the winter, all the time. And that one? Oh, you would have loved to see her play. Now, they are all gone." He looked at Baba Yaga. His mossy eyebrows swept down as he scowled. "What do you want, Grandmother?"

They weren't friends, the Leshy and Baba Yaga.

"You want to hurt the Teutonic Knights, yes?" she asked. "After what they did to your little friends. Why wouldn't you? Who doesn't love revenge?"

He came to his feet with a grunt. Soil rained down as he stirred and stomped closer to the flying Baba Yaga. "What do you want?" Now, wind rustled through the boughs and branches like Perun had sent one of his storms. But that wasn't it. There was no wind. The trees moved on their own. "You come here, while I am grieving, and talk about vengeance?"

"I am to duel the lord of these knights at dawn, O Leshy." Baba Yaga gave him her best smile, arranging her yellow teeth in a sharp grin. "I need one thing from you, to find victory. I need a seed—a seed that never stops growing." She tapped her forehead with a long nail. "I know you have it. You have no end of wonders in your forest. Give it to me, and I'll give you revenge."

"I want them back!" He roared out the words, and the forest roared with him. Wildcats and bears growled, and packs of wolves howled. Every animal in the woods called at once. Birds lifted into the sky, twittering madly. I covered my ears, and still I could hear the cacophony.

But Baba Yaga only smiled. "If I bring them back, will you give me the seed that will never stop growing?"

Another bargain. That was how Baba Yaga played her games and reeled in her victims. What did she have in mind?

Before I could warn him, the Leshy nodded.

"Good." Baba Yaga walked over to the rows of dead squirrels. "Watch and see."

She breathed in deeply and exhaled. Breath the smell of the grave—of soil and rot—left her lips. It emerged in a green cloud, and swirled and danced in the air over the clearing. Strands of the green cloud drifted down, becoming small, like eddies of water in a whirlpool, and snaked into the little mouths of all the squirrels. It slipped its way into their mouths and the bellies of those that still had flesh on their bodies pushed out with the false breath.

Baba Yaga's magic. The same that kept the skulls on her fence posts alive.

The squirrels stood. Their skeletal, charred bodies rolled over, their burnt, stick-like tails quivering in the air once again. They scampered their way up the trees and into the branches, just as they had when they were alive. Scattering their way through the trees.

But the chatter of squirrels didn't accompany them. Instead, it was the rustle of bones.

The Leshy's eyes went wide. "What have you done?"

"You don't like them?" Baba Yaga batted her eye.

One squirrel, burned completely to the bone, dropped down from a branch and landed on the Leshy's log. It crawled closer to him. He held out his hand. The mandibles drew close for a sniff. Another tear ran down the Leshy's face.

"They're still there," Baba Yaga explained. "Only different."

"Only different," he repeated. "They will find a place in the forest."

"I'm sure of it." She was all business now. "I've kept my end of the bargain. Now, you must keep up yours." She held out her hand.

He snorted and reached a hand past his beard. His stubby fingers jabbed into his flesh. Fragments drifted down like dry soil. He emerged holding a seed the size of an apple. A glistening iridescent swirl to the shell, like those of dragonflies caught in the sunlight. The Old Forest Leshy stared at the seed for a moment, sighed deeply, and dropped it into Baba Yaga's palm.

"Be careful with it."

"Oh, I will." She patted her mortar. "Come on, Dmitry. Time we were on our way."

I scrambled up the side of the mortar, my nails scratching at the polished stone. "Goodbye, Master Leshy." I waved to him. "We fly for vengeance."

He stared at us sadly, as the dead squirrels scampered and played about the clearing. "You fly to give her a victory." He tapped his head. "But I wonder what she'll do, when she gets it?" Fear in his weathered voice.

That was all I could hear before Baba Yaga beat the air with the pestle and sent us flying away. I looked at her wrinkled face, her teeth clenched as the wind blew her hair. No sympathy for the Old Forest Leshy, nor for those peasants. Or at least, none that she wanted to show to me.

"Where to now?" I asked. "You have a seed that will never stop growing. Where to now?"

"Now?" She shouted over the rush of wind. "We go to the water."

"Do you have a plan for defeating Grandmaster Gustav?"

She grinned at me. "I always have a plan, little domovoi."

Then we flew off.

The water was a tributary of the Don, or perhaps the Volga—one of the many great rivers that formed the veins of Russia. We came to a deep bend in the river, where the water ran deep and extended over rocky banks. Baba Yaga slowed the mortar and descended. We settled to a halt at the water's edge. She pushed me out, letting me fall in the mud, and hopped out to join me. The river brought cold, and my bones themselves shivered in my skin.

Across from us, a vodyanoy sat waist-deep in the water watched a Rusalka and her sisters bathing in the water. The fat frog-man had a tangled seaweed beard, which he stroked with a webbed hand as he gazed upon the water spirits. They probably hadn't noticed him—or else his leering ways would be quickly corrected.

Baba Yaga crept up behind him. "Enjoying the view?"

"Eh?" He swirled around, his fat green cheeks going bullfrog-big. "What's it to you?"

She kicked him hard. The vodyanoy gave a croaking gasp before plunging face first in the water. Then his arms lunged out and he frog-stroked away. Baba Yaga raised her voice. "Lady Rusalka! How's the water?"

The biggest of the Rusalkas paused in her bathing. She said something to her sisters and then walked back—strolling on the surface of the water. Ripples extended wherever her feet fell. She had wild, seaweed hair and skin like the polished stones at the bottom of the river. Not much clothing to speak of. She stood in front of us and gave us a wide smile, showing teeth like pearls. But she kept her distance, standing right in the center of the river, where Grandmother could not reach her.

Wary of Baba Yaga, as everyone wise must be.

"Baba Yaga. It is grand to see you." The Rusalka bowed. "What brings you to my waters, Grandmother? Do you wish to bathe?"

"Smell me, child, and ask again how often I bathe." She cackled at her joke. "No, I came to see you. To marvel at your beauty. And to ask for a small favor."

"What would that be?"

Grandmother drew a little bottle, big enough to fill a cup twice over, from her ragged garments. She tossed it to the Rusalka, who nimbly caught the bottle. "Fill this with all the waters in the rivers of Russia." She pointed to the bottle. "Make it so that it will never go empty. If you do that for me, I'll not trouble you again for many years."

The Rusalka drew out the cork and looked at the bottle. "You might as well ask for the sun in the sky."

"Can you get that for me too?"

Baba Yaga always did have a good sense of humor.

"I can fill this bottle so it will never run empty..." The Rusalka swept the bottle low, dragging it through the gray waters. Bubbles rose and she hauled it up. "But you must do something for me in return." She upended the bottle and it drained in moments.

"What do you want?"

"Hmmm." The Rusalka stroked her chin. "What can you give me?"

"Ah! I think I know." Baba Yaga strolled closer, resting her feet in the shallows. The water receded away from her. The Rusalka wanted her at a distance. "What if I brought you sunlight from the depths of this river? What if I took light out of the darkness and showed it to you? Would that be enough of a bargain, my little daughter?"

By now, the other Rusalkas had joined in. They paddled over and floated, paddling to stay in place as they listened.

The Queen of the Rusalkas nodded, keenly interested. "Sunlight from the depths, you say?"

"The very depths."

"Very well." She offered her hand. "I accept your bargain."

"Oh, no need to shake, my darling." Baba Yaga flashed her teeth. "I trust you." She grabbed my arm and hauled me down from the mortar. I had wondered why she brought me along. This must be it. "Dmitry, my faithful servant, I have a task for you. A little trickier than removing tea stains from the parlor. Do you think you could do it?"

Help Baba Yaga? Trepidation rose in me, but my head still bobbed. I was a domovoi. I did what I asked to do. "What do you need, Grandmother?"

She grabbed my scraggly beard, hauled me up, and planted her lips on my mouth. A sloppy kiss, with the sour dust of ages and the acrid, curdled rot of her last meal oozing over my lips. Her spit drifted down, into my throat—along with something else. A rotten taste. A cloud of decay, expanding to fill my lungs and make my chest burst.

I wondered if I would explode.

"Go, Dmitry!" Baba Yaga pulled me back. "Swim!" She hurled me into the center of the river.

I sunk, a dirty stone with death in my throat. The surface vanished above me as I went down. Past reeds and obese fish floating lazily by in the pellucid water. I hurtled past stones as I neared the dark bottom of the river floor. My lungs burned—but my mouth stayed shut. Trapping the decay inside. Somehow, there was no need to breathe. Baba Yaga's magic had done its job.

At the very bottom of the river, a wreck waited. A gaudy river transport, which had sunken sometime in the ancient past, perhaps when Russia styled itself as a third Rome. The banners, decayed and half-vanished, bore the Coat of Arms of the Tsars. Dead men lay sprawled over the wreck, their bones intwined with waving reeds and picked clean by the fish. They lay about the bough and the quarterdeck, wrapped around the mast or lying in the dust by the side of the ship.

What had sunk this vessel? A storm? River pirates? It was hard to say.

I floated closer. Was this part of Baba Yaga's scheme to bring sunlight from the depths? I wasn't sure how it would work.

Then my belly erupted. My mouth opened. The green cloud emerged, bursting out into the water like a fish vacating its bowels. It drifted down, snaking away into a dozen tendrils. They reached into the mouths of the skeletons.

Suddenly, those skeletal sailors sprang into action. Two dead men tugged at the lines and the sail extended. A captain worked the wheel of the boat. It careened to the side, the dust of ages falling away as it lifted up off the river floor. Silt descended in vast clouds. Other skeletons pushed it off from the bottom, and the entire vessel rose toward the surface.

That's when I realized I needed to breathe.

I opened my mouth to gasp. Water streamed in—just before I closed it. Get to the surface—get to the air. But how? I couldn't swim.

The ship. It floated up, rising with sudden speed. I paddled toward it and grabbed onto one of the lines. If the dead crew noticed, they didn't say anything. Bubbles streamed behind me as the ship went further and further up. Floating up like a cork.

My lungs burned. The dark sky drew closer. The shining moon neared us. I held tight. A little more. Just a few seconds more—

The ship erupted from the surface. Water sprayed out as the ship floated in place. I emerged with it, and gasped as I sucked in air. For a while, I just dangled from the rope, breathing in and out, with the river flowing over my waist.

Then I slipped out and paddled my way to the shore. My bones ached. Water soaked my trousers and my beard clung tightly to me. I pulled myself to the shore, river mud sticking to my toes and knees, and collapsed in front of Baba Yaga.

"Grandmother—I did it."

She glanced down at me. "Good. Here—dry yourself off." She dropped a handkerchief on top of me. Then she walked past me and approached the Rusalka. "Well? Where is my bottle? Fill it with all the rivers in Russia, so it will never go empty. You remember."

I wiped off water from my face and rolled over to watch. The Rusalka seemed less than impressed. "You promised me sunlight from the depths, Grandmother. Where is it?"

Baba Yaga laughed. She clapped her hands.

Two skeletons hauled a chest from the hold of the ruined boat. They opened the lid. It fell back to reveal a hoard of gold. Coins, of course, but countless little trinkets as well. Embossed with the seal of the Tsars.

And all gleaming.

"Sunlight from the depths." Baba Yaga pointed to the gold. "As promised."

The Rusalka looked at the gold. "That's not—you promised—" But she caught herself. Bargains were like this, for Baba Yaga and her ilk. The exact words were important. A metaphor could double as the truth. A different kind of logic than what governed the affairs of humans. Baba Yaga had promised the sun from the depths, and shining gold would be close enough. Now, the Rusalka had to obey.

She swept the bottle under the water, filled it, and held it up. She gave it a spin and the water swirled—a miniature whirlpool. "As promised." She tossed it back.

Baba Yaga caught the bottle and tucked it under her coat. "I am grateful to you, Rusalka. The waters always keep their bargain." Then she grabbed me. "And you lazy bones. Come on. We've got other places to go before this night is through." She dragged me back into the mortar, grabbed the pestle, and jabbed it into the air.

We lifted off from the ground, back into the cold sky.

The handkerchief helped a little, but the cold still clung to me. As we zoomed along, water droplets flew from my face and beard. "Did you have to do that?" I demanded. "Throwing me to the bottom of a river? Without even a warning?"

"Are you a coward, little Dmitry?" She slapped my head. "I thought you wanted to protect the people of Russia. Are you afraid of getting a little wet in order to save them?"

I fumed. "To save them? Or help you?"

"We're doing both." She spun the pestle again, sending us zooming to the side. "And you'll need all your courage before we get our next token. Then we go to Dragon Peak, and Grandmaster Gustav. You'll need your courage for that as well."

†††

This time, Baba Yaga took us to a graveyard. We flew over the rows of graves, lost in the shadow, and to the place where the tombs met the woods. We flew low, zooming under the branches of dead trees and through the shadows—until we reached a cave. Standing stones flanked the entrance, covered in ancient carvings. Dead leaves formed a carpet on the ground. In the distance, an owl hooted and a wolf howled.

The only living occupants of this place.

We descended. The mortar spilled us out. Baba Yaga and I walked closer to the cave. Blacker than night within, like the space between the stars. A chill went down my spine. Cold—and not just from the water I'd been drowning in. I shuddered as I looked into the darkness.

"Where—where are we?" I managed.

"An ancient place," Baba Yaga explained. "To see an ancient god." She raised her voice. "Chernobog. God of Darkness. I beseech you."

Two pinpricks of red flashed in the darkness. A shift in the darkness. Then silence, apart from a rush of air. They stirred the dead leaves. Chernobog—the Lord of Night—the Dark One—waited in that cave.

We were not alone in the woods. The *Nav*—the dead—crept out from under the trees. Watching us in silent ranks. Skeletons and rotting corpses. Drekavacs—unbaptized infants, their pale, curdled bodies hunched over. Luminous drool dripping down from their fangs. They hung back, awaiting their master's command.

Even Baba Yaga looked a little scared, her eyes opening. "We seek— your help, Dark One. A little gift, to free our country." She offered her hand. "Nothing valuable, for one like you. We merely want the skull of a dead man that never ceases to talk."

Silence from the cave.

"Of course, I do not come empty handed." She waltzed a little closer to the darkness. "You give me the skull, and in return, I will give you something you can never get. Would you like that, Dark One? A special treat, you bring you comfort as you squat in the night." Around the dead, rustled. Growing impatient. "All for a little skull." She held out her hand, the claws flexing. "Do we have an accord?"

Silence—and then a fluttering mass of bats hurtled their way out and shot into the sky.

"I will count that as a yes." She glanced at me. "Come, Dmitry. I have another task for you." Before I could protest, she grabbed my arm and dragged me to the mortar. Up we went, in the flying machine. It shot into the sky, and zoomed over the graveyard. Below us, the *Nav* watched with hunger in their dead eyes.

We zoomed north, passing back through the graveyard. "What are you going to do this time, Grandmother?" I let a little sourness seep into my words. After what I'd been through that long night, I think I deserved it.

"ARE YOU A COWARD, LITTLE DIMITRI?"

"Send me to the bottom of a river once more?"

"Nothing so difficult." She floated lower, humming over the graveyard, and nearing the village that rested next to it. A small settlement, consisting of a collection of wooden, cottages with thatch in the roof. Nearly lost amongst the forest and early snow. "You just have to climb down to the window and listen." She reached into her pocket and drew out an egg. The kind that would fall out of any chicken. "And hold up this."

With that, she poked a hole in the top of the egg and put it into the leather pouch dangling around my neck.

I stared down from the mortar. We hovered above the biggest building in town: the village church. It loomed tall, bright white with blue onion domes topped by a simple, multi-tiered cross. For a spirit, even a domestic spirit like myself, a church was no place to go. Baba Yaga would certainly not be welcome there. But still, she floated lower and gave me a nudge.

I stared back at her. "You'll really make me do this?"

"For Russia, little Dmitry," she said.

"Or for you." I gripped the edges of the mortar and sighed. She needed this to get Chernobog's talking skull—for whatever reason—and she needed that to defeat the Teutonic Knights. I would have to do it.

I slipped off the mortar and dropped down to the earth. Then I crept closer, one hand around the pouch dangling from my neck. I crossed the earth and arrived at the threshold of the church. The door lay open. Carefully, I poked my head inside.

There they sat—the congregation before the priest in his black robes. They packed the pews. All around them, painted ikons loomed. At the nave, behind the priest, countless more ikons looked out over the audience. Saints with gold halos about their heads. Jesus, and Mary, and all the others that I could not name. My breath fled from my mouth as I looked at them. The bottom of the river seemed preferable to this place.

These were the Gods of the people now. Baba Yaga, the Leshy, Chernobog, the Rusalka—all had been forgotten. We existed in stories alone, told to frighten the children or keep travelers wary during a night's journey through the forest. Banished from hearths to the wild places. And who would now leave a crust of bread or a glass of milk for the domovoi? They would rather pray to this new God.

And yet we remained, hidden away in the shadows and stories of the world.

I had a job to do. I drew the egg out of the pouch and held it up. The firelight of the torch shone on the egg, making the dirty shell gleam. I held it up just as the congregation began to pray. The priest led them. They joined together, old women and young children alike adding their voices to the hymn. It echoed through the church. Everyone singing together, and praising a God that I would never know.

I lowered the eggshell and went back outside. Baba Yaga waited on the mortar. She helped me aboard, her grip slack. Her usual rictus grin had faded away. "You did your job well, Dmitry. I must reward you when we're done."

"That is the future." I looked back at the church as we floated away down the village and back to the graveyard. "And we are the past."

"Oh, there will always be some who remember," Baba Yaga explained. "And there will be the tales and stories. But the days of worship for our kind are done." She sagged in the mortar for a moment, every bit of the cackling forest witch gone. She was just an old woman now, tired and defeated. "Come. Let's go back to Chernobog."

She jabbed the pestle into the air and we floated away. Back over the graveyards, and into darkness. The church shone behind us, light dancing through the windows. A place we could never go and a peace we could never have.

We zoomed through the forest and to the standing stones and the old cave. Baba Yaga halted the mortar with a jab from her pestle, and we disembarked. Once more, the dead loomed around and watched us from their places amongst the trees. Baba Yaga strolled past them and headed straight for the cave. I scampered along with her, clutching the egg. When we got close enough, she pulled the egg out of my hand.

"Chernobog." Baba Yaga held up the egg. "Here you are. Something you will never have: a Christian's prayers." She held the egg closer and let go. The prayers came out, the singing of those peasants in the church. Their chanting echoing through the dark cave. "Give it a listen, perhaps, when you are feeling rageful." She set it next to her boots and gave it a kick. The egg rolled into the dark cave and vanished. "Now, you're end of the bargain." She tapped her foot. "Well?"

Silence.

"Oh, Dark One—are you really going to break your word? We don't have much left, but we still have our words. Don't break a promise to me."

Something rustled in the darkness. A skull, caked with dirt and brown with age, rolled its way out. It rolled to a stop between Baba Yaga's feet. She picked it up, sniffed it, and opened the jaws. Whispers came out. Speaking some dead language that had once existed on the steppes, before vanishing into the dust of history.

Baba Yaga held up the skull like a glass of wine for a toast. "Thank you, Dark One."

No answer at all.

"Come, Dmitry." She tucked the skull under her arm and headed back to the mortar. "We have everything we need. Weaponry enough. Now we go to duel."

We went back into her conveyance and floated skyward. Dawn crept into the distance, the brilliant orange of new flames that marked every sunrise under the big skies of Russia. A few paddles of the pestle sent us zooming back over the countryside, heading for Dragon Peak, where the battle would be fought. We zoomed over the Russian village, their church service having just ended. They didn't know, but we were going to battle to save them.

Maybe there was something just about that.

✝✝✝

True to his word, Grandmaster Gustav had arrived at Dragon Peak—a plateau surrounded by ragged stone marked with snow, and pockmarked by numerous craters and crevices. Gustav had brought his army with him. They had set up an array of tents and formed ranks, their black and white banners fluttering in the dawn breeze. Armored knights stood in a wide circle—the place of the battle—at the center of the plateau. That's where Baba Yaga and I landed. The Teutonic Knights brandished their blades, and their crossbowmen raised their weapons. All ready to attack at a moment's notice.

"Easy." Grandmaster Gustav called some warning in German and his men lowered their weapons. He emerged from their ranks—dressed and prepared for battle. A full suit of armor, polished and shining. A crossbow on his hip, across from a massive broadsword. "You kept your word, Grandmother." Switching to Russian as he buckled a kite shield around his arm. "I was surprised." Two servants came out, bearing a helmet. Gustav knelt and they placed the milk pail helm with its massive horns on his head.

"Don't be." Baba Yaga hopped down. No armaments for her. No fancy preparations. "But did you keep yours?"

Gustav pointed to a birdcage swinging from a pole. There, the Firebird perched. A brilliant creature, big as a peacock. Its every feather pulsed with inner light—the first rays of the sun captured in those wings. It preened as we watched it, the ivory beak darting about those shimmering, glowing feathers and tucking them into place.

"May I pray before battle?" Gustav asked.

"I don't care," Baba Yaga said. "Make it fast."

He did, whispering a few words. Then he stood and drew his sword. "Very well." He walked into the center of the circle. "All right, witch. It is time for me to take your head." Then he charged, the armor surprisingly flexible as he raced for her.

Baba Yaga drew the Leshy's seed from her pocket and hurled it down. The seed slammed into the earth, and sprouted instantly. A tree burst forth, the roots snaking out and soil flying as the trunk and branches burst free. Those branches lunged for Grandmaster Gustav—a mass of punching arms. I held my breath. Would he be finished so soon?

Then his sword slashed down.

He hacked through the branches first, the broadsword cutting apart the wood. Splinters flew with each blow. Gustav took down one branch, and then the other, and then hewed into the trunk itself. It came free and tumbled to the side. He leapt over it and continued his run. Close enough for his sword to reach Grandmother now.

No! Baba Yaga had immense power, it was true. But a blow from a sword like that would still end her. I bit my fingers and whined. My mistress was in danger, and I could do nothing but watch.

She took out the bottle and pulled free the cork. A quick shake and it erupted—sending out a massive spray of water. A river burst free, running from the bottle and crashing into Gustav. He dropped down, nearly submerged. The water ran through his armor and drenched him. It spilled out, knocking over a few of the Teutonic Knights and leaving them to flounder and struggle in the mud. The new river carved its way down the hill. The Firebird, in its cage, squawked loudly and flapped its wings.

This must be Grandmother's plan. She would drown Gustav. His own armor would weigh him down and destroy him.

Gustav lay on the ground, the water spilling around him. Nearly submerged. I went to my hind legs, trying to make out the black metal and cape beneath the torrent. Gustav had dropped his sword. His hand went to his waist and he drew out the crossbow. A small weapon—capable of being used with one hand.

Which is precisely what Gustav did.

The bowstring twanged and the bolt sailed out. Not aiming at Baba Yaga, but at the bottle. The bolt hummed through the air in a gray blur, and struck into the container. It shattered in a burst of water and glass. Gouts of water spilled from the sundered bottle. Baba Yaga gave a yelp as she jumped out of the way of the growing puddle. It spread across the stone, seeped in some of the crevices—and then ended. With the bottle gone, the river would not flow.

"Well done, Baba Yaga!" Gustav pulled himself up. He let the crossbow fall to the ground and retrieved his sword. "Excellent tricks. A tree and water. It's like I am doing battle with the lands of Russia itself. Very apt, I should say."

She hurled the broken bottle at him.

Gustav brought up the kite shield and caught it. Glass shattered and hit the ground. "But that was a poor decision. What weapons do you have now, grandmother?" He walked closer, almost calmly, as his men cheered. My heart thundered. All Baba Yaga had left was the talking skull gifted by Chernobog. What good would that do against Teutonic steel?

Now, Gustav reached her. He swung the sword down, going for a head-lopping strike. Grandmother dodged out of the way. Her claws lashed out, the nails striking against Gustav's armor. They left grooves, carved in the metal—but did not pierce the breastplate.

"Look at that!" Gustav darted back and held up his shield. "Stopped by iron. You see? All the fairy tales and legends in the world mean nothing against steel."

Baba Yaga had moved further back. Now, she held the skull. The jawbone still worked, the whispering voices echoing over the plateau. Several of the Knights made the sign of the cross as the skull yammered.

"Oh, what's this?" Gustav advanced, shield and sword raised. "More sorcery? More witchcraft? More bedtime stories to frighten the children? You don't realize that those worlds are gone. No more monsters in the grove or spirits in the pantry." His eyes, behind his helmet, glanced at me. "Men with swords decide things now." Perhaps that was true. What I had seen in the church showed that, for certain.

But those men with swords were just as cruel as any fairy tale monster.

"They're not all gone." Baba Yaga took a step back. Then, her fingers opened. The talking skull fell from her hand. It dropped right into a crevice below her, and vanished from view. The echoes of its chatter slipped up the hole and vanished somewhere in the earth. Baba Yaga looked back. She grinned fiendishly. "Oops. Clumsy me."

That couldn't be right. She had to have some plan. Grandmother always a plan.

Another step brought Gustav close to her. He hoisted up the broadsword. "I'm going to split your head, devil. Have you a plea? A final prayer before I end you?"

"A question, good knight." She pointed a long finger to the stone floor below her. "Why do you think this place is called Dragon Peak?"

A rumble crept through the earth. A deep, thrumming—like the heartbeat of the world. Pebbles danced in place. The newly made tree swayed. Several of the horses whickered and a single steed bolted and galloped its way to the trail. Anything to escape.

Steam shot up from the crevice where the talking skull had vanished. A talking skull, along with rushing water and a growing tree—all making noise. All sending their echoes deep under the rock,

And waking what slumbered there.

The dragon's head burst free from one crevice, sending stone flying as it emerged roaring in the dawn sun. *Zmei Gorynich*—the great serpent. A long snake-like neck, big as a pillar, with a roaring, reptilian face on end, all in deep crimson scales. The Teutonic Knights stumbled back, reaching for their sabers and spears, as the *Zmei* faced them.

But it wasn't alone. Another dragon's head reared to the surface, ripping through the stone itself. This long neck had a purplish color to the scales, but was topped by the same snarling dragon's head.

Dragons in Russia never had just one head.

Another neck burst out of the earth, and another still. Soon, the seven heads of the *Zmei* had emerged, in a rainbow of scales—and all began to breathe fire. Their columns of flame coursed down, falling upon the Teutonic Knights and their tents and men-at-arms, and roasting everything. Knights burned in their armor, the flames cooking them as they writhed. The heat washed over me, sweat bursting to life on my thin arms. Other dragons lunged down, putting their teeth to work and crunching down metal to get at the cooked flesh within.

"*Nein!*" Gustav ran at Baba Yaga, going for his sword—but she shoved him back, right into a column of flame leaving one of the Zmei's many mouths. Fire raced up his whole body. He wailed as he dropped to his knees.

Grandmother let him burn.

She dashed past him and ran to the birdcage, which she scooped under her arm, and then came dashing back. "Dmitry—what are you waiting around for, dullard? Time to go!"

I hurried after her. Running through that fiery chaos and into the mortar. She gripped the pestle and sent us flying away from the inferno.

The Firebird screeched in its cage, its feathers going fluffy and absurd.

All the power in that magical fowl, now in Grandmother's hands.

Her attention was on the pestle, on getting us away from the fire below. I would have one chance.

Quickly, I reached over and tugged open the birdcage.

The Firebird ripped its way free, spreading its wings and soaring out from the mortar. A brighter shade of red than the fire around us.

"No!" Baba Yaga lunged for it—but her clawed fingers caught only air. The Firebird swooped down, each flap increasing its speed. Even the fastest flying mortar in the world couldn't catch the Firebird now.

It flew away, zooming into the distance and leaving us behind—with just a shimmering orange blur left in the sky.

Baba Yaga slumped in the mortar. "A waste. All of this. A waste."

"But Grandmother, you saved Russia—"

"A waste!" Then her eyes settled on me. "How did it get free?"

I clasped my hands. "I do not know, Grandmother. Perhaps, perhaps the cage was already slightly opened. It may have been jostled when you brought it to the mortar. Just an accident, I'm sure." Was that too much protest? Would she see through my lies? Maybe she'd hurl me off. Let me join the Teutonic Knights baking in dragon fire below us? "Let us go back, yes?"

"Yes." She gripped the pestle. "Back to my chicken-leg home."

✝✝✝

And so, with the battle won and the duel over, we returned. The chicken legs knelt and the gangplank extended, and Baba Yaga returned to her cottage, with her faithful domovoi alongside. She went straight to the kitchen. There, a ribcage of some unfortunate traveler waited. Baba Yaga slammed a fist into it. Bones scattered, their clatter echoing off the walls. The whole house shifted, the chicken legs moving with the blow.

Then Grandmother looked back at me. "The cage was not jostled. The lock did not open by itself."

She knew.

"No, Grandmother." I shuddered. What it would be? The cookpot? Or would she turn me into a frog?

"It could have been mine. That power—in my hands. Who knows what I would do with it." She looked at her clawed fingers. "We can be cruel to ourselves, without outsiders. I think I've proved that plenty of times." Then she sighed, and became the old woman once again—though with a hint of the jolly. "Prepare a feast for me, Dmitry. Bone marrow pie and the stewed embryos of foxes." She slapped the table. "And you may eat as much as you like."

A rare treat from Grandmother. I made up my mind to enjoy it.

THE END

Grandmother's War Explanation

When Ron Fortier offered me a chance to write a story for a pulp folklore anthology, the only question was which legend I was going to use. Folklore and myths have always inspired my writing, and I try to work the magical into every story I write, so I was spoiled for choice. A few possibilities came to mind, but the one that leapt to the forefront was the famed witch of Eastern Europe, with her chicken-leg house: the great Baba Yaga.

She's one of those characters that has nearly universal recognition. Maybe not as much as King Arthur or Robin Hood, but definitely up there, popping up in everything from *Hellboy* to *John Wick*. That's a bit odd because while most well-known legends are heroes, either mighty mythic warriors or clever tricksters, Baba Yaga's morality is much more complex. Because Baba Yaga stories have been around so long and are so widespread, there's an enormous variety in her depictions. The chicken-leg house, the skulls on the fence posts, and the mortar and pestle are common motifs, but is she an evil witch of the sort that tries to barbecue Hansel and Gretel? Or a more benevolent figure, who helps good children and vexes evil step-mothers? A child-eating bogeyman or a jolly forest trickster?

For my story, I wanted her to be somewhere in between. She'd do the right thing, but for her own reasons, and the quality of her heart would keep the reader guessing until the last page. She'd be an anti-hero, if a hero at all. Because of this, I couldn't have her be the narrator. Trying to get into Baba Yaga's head seemed to be a fool's errand. So who would be the reader's point of view? I settled on a domovoi, a house-keeping spirit, who could be Baba Yaga's long-suffering but mostly loyal assistant. Along with many other creatures from Slavic legend, like the Leshy, the Rusalka, and Chernobog, domovois have always interested me. It was an easy call to make one the pathetic narrator.

That left a villain—someone who would be far worse than Baba Yaga, so that the reader could cheer their downfall. The Teutonic Knights came instantly to mind. This Chivalric Order never really got into Russia, and though they did some terrible things, I don't know if they were as bad as the Knights depicted here. However, I went with the image of the Teutonic

Knights from the 1938 Sergei Eisenstein film *Alexander Nevsky*. The Knights there, with their fantastic horned helmets and baby-burning ways, are some of the most gruesome villains in the world of silent film, and an obvious allegory for the Nazis. The 1967 Czech film *Marketa Lazarova*, showcasing the clash between the old pagan and New Christian ways of Eastern Europe, was another major influence.

Throw in a fairy tale-style structure, the Firebird, and some dragon action at the end, and the story was ready to go. I loved my visit to Baba Yaga's chicken-legged house, and I hope you did too. I just don't want to end a skull on her fence posts.

MICHAEL PANUSH - has distinguished himself as one of Sacramento's most promising young writers. His books with Curiosity Quills include *The Stein and Candle Detective Agency, Volume 1: American Nightmares, Volume 2: Cold Wars,* and *Volume 3: Red Reunion*, all featuring a pair of occult detectives in the 1950s, *Dinosaur Jazz*— where *The Great Gatsby* meets *Jurassic Park* — a story about a Lost World battling against the forces of modernization; *El Mosaico, Volume 1: Scarred Souls, Volume 2: The Road to Hellfire,* and *El Mosaico, Volume 3: Hellfire,* a Western about a bounty hunter whose body was assembled from the remains of dead Civil War soldiers and brought to life by mad science; and Dead Man's Drive, a 1950s urban fantasy about a hot rod-riding zombie.

With Airship 27, he created the Clay Shamus—a story of a golem detective. His latest novel from Pro Se Press is *Ape's Honor: A Novel of Victoria's Ape*, the story of a gorilla lord in Victorian England. His short fiction has been published in Towers of Metropolis and George Chance: The Green Ghost from Airship 27.

Follow him on Twitter at @Michael_Panush and on the web at https://michaelpanush.com/

PECOS BILL
and the SEA HAG of
the GULF of MEXICO
BY MEL ODOM

Pecos Bill stood watering a cactus and surveying the inhospitable low, rolling, red dirt hills and plains of West Texas. Tall and rangy, with sand-colored hair that was a mite too long, he wore his Colt .44 pistols in tied-down holsters, had a Bowie knife tucked in his right boot, and had tilted his hat back so he could catch a breeze every now and again. His white cotton shirt and denim pants showed roadwear from days of hard travel, but they were relatively clean enough.

Dozens of small, irritating scratches covered his hands and forearms from all the watering he had done. A cactus wasn't generally a friendly sort no matter what a man's intentions were.

About a mile away to the west, something clawed up out of the ground and flopped around real slow like, but whatever it was looked determined to get on out of being buried.

Now, no normal man, not even a Texan who was used to looking across that great and wide land that birthed him, could have seen that far off, but Bill could. He had bright blue eyes so sharp they made hawks kick back on their tail feathers, turn green with envy, and cry crocodile tears.

He tilted back that watering can Slue-Foot Sue had made him pack with his possibles bag and shut off the water flow. When she'd found out he was bound on looking for wild horses in and around the Sangre de Cristo Mountains and would be passing through West Texas, she'd insisted he take her special watering can to help the struggling desert flowers.

Now Bill knew that Sue put a lot in store by that watering can. Not even as big as Bill's two fists mashed together and decorated with a pink petunia his wife had painted on it, the can was one of the first gifts he'd given Sue after he'd married her.

The gift had also been an apology after she'd tried to ride his horse, Widow-Maker, on their wedding day. She'd gotten thrown off on her bustle and almost bounced away. Only his skill with a lasso, and particularly his

91

skill with Shake, the rattlesnake he used in place of a rope, had saved her.

Knowing how much Sue liked gardening and how much she hated going back and forth to the well to draw water, especially in such a small can, Bill took the can to a Yowani Choctaw medicine man to make over into something special. Malata Talako, Bright Eagle, had also made Bill's possibles bag that was bigger on the inside than it was on the outside.

That shaman worked heap big magic on the watering can and made it bigger on the inside than it was on the outside. After that, the watering can held a lot more water. Still not satisfied, Bill knew he could do it even one better. He lassoed a Blue Norther in November (saved a lot of folks in the area when he did and they were mighty grateful), pulled that spiteful thunderhead out of the sky before it could tear up houses and play hob, and tucked it into that watering can.

That watering can *never* ran out of water.

Bill studied on the slowly flopping figure for a moment. The coyotes that had raised him were mighty curious, always seeing out the why and wherefore of things. That was a trait that had stuck with Bill even after he'd grown from a whelp to an adult. Now it itched at him something fierce. He looked down at the cactus he'd been watering, decided it needed a little more for good measure, and delivered another dollop.

That cactus sighed in relief and Bill smiled down at it.

"You be a good feller," Bill said. "Put on some purty blossoms. Miss Sue wants a few to brighten up her house when I get on back to home."

Satisfied he'd done all he could do for the surrounding area, which now was filled with cacti bristling yellow, pink, purple, orange, white, and red blossoms every whichway, he walked on back to his camp.

He'd set up camp on an elevated ridge where he had a good observation point. Thin, gray smoke drifted up from the campfire that had mostly burned down to ash. A few tall saguaro cacti with multiple arms stood nearby and provided narrow shade from the hot morning sun.

Myron T. Elkins, the scribe *10¢ Wild West Adventures* had sent all the way from New York City to write up Bill's latest exploits, sat brushing overeager horny toads off his britches legs and frowning. He was a certified city slicker and hadn't ever been west of the Mississippi River. In fact, he'd never been west of Hoboken, New Jersey, before his latest assignment.

He also hadn't ever seen horny toads fearful of being drowned by Bill's watering efforts. They were jumping and squirting blood from their eyes, which was a sight to see for anybody.

Skeeter-bit, sunburned, saddle-sore, and now beset by the small critters of the desert, Myron wasn't any too happy about his sojourn into the West so far. He just wanted to go home. Only, he needed a story that would satisfy his editor first.

Myron had slept in the bunkhouse during his time at the Rocking B and was sorrowful for his experience even though he hadn't had to do anything other than get up. Roughing it in the great outdoors had made him wishful for the comforts of the bunkhouse.

He was also fidgety because Bill hadn't had any adventures he could write about for the last two weeks on account of it being branding time for the new calves and that took up a lot of a cowboy's time.

A compact man still in his early years, Myron looked like a dandy in his dust-covered broadcloth suit and dark brown hair. He wore a Van Dyke beard that wasn't nearly so primly cut this morning. There wasn't an inch on him that wasn't sunburned, but before they'd left the ranch Sue had fixed him up as best as she could in medicinal salve.

Bill just made sure he rode upwind of the writer when they traveled, and he hoped the salve worked as good as it smelled bad. At least Myron didn't seem to be suffering any this morning.

He looked up at Bill's approach, which was made known by the jingling of the spurs Bill wore.

"Have you finished irrigating the local flora, Mr. Bill?" Myron sounded politely irritated, which was probably troublesome to pull off.

"I have." Bill waved back at the cacti. "Don't they look like they've done perked up a mite?"

Myron barely glanced at the flowering, prickly cacti. "They do."

"Just needed a little tendin' to, like Miss Sue said."

Morosely, Myron nodded.

"And I told you before, you can just call me Bill."

Over the last two weeks, Bill had tried to get the writer to call him by his name, but for some reason Myron just hadn't cottoned to it.

"What are our plans for today?" the writer asked.

Bill knelt and stowed Sue's watering can in his possibles bag where he stored his extra gear.

"Welp, I spotted somethin' interestin' thataway." He pointed to the west, through the tall stand of blooming cacti.

Myron took his journal from his pocket, slipped his stubby pencil from behind his ear, licked the point, and held it poised over the page half-filled with scribbling.

"What did you see? Indians? Buffalo? Bandits? Bears?"

"I don't rightly know," Bill admitted. He gazed back at the figure in the distance and it flopped again. "Looked like somethin' I probably ain't never seen before, an' I'm almighty curious about what it could be. So let's you and me go have a looksee."

Myron brushed another wave of horny toads from his pants and stood with some painful difficulty that made him wince. He picked up his bowler hat from beside the small boulder he'd been using for a chair, and, earlier, for a pillow. Using his coat sleeve, he brushed dust from the hat and clapped it on.

"Is it…dangerous?"

Bill grinned at him. "Well, if it ain't, you ain't gonna have nothin' to write about, will you?"

Myron blinked unhappily. "No, I suppose not."

"Then let's hope it's dangerous."

Myron nodded sadly. "Let's hope it's a *little* dangerous, perhaps, but we're out here in the middle of nowhere."

"This ain't nowhere," Bill stated grandly, and with no little pride, "this here's Texas, an' there ain't no finer place to be."

He turned, put his fingers into his mouth, and whistled shrilly. The sharp notes echoed over the arid land.

A moment later, hooves drummed against the hard-packed earth and Widow-Maker, Bill's horse, galloped up. The mustang stallion was tall and powerful, with a long tail and a wild mane. Widow-Maker shook his head and blew powerfully through his nostrils.

A moment later, the mule Myron had been riding trotted up, followed up by their two pack donkeys. Widow-Maker had been in charge of seeing to it all the animals found grass to graze on.

Myron eyed the mule glumly and leaned down to take up his borrowed saddle. Actually, the mule was borrowed too. Bill had loaned the mount to the writer the day he'd picked him up from the train station in town.

"Ho, boy," Bill greeted his stallion companion. He clapped the mustang on the neck and dust flew. "Let's see if we can go scare up some adventure for Myron to write up. An' we gotta run down some wild horses to take back to the ranch. Gotta get us a nest egg goin' for them young'uns Miss Sue says she's gonna have."

Widow-Maker nodded in agreement.

The imminent arrival of those young'uns had laid heavily on Bill's mind the last few weeks and made him fretful. Welping cubs was something new to him and he wasn't sure if he was up to the task.

Of course, he had Sue. She always stood by his side. That was just one of the reasons he loved her so.

According to her, she was going to have quadruplets because there was no sense in half-measures. Having one at a time seemed like an overly cautious way to approach parenthood. Either folks were going to do it or they weren't. After all, a cowboy didn't just watch over one cow.

Bill thought maybe they could approach children a little slower, but there wasn't no stopping Sue when she set her hat to something. He wasn't sure what he was going to do with a houseful of kids, or even how to take care of them properlike, but he knew they ate a lot.

He wanted to make sure he fed them, and to do that, he needed more cows and more horses for his men to ride while they saw to those cows.

With that in mind, he'd left men at home to tend to the livestock while he scouted up a herd of mustangs. He figured that him and Widow-Maker could bring in a small remuda of fresh blood to liven up things. He planned on breaking them himself on the trip back from the mountains. He didn't plan on wasting time.

Guilt chafed him a little, not quite as bad as a pair of ill-fitting boots, but enough so's it was noticeable. He knew he could have sent some of his men to round up mustangs, though no one was better at tracking and breaking wild horses than Bill, who could find them in windstorm with both eyes shut just by scent alone and feeling the ground shake from their hooves drumming against it, but he'd wanted to roam the wilderness like the old days.

Just for a little while.

He suspected Sue had known that, because she'd stocked his panniers herself and tucked in a few goodies that were his favorites. Like the bear sign and blackberry tarts they'd had the last couple of nights.

Sadly, those were gone now and he and Myron would be hunting their own grub till they reached the next town. Bill had planned for how long it would take him to travel. Myron had slowed things down.

He took a moment to throw the panniers across the backs of the donkeys, then reached down and caught up his saddle and blanket. He tossed the blanket over Widow-Maker and flipped the saddle onto the mustang's back with that little twist he'd learned early on. The saddle girth whirled around just so, ran through the billet, and drew itself taut.

Widow-Maker nodded and stamped his feet, ready to be at it. There was no finer horse.

Bill slid the bridle bit between the horse's big white teeth, stepped into the stirrup, and lighted on Widow-Maker as smoothly as a dragonfly catching a ride on a cattail. He took his makin's from his pocket, inhaled the scent of tobacco to counteract that whiff he'd gotten of the writer's burn salve, and rolled himself a cigarette. He cracked a match to life with his thumbnail and set fire to his smoke.

The thing that had come from the ground flopped a couple times more while he finished his smoke and waited on Myron to saddle the mule.

Finally, the writer was settled and they rode out to see what it was. Bill had a sneaking suspicion about its nature and he hoped he was wrong.

✝✝✝

The squirming thing was a man dressed in a Spanish navy uniform like none Bill had ever seen. Despite the red dirt of West Texas, the dark red of the heavy cloth still showed through in patches.

Stained and ripped and moldering, the uniform was filled out with shoulder pads, and coat cuffs. The collar, almost mostly intact, had a cravat that now lay slightly twisted askew. Tall gray stockings almost reaching the knees clung to the thin shinbones of the withered legs.

While Bill and his companion were still a ways off, a black vulture swooped down from the sky and landed a few feet shy of the man. Gradually, the vulture crept closer till it stood only inches from the emaciated man. Sunlight gleamed from its sharp beak and from its ebony feathers.

Bill yanked the Henry free and laid the sights over the bird, but the vulture was in line with the uniformed man. Bill swung out wide on his approach and hoped for a better angle so he wouldn't hit the bird and the man.

Pitiless, the carrion feeder darted its head forward and opened its beak. Before the cruel hook could sink into the man's puffy, green face, the man snatched the bird by the neck.

The vulture squawked and beat its wings to get free. The razor-sharp talons raked at its intended prey but only sank into the thick cloth of the uniform. The man grabbed the vulture's legs and snapped them as sharply as an alligator biting off a man's finger.

Surprised and scared, the vulture continued using its wings as feathered cudgels to no avail. The man opened his mouth, so withered and drawn-up it was almost lost in his beard, and ripped out the vulture's wattle-covered throat. Another shade of red mixed with the red Texas dirt and the maroon uniform cloth.

The vulture shivered for a moment, then went limp. The man sat up and continued to feast on the bird.

"By thunderation!" Myron croaked. He made the sign of the cross before him and hauled back on the mule's reins.

"Thinkin' maybe it's dangerous enough now?" Bill asked.

"We should turn back."

"Now?"

"We might not have the chance later. Look at that hole. More of them might come up out of it."

"I 'spect if they was any more," Bill said, "they'd have been along by now."

Myron looked like he was thinking of running for the hills, only he probably realized he didn't know which hills to run for. Bill figured it was likely the man didn't know north from south, and no way he'd know which way the ranch was.

Bill kept riding.

"What are you doing, Mr. Bill?" Myron asked.

"A man comes up outta the ground, an' him lookin' like that? Like death warmed over? Dressed in those clothes? Don't that make you a mite curious?"

"No."

"Well, sir, it's enough for me, an' it's probably enough for them folks you hope will be readin' what you're writin' about me."

Bill halted a few feet shy of the uniformed man and his grisly meal. He adjusted his hat better to shade his eyes and pondered the man who watched him with a dead-eyed gaze.

Blood covered the man's round face, which looked even more odd considering his bones showed through gaps in his flesh. However, a scorpion crawled out of the empty socket where his left eye was supposed to be.

"I will not share," the man said in Spanish. "You have to seek your own repast."

"I et my fill of vulture a long time ago," Bill admitted.

The man spoke Spanish like a native, but this Spanish was different, more highfalutin. On occasion, Bill had talked with men from Spain and believed this man might be one of those, but even those men had sounded different than this one.

Bill held onto the Henry, pulled his right leg over the saddle horn, and kicked his left foot free of the stirrup. He dropped to the ground and held the rifle not quite pointed at the man.

Slowly, not trying to antagonize anything, Bill walked over to the man, stayed back just out of arm's reach, and pondered him.

"Thought maybe we could talk for a mite," Bill suggested.

Casually, the man glanced around, then looked back up to Bill. "I find myself not overburdened with compulsory tasks at the moment. Since I am free, you may speak to me."

"What are you doin' out here? Other than eatin' one of the worst tastin' birds I've ever et?"

The man squinted his good eye up at Bill. "To whom do I speak?"

"My name's Bill."

After a brief wait, the man looked puzzled. "Just...*Bill*? Nothing more? No title?"

"Pecos Bill," Bill said, because there were a lot of men who knew him by that name.

"All right then, Mr. Bill..."

"You can just call me Bill."

"Bill." The man tried to sit up a little straighter. "I, myself, am Captain Fernando de Alfaro Naranjo. I lament that, at this precise moment, I am unable to afford even the most modest of hospitalities for a guest. I find myself greatly embarrassed."

"Well, Captain, it seems to me you've come up on some mighty hard times, so I don't hold the lack against you."

"You are a gentleman, sir, and you offer me a kindness that I wish I might repay."

"Perhaps you can," Bill said boldly.

"How so?"

"Like I said, I'm mighty curious as to how you ended up out here."

"Please give me a moment and let me quench this infernal thirst that has plagued me for..." De Alfaro shook his head and drank blood from the stump of the vulture's neck. He wiped his mouth with a holey sleeve that revealed rotted flesh and ivory bone. "For how long I was buried I must sorrowfully admit I do not know. What is now the year?"

Bill reflected a moment and realized he wasn't even sure of the month or day. "It's 1867, Captain."

"It's 1868," Myron called from where he sat on his mule fifty yards back.

"Okay," Bill said and shrugged, "it's 1868. I don't keep track of years so good. Don't see how it matters. They tend to lead one into another—until they don't, an' then I reckon a body just don't care no more at all."

"My god!" the captain said in disbelief. "So long! I have been in the ground for so long! For ninety-eight years I have battled the worms and other vermin of the earth for what little spark of a soul that remains housed within this frail flesh."

"For how long?" Myron asked. He sat on his horse with his journal in one hand and his pencil in the other. He wrote furiously. "I'm sorry, but my Spanish is rusty, and Spanish in New Jersey doesn't sound much like what he's using."

"Ninety-eight years," Bill said in English and swapped back to Spanish. "What happened, Captain?"

"The ocean drank down my good ship, *Swan*, in 1770 after I crossed paths with a most treacherous witch."

"'*Cisne?*'" Myron repeated the Spanish word for swan that de Alfaro had used.

"Swan," Bill said, but he kept his attention on de Alfaro. "If you sank in the ocean, how'd you end up in West Texas?"

The dead sea captain turned his stiff neck as much as he was able. "Is that where we are? I thought surely from the heat and the appearance of the environment we must be in Hell."

"No," Bill said. "This here's Texas. It just draws up men to be strong an' tough, just like the land. What was that you said about a witch?"

"Have you ever entered into a détente with a witch, Bill?"

Uneasiness stole through Bill then, because, while he'd been able to do some powerful and bodacious things, anything smacking of magic gave him the willies.

"I've palavered with a couple now and again," the Texan said. "I don't go outta my way to do it."

Various Indian tribes Bill had had dealings with had witches, male and female, and skinwalkers.

A bloody smile twisted de Alfaro's face, but the flesh it rested on was weathered and dry so that it only looked like an old scar in the middle of the captain's dry, broken whiskers.

"Speaking to a witch, even when you think you love her, never bodes well, my friend. This I know. And I thought I loved Marguerite Darcantel." De Alfaro contemplated the dead vulture he held in his hands. "Perhaps I did love her, too much, but, alas, I see from my unfortunate condition that she did not love me."

"What happened?" Bill asked.

"I sailed for King Charles III, the ruler of all Spain," de Alfaro said. "My time was not my own. Unfortunately, lovely young women do not always understand that a man is not captain of the hours of his day. She grew jealous and assumed that I was trifling with another woman on my voyages between New Orleans and Spain."

"Were you?" Myron asked.

Bill looked at the writer. That hadn't been a polite question, certainly not one Bill would have asked.

For a moment, the dead captain's good eye squinted a little and he might have gotten a full-blown mad on, but he caught himself and heaved a sigh.

"I dare not lie," de Alfaro said. "I did once, and that is how I came to be here. Perhaps if I tell another falsehood, another, even more hideous, situation might lie ahead of me. I cannot risk that. I have not much of myself left."

The captain looked so despondent that Bill felt sorry for him.

"There were indeed other women," de Alfaro said. "Many such women. Though you cast your eyes on the wreckage of a man before you, I was once a handsome young sea captain. A man of leisure who could easily navigate the deep waters of a woman's heart for his own pleasures."

"How many women?" Myron asked.

"Surely no more than a dozen," the captain said. "Sometimes I forget who was before Marguerite and who came after her. Those were exceedingly busy times for me, and after a hundred years of burial in this roasting furnace—"

"Easy there," Bill cautioned. "This here's Texas. You can't go around bad-mouthing Texas. Not around me. There ain't no finer place than Texas."

De Alfaro shot him an apologetic look and nodded courteously. "I beg your forgiveness, my friend. I blame it on the horrors I have suffered for so long."

Bill nodded. "So this witch found out you'd been two-timin' her."

"She did, and it broke her heart," de Alfaro said. "Shattered it beyond repair. I kept hoping I might forestall her wrath, and I did for a time. I was on my way out of New Orleans and back to Spain when she found out I had no plans to return. I had new opportunities in California, and I intended to avail myself of them."

"You were in the Gulf of Mexico," Myron said.

"I was."

"And she was back in New Orleans."

"She was."

Myron scratched his head with his pencil. "Why didn't you get away?"

"I could not. She found me and cursed me and my ship, which she said I loved more than her."

"She took passage on another ship?"

"No." De Alfaro shook his head slowly and with great sadness. "She ran across the waves, sir. Like a gazelle she was."

"Ran across the waves?"

De Alfaro nodded.

Myron looked at Bill. "Have you ever heard of such a thing?" the reporter asked.

"Nope," Bill said. "Can't say that I have. The hardest thing I've ever done was run between the raindrops durin' a thunderstorm that's come up a toad strangler. I had a sack of goods I couldn't let get wet."

"That sounds like quite a feat. I should like to hear of it."

"I'd be happy to tell you about it."

"I fear that I won't have the time to hear your wondrous story."

Bill focused on the sea captain. "So the witch caught up with you an' she cursed you."

De Alfaro nodded solemnly. "She did that, my friend. That was when I found out she was a witch. She called down the wrath of the storm and the fury of the ocean. *Boom!* And like that," he snapped his fingers and blood flew from the dead vulture, "my beautiful *Swan* shattered and sank beneath the waves."

"Okay, but how did you get to Texas?"

"I went down with my ship, as a good captain must, especially when he is cursed by a vengeful witch who locks him to his vessel, and blamed by his crew, rightfully so, I must admit, for the misfortune that befell them. They wouldn't let me into one of the longboats. The witch's last words to me were that my final resting place would be filled with misery." De Alfaro grew quiet for a moment. "I mean no harm to your great state of Texas, of course."

Bill nodded.

"After that," de Alfaro continued, "I knew only the worms and the other despicable vermin that haunted me and ate into my body. Those were hard and difficult years. I truly cannot recommend such an experience."

"But it's been almost a hundred years," Myron said. He hadn't come any closer and had to speak loudly to be heard. His Spanish was getting worse too. "Why did you pick today of all days to crawl out of the ground?"

De Alfaro shook his head and looked puzzled. "I do not know. Until today I was not able to move so very much. But today, I was stronger. Something called to me."

Myron looked at Bill. There were some who said Bill was so powerful as a man and as a Texan that folks around him sometimes found they were capable of doing great things, impossible things. Maybe this was one of those times.

The Yowani Choctaw medicine man who helped make Slue-Foot Sue's watering can once upon a time told Bill that the spirits looked out for him and sometimes acted through him. Maybe it was that capacity in Bill that drew the dead sea captain to him that day. It was surely what allowed Bill to talk to the dead as he had on other occasions.

"Welp," Bill said, "at least you're out of there now."

"I am." De Alfaro smiled. "And now that I am, I would ask a favor of you, if I may."

"If I can," Bill said. "Right now I'm out here lookin' for wild horses. I need to add to my string on my ranch. I'm soon to be a daddy an' I want to provide a future for my young'uns."

"Ah, my friend," de Alfaro exclaimed in delight, "congratulations! I wish you great success in your endeavors!"

Bill grinned. "Thank you."

He tried not to ponder what good wishes from an undead and dying man might be worth. It was the intention behind those wishes that mattered after all. He believed de Alfaro was a good man because even though he was dead, he had offered no harm.

"And perhaps I can offer you more than merely good wishes," the dead sea captain said and lowered his voice. "I have in my possession a document that reveals where a fabulous treasure lies."

Treasure? Bill's ears perked up and his nostrils flared.

"Treasure?" Myron T. Elkins echoed. And in that moment he sounded more alive than he had at any time.

Excitement ran through Bill like red ants chased out of their hill with boiling water. A man could do a lot for young'uns if he had himself a treasure.

"Yes," the dead sea captain said. "As I said, I have in my possession such a document. One that I got from a French privateer I sank in a mighty battle just off the coast of New Orleans. He, himself, got it from a sailor who told him the map belonged to Anne Bonny, one of the most infamous pirates ever to sail the seas."

"You're still livin' right now," Bill pointed out. "A treasure might just fix you right on up."

"Alas, my friend, that will not last. All good things must come to an end." De Alfaro frowned and held up the dead vulture. "And so that we may be clear, this is *not* a good thing. This is merely a thing that happened."

"You want to give me the document?" Bill asked.

"Yes," de Alfaro said, "and I wish to exact from you a promise in exchange, if I may."

"You can ask." Bill had learned the hard way not to make promises any too quickly with men, and dying ones would likely be even harder to trust.

"I will expire soon."

"If you're feeling a mite sickly, I could fetch you another vulture. There's plenty of them around." Bill pointed his Henry up to the wide blue sky where a half-dozen of the carrion feeders glided on the winds.

"No, my friend, I appreciate your generous offer to provide me with sustenance, but I will not trouble you to do that because such an effort will not work. Whatever dark sorcery that has allowed me to live in such misery for so long is at its end. Do not ask me how I know this is so, but I do."

The sea captain was looking weaker and paler.

"Welp," Bill said, "I'm mighty sorry to hear it. What are you wantin' to ask?"

"Simply this: after I perish, when I am completely dead and not as you see me before you, will you see to it that my body is returned to Spain? I wish to lie in the same ground as my forebears. It seems only fitting."

Bill didn't have to think on that overmuch. It seemed such a simple thing to do, and a kindly thing at that. Sue, had she heard de Alfaro's story, would have insisted.

"I'll do it," he agreed. "I'll see to it your body gets on back to Spain."

De Alfaro smiled. "For someone I have only just met, Bill, you are a good and true friend. Thank you."

The dead sea captain offered his hand.

Bill shook hands and de Alfaro's arm came off at the elbow and his fingers dropped to the ground. The fingers wriggled like field mice scattering from a nest that had been invaded by a prairie kingsnake.

"Sorry 'bout that," Bill said.

"That was not your fault, my friend."

Gently, Bill laid the forearm and fingerless hand in the dead sea captain's lap. The fingers scratched across the dirt to de Alfaro like chicks looking for their ma.

"I grow weaker still," de Alfaro said. His remaining eye fluttered. "But before I go, I must tell you about the document you must seek."

Bill leaned in closer to hear the dying man's faltering voice.

"It is in the *Swan*," de Alfaro declared in a voice that was little more than a whisper.

"The *Swan*? But that's at the bottom of the ocean."

De Alfaro smiled. "No, she's not. My ship is *here*, my friend. All ninety feet of her with her square-rigged masts."

With his good hand, the dead sea captain scrabbled through the dirt piled around the hole through which he had escaped his burial. With only a couple of scrapes, he revealed a wooden timber buried beneath the red West Texas dirt.

"See? Here she is," de Alfaro said.

"That's the ship?" Bill asked in disbelief. He tried to imagine a ninety-foot long sailing vessel buried in the ground and his mind boggled.

"This is the ship," de Alfaro gasped. "The witch buried me inside the *Swan*. You will find the map in the desk in my quarters. It's in a plain brown bamboo tube with a swan in full flight carved into it. Thank you for all that you have…"

The dead sea captain fell silent, slumped, and his remaining eyeball popped out of his head. A baby Gila monster, mottled in black and white beaded scales, clambered through the eye socket and three small, brown rattlesnakes slithered out of de Alfaro's left nostril, his right ear, and his mouth.

Myron threw up.

Bill's stomach was fine. His thoughts were focused solely on the treasure that would soon be his and Sue's and their young'uns'.

†††

Bill acted in good faith on his promise to the Spanish captain, something he always did. He wrapped de Alfaro's mortal remains, even gathered up the fingers, in a blue blanket Sue had made him against the chill that haunted the Sangre de Cristo Mountains. Once he was sure he had all the man more or less in one spot, he tied it all up with rope so he wouldn't lose any bit of the captain.

That was just in case de Alfaro, or the bits of him that might shake loose during the ride, decided to look him up later.

Myron sat in the shade of his mule and worked at the notes he'd taken in his journal. The writer didn't offer to help Bill with the sorrowful task of tending to the dead man.

Bill didn't care. His thoughts were plumb eat up with the idea of that

"SEE ? HERE SHE IS" DE ALFARO SAID.

treasure and what he could do with it toward making a finer home for Sue and the young'uns that were coming.

He took a shovel from one of the donkeys and dug out around the timber de Alfaro had pointed out to him. The work went quickly despite the hard ground, because Bill was enthusiastic and hopeful at his prospects, and he soon found himself six feet below the ground level.

"Do you reckon the whole ship is down here?" Myron stood at the edge of the big hole Bill had dug.

"I'm tryin' to find out," Bill said. "Why don't you go fetch that other shovel? Might be we'll find out faster together."

"Sorry," Myron said. "Can't. These hands need to be protected. I have a lot of stories to tell."

The writer backed away from the hole's edge a little, but he didn't pull a full retreat. He stood on tiptoes and watched Bill labor.

Growling in disgust, Bill cursed and kept digging. He tried to remember how big sailing ships were. It had been a long time since he'd seen one. Maybe the *Swan* was ninety feet long, but de Alfaro hadn't mentioned how wide she was. The ship turned out to be of considerable size.

He was twenty feet down and covered in sweat and dirt that had turned to mud when he figured he was sure the *Swan* stood buried straight up while standing on her stern. She was a big ship and broad, with tall masts, at least one, anyway, because he had unearthed part of it.

Eyeballing the twenty feet he'd dug out, he guessed he had another seventy feet to go. Probably less if he only wanted to reach the captain's quarters where the map was supposed to be.

With the way the sun was sinking to the west, it only took a little ciphering for him to know he wasn't going dig the *Swan* out before nightfall. Especially not if he had to throw dirt up forty or fifty feet out of the hole. Even digging out following the hole the dead sea captain had made didn't lighten the load any too much.

On top of that, now that de Alfaro was no longer only somewhat alive and was now all dead instead of mostly dead, the remains were stinking something fierce. It was strong enough to put a rough and tough cowboy plumb off his feed.

A horse neighed.

Bill threw his latest shovelful of dirt up over the rim of the hole and looked up a Widow-Maker.

The horse blew out his breath in a bored fashion, then placed his nose against the ship's timbers and pushed.

The *Swan* quaked in her grave, like she was loose now. Widow-Maker was a strong horse.

Excitement flared through Bill again as an idea lit in his head. He always tried to grab hold of the good ones quick.

"Hey boy," Bill called up, "you reckon me an' you might get this ship out of here together?"

Widow-Maker nodded and reared excitedly.

Thinking happy thoughts about the map all over again, Bill clambered up the side of the hole he'd dug.

"You realize this is foolishness," Myron asserted.

"If you ask me, burying de Alfaro in West Texas was foolishness, but that was done by a witch with a broken heart, so I can kind of understand that."

Bill continued walking around and checking the block-and-tackle he'd threaded through a half-dozen saguaro and sycamore trees not too far back of where the *Swan* was buried.

He'd used ropes he'd carried with him to take back a string of wild mustangs and tied them into a wild concoction of angles that took advantage of the surround saguaros and boulders. If everything worked as he thought it should, the block-and-tackle would make hauling the *Swan* up from the ground a sight easier.

"There's no way, even with this," Myron pulled on one of the ropes Bill had tied and it was so tight it *twanged*, "that a horse can pull that ship out of the ground."

"There's your mistake," Bill said. "Widow-Maker ain't a horse. He's a mustang with a heart as big as all outdoors, an' there ain't another like him. Not even in this great state of Texas where a man can get anythin' he's a mind to."

Widow-Maker neighed and drummed his hooves in agreement.

"You know, maybe if you dug some more," Myron said, "you might get back to the stern where the captain's quarters are. Then you could get that document without having to dig up the ship. Or maybe you could break into the hold and work your way back from there to a spot under the captain's quarters and break in."

"Goin' through the hold's not gonna work," Bill said. "I already thought of goin' through there myownself. There's a whole mess of critters stuck in there, some of them that crawled in from the land, an' some of them that got there most likely from the sea from when the *Swan* went down. Some of that witch's magic must still be workin', because most of them critters, includin' one shark with a bad attitude an' a squid that likes puttin' its tentacles on a man's face, are still kickin' an' bitin' an' suckin'."

Bill touched a sore spot on his left cheek. One of the squid's tentacles had caught hold of him so tightly he'd pulled off a patch of hide getting it loose.

"I ain't goin' back in there without throwin' in a stick of dynamite first," Bill said, "an' that might destroy de Alfaro's quarters an' them directions to the treasure. *An'* there ain't no guarantees that explosion will kill them blasted things. They've lived a hunnerd years down there. No sir, I ain't takin' the chance on it not killin' them an' them comin' after us."

Satisfied with the block-and-tackle and the placement of all the ropes, Bill held up the harness he'd rigged for Widow-Maker and called the mustang over.

Frisky as a newborn foal, Widow-Maker slipped his head right through that harness and took up the slack. With all four hooves planted solidly on the ground, the mustang leaned forward and snorted. He lifted one hoof and stepped forward.

The *Swan* quivered and a heap of dirt slid back down into the hole Bill had spent hours digging. His confidence broke just a little bit because he knew Widow-Maker was straining to pull the load. He feared for a moment he might have set his mount to a task so big that even Widow-Maker might not be able to do it.

Bill fretted what getting defeated would do to his old friend. Widow-Maker was mighty sorrowful about nearly causing Sue to bounce away on Bill's wedding day and had done everything he'd been asked to do ever since.

Timbers cracked down in the hole, thundering like a bunch of cannons going off, and the terrifying noise echoed all around Bill and nearly shook his teeth loose. He gritted them to make sure they stayed in his head.

"It isn't going to work!" Myron shouted. "That ship is going to shatter and the loose ground will fill in the hole again! Or your horse is going to kill himself trying to pull it from there!"

Stubbornly, Bill strode over to Widow-Maker and gripped one of the ropes tied onto the harness. He wasn't going to allow Widow-Maker to fail. Not when there was a handhold left on that rope.

He dug his boots in, rocked back so his spurs dug in too, and pulled hard. Black circles filled his vision and he thought he was going to kill himself right alongside his horse. It might even be a race between him and Widow-Maker as to who gave up the ghost first.

Widow-Maker whinnied and threw himself even harder against the harness.

"For Pete's sake!" Myron bellowed. "You two are about the most stubborn I've ever seen!"

The writer grabbed a rope on the other side of Widow-Maker and heaved to as well.

Maybe it was just that little bit of help that tipped the scales, or maybe somehow being around Pecos Bill inspired Myron T. Elkins and made him stronger, for a little while, than he'd ever been at any other time in his life. Or maybe even the red earth in West Texas realized it couldn't hang onto something when Pecos Bill was on the other end of the tug of war.

Whatever it was, the three put forth a monumental effort that ended in success but left them winded and all but spent.

The *Swan*, landlocked for almost a hundred years, jerked free of her earthen tomb with lots of rattling, squeaking, creaking, and cracking. Piles of dirt that looked like giant gopher hills and boulders rolled up out of the ground with the vessel, and settled around the excavation site for a mite, then tumbled back into the hole with enough force to jar the surrounding countryside and set tall cacti to quivering like runny-nosed pups scared by a chicken hawk.

Widow-Maker, Myron, and Bill kept right on pulling till the Spanish ship came up on level ground and skidded a few feet more while ragged and dirty sheets of canvas hanging from the broken masts and 'yards fluttered in the wind.

"I did it!" Myron screamed and dropped the rope he'd been holding. "Oh my god, would you look at that! I pulled a pirate ship out of the hardscrabble earthen loins of West Texas!"

Bill, being of generous mind and heart at the moment, patted the scrawny writer on the shoulder and said, "You done good."

He didn't bother telling Myron that the ship came free only because him and Widow-Maker had grabbed a second wind and dug in harder.

†††

After much celebrating, drinking a few gallons of water, and a quick lunch of cold flapjacks and jerked beef left over from breakfast for Bill and Myron, and some oats for Widow-Maker, the mule, and the pack donkeys, Bill took up his shovel again, marched over to the *Swan*, and clambered aboard.

Red dirt still covered the ship's deck in huge mounds and Bill commenced to shoveling it over the side like a man possessed. And he was possessed—possessed of thoughts of riding back the ranch with gunny sacks full of pirate treasure in each hand and telling Sue she could have as many young'uns as she wanted.

The shovel bit into the dirt again and it jarred him into thinking. On second thought, he figured he might just tell Sue they could now afford the first batch of young'uns they were having. No sense in putting ideas into her pretty little head. She had enough ideas all on her own and kept Bill hopping around the ranch like his tail was on fire and his head was catching.

After a few minutes, Bill worked on unearthing the door to the captain's quarters. It was located beneath the stern deck. Overhead, on the stern deck, the ship's great wheel spun a little in the breeze and squeaked enough to accompany the tattered canvas popping overhead. Bill's shovel *chuffed* into the red dirt and kept up a steady rhythm with the other noises.

"I can't wait to see what we found." Myron stood on the ship's warped and dirt-covered deck a few feet out of the way and out of the line of fire as Bill managed the working end of the shovel. The writer rubbed his hands together in anticipation. "Anne Bonny's treasure. Just think of it. Do you know that no one knows whatever happened to Anne Bonny?"

"Nope." Bill shoveled more dirt. He didn't even know who Anne Bonny was, aside from what de Alfaro mentioned. At the moment, he didn't care. He just hoped she'd buried a big treasure.

"She and Mary Read plundered ships down in the Caribbean with such disreputable corsairs as Calico Jack and others just as ill-natured," Myron went on. "Calico Jack died at the end of a hangman's noose and was thereafter gibbeted for all to see and to strike terror in the hearts of pirates everywhere. Mary Read was captured and died in prison. Even to this day, no one knows what happened to Anne Bonny."

"Welp," Bill said, "that was a hundred years ago, so I'm bettin' she's dead by now, an' all that gold an' jewels she's left in hidin' is mine. As soon's I find it an' dig it up."

With a few more mighty shovelfuls that set dirt to flying in long streams through the air, Bill uncovered the door to the captain's quarters. He put down his shovel, thought about the critters still fighting one another in the ship's hold, pondered whether there might be any behind the door, and took the shovel right back up in his callused hands.

Battered and worn from being buried near to a hundred years, and after no telling how many years before that surviving everything the sea could throw at it, the door to the captain's quarters still hung tight. That was a sure sign of craftsmanship, and Bill respected it. Red dirt and sea flotsam filled the cracks between the door and the jamb.

Bill reached for the brass door handle, yanked, and was disappointed when the door didn't open. He tried again with the same results.

"Perhaps you should *twist* the handle," Myron advised. He pantomimed the action.

Bill twisted and pulled, and the door sprang open. He was caught flatfooted by the ten-foot-long devil ray that exploded out of the room along with a couple barrels of seawater. The creature was deep blue-mauve on its back and the color of old ivory on its front, and it was madder than an old wet hen.

The devil-tail commenced to battering Bill with its heavy side fins and trying to chew his face off with its mouthful of fangs. He hadn't known that devil rays had fangs, but this one surely did and was excited to use them.

Spluttering, his eyes and nose burning from the saltwater, Bill staggered back. For a moment, when the devil ray balanced on its forked tail and attacked him again, Bill stood frozen, pure-dee confounded by the monster in front of him because he'd never seen such a thing on land. It spread its wings and lunged forward, mouth open wide to expose its fangs in a horrifying fashion.

Quick on the draw, Bill beaned the monster with the shovel he was holding right between its widely separated eyes just before it reached him. The fleshy *clunk* shut down the devil ray's charge immediately. It locked up and teetered precariously on its tail, frozen and unable to move. It mewed sorrowfully like a cat with a sore throat.

Bill frowned at it and pushed it aside with the shovel. The devil ray *splatted* against the now-muddy ship's deck and lay there trembling like it had a case of the vapors.

Wet and just this side of mad at the whole ordeal because the saltwater aggravated all the scratches he'd gotten while watering cacti, Bill rolled up his sleeves, took a firm grip on the shovel, and stepped inside the captain's quarters.

The space was small and had a low ceiling, filled with a bed, a shelf of charts and maps and a few books, a few interesting knickknacks and shells and such, and a couple of shrunken heads with drenched feathers clinging to their stitched-together lips. Beneath the shelf of charts and maps stood a fine desk with brass and marble inlays.

He yanked the desk drawer open and found the bamboo tube with the flying swan carved into it. The tube was as long as Bill's arm from his elbow to his fingertips. With his heart beating wildly as a New Orleans voodoo priestess's drum, Bill opened the tube. The container buzzed and jumped in his hand for a moment, like someone had thrown a lasso over it and tried to yank it away, but he held on tight and the tube settled down.

Gleefully, he walked outside onto the ship's deck so he could see what was inside the tube. He didn't want to blindly stick a finger in because the day had already been filled with too many nasty surprises.

Only rolled parchment was inside. It looked like aged, hard-used, and smelled faintly of cloves.

Bill dumped the map out into his palm, looked it over, and saw the big red X marked on a small island in what appeared to be off the Gulf of Mexico somewhere south of Galveston.

"Did you get it?" Myron asked.

"I sure did," Bill said. He studied the red X and tried to figure out where the island was. "I got the map an' it weren't hardly no trouble a-tall."

The devil ray flopped weakly.

Myron came over and peered around Bill's shoulder, him not being tall enough to peer over, and looked at the map.

"That's not a map," Myron said.

"It's a map," Bill insisted. He pointed with a forefinger. "Right there's the X. X marks the spot ever' time on a pirate map."

He assumed that was true. He'd never seen one himself, but that was the way all the stories had it.

"A map relays information about land," Myron explained distractedly. His gaze was fixed on the parchment. "A chart relays information about oceans. See here where the depths are noted? The coral reefs that might take out the bottom of a ship? That's a chart."

"Except for the island where the treasure is," Bill said stubbornly. "There it becomes a map again because that's land." He tapped the island with his forefinger.

"I suppose," the writer said, "but I still think this qualifies as—"

Horrendous growling and grating interrupted Myron and drew rapidly closer to the beached *Swan*.

Bill looked up from the parchment and eyeballed the horizon. East by southeast, a cloud of red dust rose up from the flat West Texas land and came closer and closer, like it was being blown by a fierce hurricane.

"What in tarnation?" Bill asked. He rolled the parchment, shoved it back inside the bamboo tube, and then shoved the tube through his belt so his hands would be free. He picked up the shovel again and lamented the fact he'd left the Henry in the scabbard on Widow-Maker.

"Whatever it is, it's coming this way," Myron said, "and it's coming mighty fast."

"I can see that for myself."

"What is it?"

Bill squinted and made out three tall masts and full-bellied sails that looked as full as proud pigeons that hung over the ship that somehow plowed across West Texas. A flag showing three broad stripes of red, white, and blue, with a huge V overlaid by a smaller O and a C flew from the topmost mast.

"My god," Myron said. "That's a ship!"

"I can see that for myownself," Bill growled. "I ain't blind."

What he wanted to know was what it was doing there, and why it was headed for them.

Since the writer could now see the ship, Bill knew the vessel had gotten mighty close mighty quick. He didn't know how it navigated the land, but there wasn't no sense in trying to outrun it. Not even with Widow-Maker. The ship was too blamed fast.

The mule and the donkeys cowered back against their lead ropes that held them to saguaros. Widow-Maker laid his ears back, bared his teeth, and kept an eye on Bill, ready to take his lead from him.

Bill wished again he'd brought his Henry onto the *Swan*, but he had no time to get to the rifle now. He figured his pistols would do in a pinch. He walked over the ship's side and peered out across West Texas as the ship halted alongside the *Swan*.

The new ship was easily twice as long as Captain de Alfaro's vessel, taller, and bigger. Several sailors aboard the ship scurried around the deck and clambered through the rigging. Some drew up the sails and stowed them.

One threw out an anchor that *plunked* onto the hard-packed red earth and smashed a half-dozen saguaros into green and white paste.

Others ran out cannons and adjusted the weapons so they pointed down at the *Swan*. Even though the sun was to the west and it was still daylight, the ship glowed like a lightning bug, only it was gold, not green.

Three large gray, black, and white birds sat on the rigging near the crow's nest.

Bill swore. Sweat trickled down the back of his neck. It had been a long time since he'd been outgunned, but he was surely outgunned now.

But he wasn't ready to give up.

A slender man dressed in a dark green uniform and wearing a hat sporting a white ostrich feather stepped up to the side of the big ship and struck a jaunty pose. He wore a full beard and mustache, and his dark hair brushed his shoulders. He looked like a man who knew his business and had been at it a while. A sword hung at his hip and a brace of flintlock pistols sheathed on a wide leather belt hung over his left shoulder.

"That's no place to leave a ship," the man called.

"I didn't leave it here," Bill replied. "I was the one who dug it up."

The man frowned and looked mighty perplexed. "You dug it up?"

"It was buried."

"For heaven's sake, why would anyone bury a sailing ship?"

"Mister," Bill said, "that there's a long story an' I ain't got time to tell it. What are you doin' here? I suppose you ain't sailed across West Texas for nothin'. Are you lost? Need directions? Maybe you took a wrong turn at Albuquerque."

"I most certainly am not lost and I know not of any port called Albuquerque," the man retorted. "I am Captain Barend Fockesz. This is my ship." He waved at the crew spread out around him. "And these are my men."

Beside Bill, Myron gasped. "I know that name. He's the captain of the *Flying Dutchman*."

Bill couldn't quite place the name, but he knew he'd heard it.

Fockesz grimaced. "Some people have given my ship that accursed and salacious sobriquet, but that is not her true name. She is the *Gelukseend*, and she is the fastest ship upon any ocean."

"Fastest ship in West Texas too," Bill said, though it hurt his pride to admit it. He figured he could work at the *Swan* and have it ready to race when he had some new sails. He wasn't a man to ignore a challenge. No Texan was.

Fockesz smiled and doffed his hat in an elegant manner that made his plume swish through the air in an elegant manner. "Thank you for your praise."

"It's the *only* ship sailing in West Texas," Bill said, "so there ain't much competition."

"There's a problem you're not seeing, Bill," Myron said quietly and with some trepidation.

"What problem?" Bill asked.

"*The Flying Dutchman* is a ghost ship. It was supposed to have sunk somewhere around the Cape of Good Hope down by Africa. Every man on that ship was believed to have drowned. Only now it sails around the world and every sailor aboard it is dead. Including the captain. I just read an old article on it in *Blackwood's Edinburgh Magazine.*"

A cold wind blew across Bill's spine and raised his hackles.

"We sure are crossin' paths with a lot of dead folks today," he muttered. Captain Fockesz showing up about now couldn't mean anything good.

"That's not the worst part," Myron confided. "*The Flying Dutchman* has a nasty habit of showing up right before some disaster at sea."

Bill relaxed a mite. "Welp, it's a good thing we ain't at sea, ain't it?"

"If I can interrupt your conversation for a moment," Fockesz said, "pray tell me who you might be."

"I'm Bill," Bill said.

Fockesz paused for a moment. "Bill? That's it? Just Bill? Captain Bill?"

"This is *Pecos* Bill," Myron shouted at the sea captain. "He's the greatest cowboy in all of Texas."

Although he didn't want to show off too much, Bill puffed out his chest a little.

"Hmmphh," Fockesz responded, and he didn't look impressed. "Congratulations on achieving that recognition, Captain Bill. I am very happy for you and I am sure I celebrate your many fascinating successes. However, time is of the essence, even for a phantom, so I must attend to what brings me here."

"What would that be?" Bill asked.

"I've come for the treasure map, of course," Fockesz answered.

Bill pondered the request for a moment. Dead folks had a way of putting pressure on a feller and he wanted to know what might be coming.

"Tell him there's no map," Myron whispered.

"I don't lie," Bill told the writer. Then he realized something and he raised his voice. "I ain't got no map, Captain Fockesz."

"I thought you didn't lie," Myron whispered.

"I didn't lie," Bill said from the corner of his mouth. "It's a chart, not a map." He thought he was pretty clever for figuring out that loophole because he was certain Fockesz was trouble. He would have known that even without the huge ship laying at anchor in front of him. "Now hush an' let me palaver."

"That," Fockesz declared haughtily, "is a contemptable falsehood. I know you have the map. I have got the skull of a Phoenician sailor in my quarters that tells me when such things have been found and summons me to their locations. That skull has never been wrong. So give me the map!"

Anger swarmed over Bill then. No man called him a liar. Especially not when he'd skated the truth so well. It took everything he had to keep from heaving himself over the *Swan's* side and clambering up the anchor rope to get at the ghostly Dutch captain.

It was only the look of those cannons, all staring at him like the eyes of a dozen polliwogs, and thoughts of Sue and his young'uns that held him in check. Still, he was mighty tempted.

Fockesz must have seen the look on Bill's face because he spoke up quickly. "Don't even think about it, Captain Bill. Before you can clear yourself from that deck, perhaps only the heartbeat after, I'll have my men open fire and reduce that beached whale you call a ship into kindling spread all over this sordid place. I daresay you and your friend won't survive a broadside of grapeshot from the *Gelukseend*."

"*Sordid place?*" Bill could scarce control his outrage. "Why this here is Texas, mister! The Good Lord blessed Texas with his own hand! You won't be talkin' bad about the place of my birth!"

"I will have that map," Fockesz said. "You have until the count of three."

"I only need until the count of two, you big galoot! I'll trounce you!" No longer quite in control of his temper, Bill reached for his pistols.

"BILL!" Myron grabbed Bill's left arm and stilled his hand. "How do you expect to kill a ghost?"

"Put enough lead into anything an' it'll die."

"Have you ever shot a ghost?"

"No."

"Well you can't shoot that ghost."

"I can. He's only standin' right there. I can't hardly miss at this distance."

"You got to think of your young'uns! You don't want your pretty young wife raising them as orphans because you went and got yourself blown to flinders!"

Well, that thought spiked Bill's heart with cold fear, and he felt like they'd been driven deep by a hammer John Henry hisownself swung. Bill had never worried none about dying. A man, especially a Texan, couldn't court notions like that because it would make him hesitate or freeze him in his tracks.

He knew what growing up without a daddy was like. Coyotes had raised him. He hadn't found his natural family until a long time after he was a full-grown man. He'd missed out on a lot of things a true daddy could provide. Things that he wanted to provide to his own now that Sue had put the notion into his head.

"Think of your young'uns, Bill!" Myron pleaded. He still gripped the Texan's arm in a death grip.

In reality, the writer wasn't so worried about Bill's children. He was just hoping to save his own neck.

Bill didn't know that, however, but he thought about them young'uns growing up and not knowing their daddy, and he thought of Sue working her fingers to the bone after he'd promised he'd be there to help with them. It was godawful terrible to consider.

"One!" Fockesz shouted.

The pirates manning the cannons held smoldering slow matches and looked eager to be about their violent trade.

"All right, dadblame you," Bill replied. "I'll give it up."

The crew of *The Flying Dutchman* looked mighty disappointed at Bill's decision.

The Texan pulled out the tube that contained the chart to Anne Bonny's treasure from his belt. "Come an' fetch it."

Fockesz looked up at the ugly birds gathered at the crow's nest, gave a sharp command, and one of them fell from the rigging and spread its wings. Quick as a wink, the bird sailed across the distance between the ships.

Myron dove to the deck and pulled his hat down good and tight over his head. "Look out for that albatross, Bill!"

Bill had never seen an albatross because they didn't live around Texas or the Gulf of Mexico, but he'd heard a few stories about them here and there. Sue favored and sometimes read *The Rime of the Ancient Mariner* by Samuel Taylor Coleridge to Bill on occasion when they were rocking in their chairs on the front porch of an evening. He liked hearing her read, although he didn't remember all the story.

He did remember how shooting the albatross brought bad luck to the ship's crew and they all died as a result. On account of that, Bill didn't draw one of his shooting irons out of pure reflex and put an end to the bird before it reached him.

The albatross flapped its wings, arced up a little, and snatched the chart tube right out of Bill's fingers with its jagged claws. It flapped again and swooped in a tight circle back to the *The Flying Dutchman*. With unerring accuracy, the albatross dropped the tube into Fockesz's hand and flapped on up to the crow's nest.

Fockesz opened the tube and unfurled the parchment. When he saw what was there, he smiled. Then he rolled the chart back up, put it back into the tube, and slid it into his coat.

"Alas, Captain Bill," the Dutch sea captain said, "would that I could, but I dare not tarry. I must needs be on my way. The Devil is a most unkind taskmaster. I wish you the best of luck on the birth of your children."

"No you don't, you thief!" Bill roared and shook his fist. "You're takin' their birthright! That there's my chart! I found it! That treasure belongs to my young'uns!"

Fockesz called out to his crew. The canvas sheets were once more unfurled, the anchor hauled up, and *The Flying Dutchman* lurched forward. The ship inscribed a great semi-circle and left a furrow in the red West Texas ground nearly as wide as a man was tall.

Bill cussed a blue streak and dropped over the *Swan's* side. The ship dragged a cloud of red dust after it and quickly vanished from sight till it was only a puff of red on the horizon.

Myron climbed down from the *Swan* carefully.

"I can't believe I just let him run off like that," Bill growled. "I should have grabbed hold of him an' stomped on him."

"I'm not sure that you can stomp a ghost, Bill."

"Welp, I wish I'd found out."

"He had cannons," Myron said. "A *lot* of cannons."

"But he didn't even fire a-one of them."

"Bill," Myron said gently, "Captain Fockesz wouldn't have fired one of them. He would have fired *all* of them. You heard him. He was prepared to destroy everything if he couldn't get what he wanted. Ghost, phantom, whatever he might be, he's insane." He put a cautious hand on Bill's shoulder. "You did the right thing. This way you get to go home to your wife and your children."

"No sir!" Bill exploded. "I had a treasure right there in the palm of my hand." He held out a hand to show where that treasure had briefly rested. "I wasn't even man enough to curl up my fingers an' hold onto it."

That hurt Bill an awful lot to say, and it was even worse hearing him say it.

"That was *The Flying Dutchman*," Myron cried. "The most cursed ship on all the seas. Captain Fockesz was the fastest ship's captain who sailed for the Dutch East India Company. Rumor had it that Fockesz made a deal with the Devil himself to achieve that speed. You can't take on someone like that who bargains with the Devil."

"THAT TREASURE BELONGS TO MY YOUNG 'UNS!"

Well, Bill liked that being said by the reporter even worse than admitting it to himself.

"I could have if Daniel Webster was still alive," Bill groused. "Old Daniel woulda figured out a way to break a bargain with the Devil. He done it before."

Myron didn't say anything to that.

Fretting and fuming, Bill paced amid a patch of splintered saguaro left by the *The Flying Dutchman*. Back and forth he went, oblivious to the world around him. He thought about how he'd crawfished to Fockesz, and he thought about how ending up dead wasn't going to help Sue or them young'uns.

He thought about having to go back to Sue without a string of green-broke mustangs. He thought about going back to Sue with his tail between his legs and him never again capable of being the cowboy he set out to be.

He thought about getting killed and not going back to Sue a-tall.

That would be bad and didn't set well with him.

Then he thought again about how he'd crawfished, and on and on it went, faster and faster till it was a swarm of whirling bullets ricocheting inside his skull. He lost sight of everything till all he knew was the thoughts running screaming around and around till it made him dizzy and he had to force himself to think clearly.

"I ain't no coward," Bill said. "I was only thinkin' of them young'uns an' them not havin' no daddy. That's what I done."

He rolled and smoked a cigarette and pondered some more on his recent actions.

"I didn't see Captain Fockesz comin'," he said. "That's what discom-bobulated me. I got ambushed good an' proper because I didn't know anybody else knew about the chart."

"Captain Fockesz has the skull of a dead Phoenician telling him things," Myron said. "There's no way you could have known that. Those stories I've heard about *The Flying Dutchman*? Not a one of them mentions that. You didn't know. I didn't know. Captain de Alfaro didn't know. None of us could have known that."

Round and round things went inside Bill's head.

"Is it better to be a dead cowboy or a live daddy?" Bill asked himself and kept pacing.

When it got dark, he rolled himself another cigarette and struck a match with his thumbnail. The sudden burst of light reflected from the earthen walls that had raised up around him.

Confused, Bill looked around and saw that earthen walls hadn't just raised up around him. He was pacing in a long trench. He wondered how that could have happened. Widow-Maker and Myron and the mule and the donkeys, and even the *Swan,* were no longer in sight. Overhead was a rectangular slice of blue sky and dust devils playing at the edges of the hole he was standing in.

"Myron?" he called up.

"I'm here, Bill." The writer stuck his head over the crumbly edge of the hole. He looked fretful.

"What happened?" Bill asked.

"You wore out the ground under your boots," Myron said. "Just walked a big hole in the earth."

Bill looked around and decided that was true. The trench was about twenty feet long and likely a good ten or twelve feet deep. He'd been doing some serious pacing.

"I guess I had me some ponderin' to do," Bill admitted.

"I guess you did."

"But I got it all ciphered out now."

"Good." Myron smiled hopefully. "Are we going back to the ranch now?"

"Nope."

Myron lifted his eyebrows and looked a mite worried. "We're going after the mustangs then?"

"No sir," Bill replied.

Myron closed his eyes. "Then, pray tell, what are we going to do?"

"We're gonna corral us some ghost pirates is what we're gonna do, an' we're gonna get my young'uns' treasure back. Ain't no other way this can be done that won't knot up in my craw."

"What about your young'uns?"

"I've pondered on that an' the only right answer to that question is they got to have a daddy they can look up to. Not one that showed back up to home with his tail a-draggin' after losin' their inheitance. No sir. I ain't gonna give them that kinda daddy. They deserve better."

Widow-Maker whinnied not too far away, and he drummed his hooves in that way he had of showing his approval. Bill reckoned it was possible that if Fockesz had gotten the better of him, Widow-Maker would have made his master walk back to the ranch on his own two feet and he might never have rode with Bill again.

"You'll want to move on back a mite," Bill advised. "I'm comin' outta this here hole."

Myron hastily pulled back from the edge.

With a mighty leap, Bill hurled himself out of the hole he'd walked in the ground and landed near the *Swan*. He shaded his eyes and glanced up at the sun.

It didn't look like it had moved much, but it was in the west still above the horizon. Night would come on soon.

The furrow in the ground still marked the path *The Flying Dutchman* had taken. Tracking the ship wasn't going to be an ordeal.

"How long have they been gone?" Bill asked.

Myron took out his pocket watch. "About five minutes."

Bill glanced at the hole he'd walked in the ground and breathed a wistful sigh. "That was the longest I ever spent tryin' to make up my mind about somethin'. I sure hope I never get stuck like that again. Life ought to be simpler."

"I sure wish you'd give this plan of action another thought," Myron said.

"Can't," Bill growled. "I done wasted too much time. Get mounted. There's a town not too far from here. We'll take Captain de Alfaro's body there an' leave it till we come back to fetch it."

Myron hurried to his mule. "You think we're coming back?"

"After we get that map an' my treasure?" Bill nodded. "I surely do. I'm gonna keep my promise to de Alfaro."

"You do realize if Fockesz kills you, you won't be coming back?"

Bill shook his head. "That's not gonna happen neither. I promised Sue I'd be back on to the house directly, an' that's what I mean to do."

Bill stepped into the stirrup and hauled himself into the saddle.

"How are you going to deal with Fockesz and *The Flying Dutchman*?"

"That," Bill growled, "is somethin' Sue would call a work in progress. Let's ride."

✝✝✝

Just after nightfall, Bill reached a little town called Scant, which was named after itself on account of there being only a scant few folks, a scant few cows, and a scant few houses. The town was only a little out from the trail left by *The Flying Dutchman*.

Bill left Captain de Alfaro's remains with the hostler, a man he'd met in past wanderings and trusted, and he left the donkeys and the mule as well.

"My mule?" Myron asked. "Do you expect me to walk?"

"Nope," Bill said. "You're gonna ride double with me. Widow-Maker can carry both of us an' cover more ground than if we try to take that mule."

They took on a few provisions and rode off into the night. The moonlight was bright enough for Bill to follow the groove torn across West Texas that headed east, southeast. The Gulf of Mexico lay that way, so Bill figured Fockesz was headed thataway instead of California and the Pacific Ocean.

The Texan rode with his thoughts fixed only on one thing: being the best dadblamed daddy any young'un could ever want.

And he was going to do that by bringing them back a treasure before their first birthday.

†††

Three days later, arriving at night only just this side of the witching hour after traveling nonstop at a full gallop and pausing only a few times out of necessity, Bill reined in at the edge of the Gulf of Mexico and stared at the single scar along the sandy beach that showed where *The Flying Dutchman* had passed and kept on going.

The track led right on out into the sea and vanished under the dark water and moonlight-kissed white curlers that slapped the shoreline in a timeless rhythm.

It was the end of the trail.

"We lost him." Myron sounded disgusted, tired, and all but exhausted. He might have sighed a little in relief.

Bill didn't say anything and swallowed his own frustration. He knew what the writer had said was true.

He had lost the ship.

He had lost the chart that led to Anne Bonny's treasure.

Widow-Maker was tuckered too. He stood there and had himself a blow and white flecks of sweat showed along his coat, proof of how hard he'd tried to catch *The Flying Dutchman*.

"Dagnab it," Bill growled. Cold fury battled deep, dark despair and neither one of them would have been a good winter.

He got down from Widow-Maker, got one of the canteens they carried, and watered his horse. Widow-Maker drank greedily from Bill's hat and slurped noisily. His whiskers wetted down and trickled drops over Bill's hands and forearms.

"It wasn't you," Bill told his horse. "You did good. I ain't gonna ever say otherwise. That blamed ghost ship was just too fast."

Widow-Maker whinnied and shook out his mane.

"It was them five minutes I spent frettin' about things," Bill said. "If I hadn't done that, if I hadn't delayed on figurin' out what was what, you'd have caught him. Look at how fresh that there track in the sand is."

Widow-Maker butted Bill with his head to show support.

Myron was so saddle-sore he couldn't hardly walk.

"What are we going to do now?" Myron asked.

"We're gonna have dinner," Bill said. "All of us. I'm feelin' hollow. While we're eatin', I'm gonna be ponderin' what it is we need to do next."

Myron waved toward the Gulf. "It's apparent what happened. Fockesz sailed his haunted ship right off into the ocean. He's probably digging that treasure up even as we speak."

"He ain't had the time, I'll promise you that. An' even if he was, it woud save us the trouble of diggin' it up our ownselves. We're gonna catch up to him yet."

Myron shook his head and looked apoplectic. "How do you figure on chasing *The Flying Dutchman* into the Gulf of Mexico, Bill?"

"Welp, that's what I'll ponder on while we build us a fire. If I keep my hands busy, my head will work it all out."

Finished watering his horse, Bill clapped his wet hat back on and went in search of dry driftwood to use for a fire. Thankfully, finding wood was no problem because lots of it had piled up in this area, likely because no one had ever been there before, or at least not in a long time, and the writer proved himself useful.

Bill dug a hole in the sand for the fire not far from the waterline, set the wood in place, scraped up some kindling from a branch with his Bowie knife, and lit the woody curls with a match. In practically no time at all, he had a cheery little campfire going. That made him somewhat more accomplished and hopeful. He would find a way to catch the ghost ship.

Myron stood staring into the thin saddlebags he'd taken from Widow-Maker. "We don't have anything to cook. We already ate everything except a little bit of cornmeal and some bacon grease you saved back."

"I know." Bill nodded toward the Gulf. "Don't you worry none. That there ocean has plenty of fish in it. We'll catch what we need an' we'll eat like kings."

"Did you bring any fishing poles?"

"Nope. But I got a spool of string an' hooks 'cause I always travel with those for when I want to do a little fishin', an' we can use twigs as floats."

"That water's so dark I can't see anything, and I've never fished in my life."

"Welp, it's a good thing I can see an' I can fish. Otherwise you'd be goin' hungry."

Bill whipped up three lines with hooks, found a crab walking on the sand and cracked it open, and baited the hooks with meat from the crab. He cut branches with his Bowie knife because he didn't want to try to find a suitable young sapling to use as a pole. He shoved the branches into the sand and staked his lines the shoreline.

Satisfied with his anchoring points, he twirled the baited hooks overhead and heaved them as far out into the dark ocean as he could, which was mighty far because he still felt awful frustrated.

When he sat down to watch over the lines, the campfire warmed his back and made him think of home while he sat there waiting for a fish to bite.

He missed Sue something fierce, and he didn't know how he was going to tell her he'd had a treasure—a surefire way for them to take care of the coming young'uns—and let it slip right through his fingers.

Myron snored. He lay curled up on a blanket on the other side of the campfire. Probably the writer hadn't intended to fall asleep, but he had.

Bill wondered if the writer had gotten enough stories to write about. Not much had happened until they'd found de Alfaro and the *Swan*, and the things that came after that meeting didn't rightly have endings. At least, not good ones.

It was disappointing, and Bill worried about Myron writing a story that told about how Pecos Bill got licked by a phantom captain and his crew of ghosts.

Nope, that wasn't a good story at all, and he didn't want it out there. Enough foolishness was said about him as it was.

He teased the lines, then got back to pondering about Fockesz and *The Flying Dutchman*. He couldn't imagine what it would be like to be a ghost sailing around the world and bringing nothing but doom and gloom to folks. That had to be depressing. Of course, Fockesz seemed like he enjoyed what he was doing. All those years had made *The Flying Dutchman's* captain a mighty cold and ruthless man.

Bill wanted to bring Fockesz down a peg or two.

But how was he going to get the better of a ghost?

One of the twigs floating out on the ocean surface jerked a little.

Something had taken an interest in the crab meat. He leaned forward, took up tension on the line with his fingers, then, when he got a definite bite, he twitched his fingers and set the hook.

Thirty yards from the shore, the hooked fish broke the ocean's surface in a mad struggle to escape. The fish looked silver in the moonlight instead of its usual blue-gray or dark brown, and the pronounced serrated spines and forked tail told Bill exactly what he'd got hold of.

The gafftopsail catfish flipped and flopped around like a stubborn hammerheaded stallion refusing to be broken. When it came back down, the catfish landed in the water with a large splash.

Hoping for the best, he played the fish, let out line and took it back in, so he wouldn't break the string and lose his catch. His mouth watered in eagerness for the coming meal. Gafftopsail weren't the best fish for eating, but it would do tonight. Slowly, he brought the fish in.

Only a few minutes later, he filleted it with the Bowie knife. The keen blade passed right through the meat and in short order he had a couple sizeable fillets. He threaded them onto sticks and set them by the fire to cook.

Not many more minutes passed before he had two other fish to join the first. He seasoned his catch with yellow flowered onions, wild garlic, purple sage, and a pinch of salt left over in his possibles bag.

It didn't take long before the fish all smelled mighty fine. Bill's stomach rumbled in anticipation. He mixed up some cornmeal to fry up a pan of cornbread.

"Help!"

When Bill first heard the girl crying out, he thought he was just tired and imagining things, or that maybe his stomach was truly desperate and crying out for relief.

After hearing her call out again, though, he stood, held up a flaming brand from the campfire, and searched the treeline on the other end of the sandy beach.

He didn't see anything, convinced himself he was imagining things, and was just about to sit back down when she called out again, even more desperate this time.

"Help! Please!"

This time, Bill knew the girl's voice carried over the gentle swell of the tide. He turned and spotted the pale oval of her face just above the water's surface fifty yards out. Something was wrapped around her head.

"Help!" she cried and went under for a moment.

Bill kicked off his boots, thrust his Bowie into his belt, and shucked his pistols. He ran into the surf up to his knees, then dove headfirst when the bottom fell away and the cold water got deeper. He surfaced, took a breath, got his bearings, and spotted the girl.

A dozen feet away from the girl, a large triangular fin broke the water's surface and circled her.

Bill swam with the heart and speed of a salmon swimming upstream in spawning season. As he neared the girl, the triangular fin changed directions and headed for him.

"Look out!" the girl screamed.

Bill had tangled with a shark before, and he'd battled alligators down in the swamps of East Texas and over to New Orleans. He knew how to bob and weave when he was up against critters that seemed to be equal parts teeth and pure nasty mean. Even in the water the Texan was quicker than a panther.

As the shark closed on him, Bill juked to the side and reached down for the Bowie knife at his belt. The blade came free in his hand and gleamed for an instant in the moonlight that penetrated the Gulf water.

When the shark shot by and narrowly missed him, Bill caught hold of that fin in his left hand and hauled himself aboard the shark like he was climbing aboard a rowdy bronc in a holding pen and headed into a bucking tussle.

Suddenly aware it was carrying a rider; the shark headed for deeper water and pulled Bill under with it. Everything got cold and black around Bill, but he stuck like a burr. He fisted that Bowie and stabbed the shark repeatedly. When it finally went limp beneath him, he turned it loose and swam to the surface.

The girl still had to be saved from whatever was holding her.

He popped up, took a deep breath, and spotted her floating ten yards away. Only her face was out of the water. She looked frightened.

"Where's the shark?" she asked and peered around anxiously

"Dead," Bill said. "I done for it. Ain't gonna be no more bother."

He slipped the Bowie behind his belt again and swam toward her.

When he reached her, he discovered she was caught up in a fishing net used by trawlers in the area. The twisted strands were shot through with water plants and covered in barnacles.

"How'd you get out here?" Bill asked.

"I was out for a night swim and got caught up in a net some fisherman must have tossed into the Gulf."

Bill slid the Bowie in among the net strands and whittled away at the net holding her prisoner. "Why in tarnation would you be out swimmin' at night?"

"That's when I do my best thinking," she said.

"Musta had to do some powerful thinkin'."

"I did. I had things on my mind."

"You coulda took a stroll along the beach. I hear tell some folks enjoy that."

"I'm not much into strolling." She looked a little put-out, then her features softened.

Bill guessed she was embarrassed about getting caught up in the net.

"My name is Aeliana," she said in a gentler tone.

"I'm Bill. Pleased it meet you."

She favored him with a smile then, and it was the best smile he'd seen in days, since he'd left Sue back at the ranch.

"It's nice to meet you, Bill. I'm sure glad you happened along."

"Was there anybody else with you, Miss Aeliana?"

"No, just me and my thoughts, and after a while, that shark."

"I don't suppose he had friends with him." Bill studied the water carefully and kept cutting. The net was purely a mess. The barnacles and kelp made handling it even harder.

"No. Just the one you saw. He was bad enough. I thought he had me for sure. He just couldn't quite figure out how to get at me through the net, and I couldn't get away. If I'd been able to get free, I'd have given him a run for his money."

Bill glanced at the girl. She was a pretty little thing, redheaded like Sue was, only her color was darker, and her hair was longer and pooled out across the water. Her cute little nose was freckled and gave her a stubborn look. Her eyes were the same gray and silver as an early morning fog kissed by the rising sun.

After Bill freed her head and shoulders, he hesitated about feeling around her body to get at more netting.

Aeliana smiled at him, evidently amused by Bill's modest ways.

"If you'll let me borrow your knife, cowboy, I think I can manage the rest myself," the girl suggested.

Bill held the Bowie by its blade and handed it over.

Aeliana took the knife, hefted it for a moment, and nodded. "This'll do."

"Do?" Ben echoed. "That there is a *fine* knife, one of the best ever made. It was forged an' given an edge by Jim Bowie hisownself. One of his kin gave it to me for savin' his neck from a Wendigo a few years back."

She ducked under the water for a long minute, long enough that Bill worried an undertow might have snatched her away. Then she surfaced, swept her long hair back, which he could now see was decorated with tiny shells and bits of white and blue coral, and handed him the knife.

"Thank you," she said. "I don't know where I'd have been without you."

"I'm just glad I happened to be around when I was," Bill said.

"Things might have been different if I could have gotten to my spear, but that net trapped my arms and I couldn't reach it." She reached over her back and pulled up a short shank of wood about as long as Bill's arm. An edged piece of hooked red coral gave it a dangerous point that gleamed in the moonlight. "I use this mostly for fishing, but it's a good weapon too. The shark would have at least been in for a fight."

"Yes, ma'am, he would have," Bill agreed, but he was wondering why a young lady would go for a swim carrying a spear.

"Bill!" Myron stood on the beach and hollered through his cupped hands. Evidently there'd been enough of a commotion to wake him. "Are you all right?"

"I'm fine," Bill called back. He waved.

"What are you doing in the water?" Myron asked.

"He was helping me," Aeliana shouted.

Myron straightened in surprise, leaned forward, and widened his eyes. "A girl? You found a girl out there?"

Aeliana laughed and the sound was musical. "He did, and just in time too. The shark almost had me."

"*Shark?*"

"We'll tell you all about it in a minute." Aeliana looked at Bill. "That's your campsite?"

"It is. I got some coffee on. Might warm you up some."

The girl grinned. "All right. I like coffee just fine. Don't get to drink much."

Bill swam for shore and the girl swam alongside him so smoothly it was clear she was good at swimming. He didn't worry about her until she slowed down at the shore's edge.

"Somethin' wrong?" Bill asked. He stood there, able to touch bottom and keep his chin up out of the water except for the occasional small curler that rolled in. "You got a cramp?"

"No." She pursed her lips and looked uncertain. "There might be something I need to explain."

"Is that so?" Bill was curious.

Now that her head and shoulders were clear of the water, the two large clamshells she wore to preserve her modesty gleamed against her olive skin. She carried the spear in one hand.

"Yes," she said.

A fluked tail broke the surface near Bill and flicked away seawater droplets.

"Strolling along the beach isn't something I do because I'm not built for that," Aeliana said.

"Have long have you been a mermaid?" Myron asked.

Aeliana frowned at the writer. "Now how long would you think I've been a mermaid?"

"Sorry." Embarrassment turned Myron's face red. "I suppose that was a foolish question. I don't usually ask foolish questions, but I don't often meet mermaids. Or ghosts, either." He took a deep breath and sighed. "The last few days have been more interesting than I ever could have imagined. Of course, when you're riding with Pecos Bill, I guess you should expect anything."

"Pecos Bill!" Aeliana smiled excitedly and riveted her gaze on Bill. "I've heard of you! You're a Texas legend! You married Slue-Foot Sue!"

"Yes, ma'am," Bill said. He tried to downplay his fame, but he soaked it up all the same. Getting recognized by folks was a guilty pleasure.

He was still amazed by the sight of the half-girl, half-fish in front of him. From the waist up, Aeliana was as pretty a girl as a man could hope for, but from the waist below, she was covered in blue-green scales and sported flukes instead of feet.

A coil of netting covered her hips. The clam shells barely hid her charms and the black pearl in her belly button enhanced them. The flickering flames from the campfire somehow her even more mesmerizing.

She sat with her back to a boulder in the sand; her lower half folded up, and held a tin coffee cup in her hands.

They'd eaten supper, such as it was, of fish and cornbread Bill had fried in the frying pan, and they were enjoying a pot of coffee afterward.

"I met Sue when she was a girl, when she wasn't nothing but a hank of hair, skin and bones, and huge feet," Aeliana said. "Such an adventurous thing, but I had a feeling she'd grow into her feet. They were so big. By Poseidon's beard, I never saw such big feet."

Bill nodded. Sue did have some big feet, and she was a mite self-conscious of it, so he never mentioned their size around her.

"I first met her when she was a girl," Aeliana said, "back when she rode her first catfish all the way down from Colorado to the Gulf of Mexico just to prove it could be done. She was always up to doing things. Is she still fun and exciting? You have to tell me."

"She is," Bill admitted and felt a little pride.

"Well, when you get on back home, tell her Aeliana says hey and that she should come on down and see me sometime."

"I will," Bill promised. "She'll probably want to bring the young'uns when she does."

"Y'all have young'uns?" Aeliana asked, and her eyes gleamed.

"Fixin' to have 'em," Bill said. "A whole passel."

"Young'uns are always so much fun. Especially with the way they are so curious and swim around."

"Uh," Myron said, "Bill and his wife are going to have human children."

Aeliana frowned. "Oh, that's too bad. I don't see how human children can be happy with such a flat world or not being able to breathe underwater."

Myron scratched his head. "A flat world?"

"Yes, only able to go to and fro, and back and forth across land. At least if they lived in the sea, they could easily go up and down in the water instead of having to climb hills and mountains to get any variety. Without mountains and hills, the dry world would be a lot flatter."

"I hadn't thought of that," Myron admitted.

"I have to tell you, I wouldn't ever want to live the way you folks do," Aeliana said. "I don't mean no harm when I say that."

"None taken," Bill said.

"Good." Aeliana smiled brightly, then sobered. "If Sue is about to have young'uns, what are you doing all the way out here? Shouldn't you be home with her?"

"We ain't gonna be havin' 'em for a little while. Sue give me leave to go out on an adventure with Myron before them young'uns come."

"That's sweet of her, and right smart knowing how an adventuring man doesn't quite get over hearing that call to the wild and unknown. I see men like that out on the Gulf and in the Atlantic all the time. Always going one place or another and chasing adventures." Aeliana sipped her coffee. "So you decided to come on down to the Gulf to stretch your legs?

What are you planning to do down here?"

"Actually," Bill admitted, "I meant to be throwin' a lasso over a few head of wild mustangs over in the Sangre de Cristo Mountains, only I crossed paths with a Spanish sea captain buried in West Texas."

Aeliana wrinkled her pert little nose and glared at the track *The Flying Dutchman* had left when it sailed into the Gulf of Mexico.

"Well, Bill, I was purely hoping that you being here had nothing to do with that old pirate who left that track," she declared. The pointed at the wide mark across the beach. "He's nothing but trouble with a capital T."

Surprised, Bill asked, "You know him?"

"I do, and I'm here to tell you he's purely not worth knowing." She looked back at Bill. "How did you run into Fockesz all the way up in West Texas?"

"We found a treasure map," Myron said.

"A treasure *chart*," Bill said.

Myron sighed. "I get excited. *Map* just rolls to trippingly off the tongue. Treasure map. See?"

"Treasure?" Aeliana's eyebrows shot up. "Where did you find a treasure map in West Texas?"

"It belonged to that Spanish captain," Myron said. "That poor soul was buried with his ship in West Texas as the result of a witch's curse."

"I promised Captain de Alfaro I'd see to it his body got buried in Spain," Bill said. "He give me the map to the treasure, which I planned on findin' an' givin' to my young'uns as their inheritance. Then Fockesz sailed up in *The Flying Dutchman* an' stole it away like a...well, like a pirate."

"Fockesz does like to get his hands on treasure," Aeliana mused. "It's the only way he can pay off the Devil for helping him so much during his mortal years while he was running cargos. Only the stories I hear say Fockesz owes a lot more to the Devil than he'll ever be able to pay no matter how long he sails. His pride and desperation just won't let him admit it so he keeps on pirating."

"I should imagine he doesn't want to forfeit his soul to the Devil," Myron said. He shivered. "I can't fault a man for that."

"No," Bill agreed, "but I can fault him for takin' my young'uns' inheritance. If I could find him, I'd take my chart back an' go fetch my treasure."

Aeliana tapped her tin coffee cup thoughtfully. "I might be able to help you find your treasure chart."

That caught Bill's attention and he perked right up. "You know where Fockesz is?"

"...SEE TO IT HIS BODY GOT BURIED IN SPAIN."

"I know where the chart might be," the pretty young mermaid said. "You see, Fockesz might be buying his soul back from the Devil, but Cressida the Cold is the one he has to deal with."

"Who's she?" Myron had his journal back out.

"Let me have a little bit more of that coffee, if there is any," Aeliana said. "It's going to take something strong to wash the bitter out of my mouth after I tell this."

Bill picked up the coffee pot sitting near the campfire and poured another cupful of coffee into Aeliana's cup.

"Cressida the Cold is the Sea Hag of the Gulf of Mexico," Aeliana said. "She settled into the area about a thousand years ago and has made life terrible for the local mermaids by conning them out of their powers for the promise of true love with a human they've chosen to fancy. That's why folks see so few of us. We avoid the Sea Hag. She's just mean-tempered and vicious. She's also in league with the Devil, which puts her in business with Fockesz."

"Why is she workin' with the Devil?" Bill asked.

"Cressida is the granddaughter of Hades, the god of the Underworld, which, as it turns out, is just a branch office under the Devil. Her mother was Melinoe, who was the goddess of ghosts and the bringer of nightmares and madness. I'll tell you, the apple didn't fall far from the tree with Cressida. She's nothing but evil. Since Fockesz made it this far, I'm willing to bet he's delivered that chart to the Sea Hag because she handles goods meant for the Devil. She's one of his managers."

"Where can I find her?" Bill asked.

Aeliana pointed south, far away across the dark, rolling waves of the Gulf of Mexico.

"Out there," she told Bill, "in a cave deep under the sea with captive ghosts of sailors she's taken from doomed ships over the years. There she conducts business with Fockesz and others of his ilk who trade other people's sorrows to pay for their own." She hesitated and looked at the Texan with soft, liquid eyes. "It's not a place for anyone who still maintains the breath of life within them, Bill. If you go to her, there's a good chance you won't return and you might end up trapped there forever."

Bill pondered that for a moment.

"If she's deep under the sea," Myron said quietly, "you'll never reach her, Bill. It might be best to let this go and be glad we're all still alive."

The writer's words made good sense, and Bill knew that. But he just couldn't bring himself to give in.

"I can hold my breath a powerful long time," Bill said contemplatively, and partly he was convincing himself. "I can make it."

"Bill," Myron said, "nobody can dive to the bottom of the Gulf of Mexico, fight with a Sea Hag—"

"And her ghosts and monsters," Aeliana added.

"Right," Myron agreed. "All of that. Then fight the Sea Hag, get the chart, and come back up before you drown. It's too much even for you, Bill."

"It can't be," Bill said. He shook his head. "I won't let it be. I ain't gonna let nothin' stop me. I never have. It just ain't been my way, an' I ain't gonna start now."

Aeliana reached out and took Bill's hand. "Are you sure you want to do this?"

Bill looked into the young mermaid's silver-gray eyes. "I got it to do. For my young'uns. It's a promise I made to myself, an' I don't go back on my word, especially not to myownself."

Aeliana squeezed his hand, then she released it and studied him. "There might be a way."

Bill tied onto her words with the desperation of a calf that had lost his momma. "How?"

"These." The mermaid reached up to her ears and removed her black pearl earrings. "These were crafted by Daedalus, the greatest inventor of all time. He was the man who built the Labyrinth where Minos kept his minotaur stepson. Later, Daedalus also constructed wings so he and his son could escape Crete." Sadness showed in her silver-gray eyes. "Only that didn't turn out so well. Maybe you've heard the tale."

"Icarus, Daedalus's son, fell into the Aegean Sea," Myron said.

Bill didn't know the story, but it sounded heartbreaking to him.

"That's right," Aeliana said. "Icarus." She held the pearls between her forefinger and thumb. "One of these gives the gift of water-breathing to humans as long as that human holds the pearl in his or her mouth. It also protects that person from the crushing depths of the sea. Otherwise the swimmer would get smashed."

"Surely you're joking," Myron said. "You can't expect us to believe one of those pearl earrings can allow a man—one of *us*—to breathe underwater."

Paying the writer no nevermind, Bill graciously took one of the offered pearls and popped it into his mouth. It tasted salty and sweet at the same time, like pulled taffy. He walked straight out into the Gulf, took off his hat, and stuck his head under the water. He tried to take a breath and couldn't bring himself to do it.

"You need to relax, Bill," Aeliana coaxed. She'd flicked her flukes and swam over to join him. "Taking a breath underwater isn't natural for you, but you can do it."

The water in Bill's ears made the mermaid sound like she was far away even though she took hold of his elbow.

She put her head down in the water beside his and took a breath. "Just like that."

Overcoming his fears and all his natural-born instincts, Bill took in a big sniff of the water. The salt stung his nostrils for just a moment, but that quickly passed. Somewhere along the way, the sea stopped being water and became air in his lungs.

Feeling near pole-axed with surprise, he yanked his head up from the water and smiled from ear to ear. "It works! I can breathe underwater!"

Aeliana pulled her head up from the water as well and clapped her hands in delight. "I'm so glad it works!"

"Wait," Myron said suspiciously. "I thought you knew these pearls would work. You sound too surprised that this one did to my way of thinking."

Aeliana smiled. "They were given to me by my granny, who told me the story. I've never given them to anyone to use before. She told me I should only trust them to somebody good, that they wouldn't work for someone who had evil in his or her heart. She gave them to me so I could use them to know that." She looked at Bill. "I just haven't ever met anybody I wanted to trust that much until tonight."

A smidge of discomfort trickled through Bill, but he knew wasn't going to do anything wrong. He didn't think Aeliana would either. But her admission touched him.

"So the pearl lets you know if someone was evil?" Myron asked. He was oblivious to the whole meaningful look Aeliana shared with Bill.

The mermaid blinked shyly for a minute. "My granny told me the pearl would help me know if someone I ended up setting my cap for turned out to be not as good as he should be. She was protective like that, especially after my momma...died."

"I'm sorry to hear that," Bill said.

"Thank you," Aeliana said and blinked away tears. "It was a long time ago. Anyway, Granny married a human and they had a child who had legs instead of flukes and couldn't breathe water. The other three, including my momma could breathe water just fine. She asked Daedalus to make her the pearls for her husband and son so they could be together."

"Your grandmother knew Daedalus?" Myron's eyebrows were about to jump off his head and take flight.

"She did," Aeliana said.

"But that was thousands of years ago."

"Mermaids live long lives," Aeliana said, "but they're trapped in a lot of loneliness because they have to give up so much for the love of a good man. Maybe not ever being able to return to the sea as a mermaid is the hardest. That sometimes happens. And it turns out, not many men are all that good. There are lots of mermaids and only a few mermen because that's how we're born. Doesn't seem fair from the get-go, if you ask me. On top of that, Cressida makes things worse around the Gulf by killing and eating mermaids, and she takes hunting merman as a special joy."

"She eats mermaids?" Bill asked.

"She does. We're one of her favorite snacks. She's always hungry."

"Welp, that's a special kind of evil right there."

Myron peered at the mermaid more closely. "How old are you?"

Aeliana shot him a coy glance. "A girl never tells, and a man shouldn't ask." She looked at Bill. "You saved me, and you're Sue's husband and a soon-to-be daddy. If I can't trust you to be a good man, then who can I trust?"

"But those pearls might not have worked," Myron protested.

The mermaid frowned at the writer. "My granny would never have given me something that didn't work, and when she said something was special, it was special."

"Welp, them pearls do work an' I was breathin' water just fine," Bill declared before Myron could say anything else.

Aeliana flicked her flukes and looked at Myron. "Maybe you should try the other pearl and see if it works for you. I knew Bill was a good man, but I don't know you at all. Can't judge you for good or ill from the company you keep. But you're with Bill, so that's why I'm even letting you borrow my pearl."

She held it out to him.

Grimacing, Myron took the other pearl and placed it in his mouth. He grimaced fearfully like it was going to explode his head or something, closed his eyes, and shoved his head underwater. He tried to come back up, but Aeliana pounced on him and held up under.

Bill took a step toward them.

Aeliana looked up at Bill and smiled. "Give it a minute," the mermaid said. "He's fighting and not able to take a breath. I'm just helping him convince himself. He'll come around."

Myron waved his arms wildly and tried to push Aeliana away, but the mermaid was too strong.

She grinned. "He's pretty spirited, isn't he?"

"He's come a far piece with me," Bill acknowledged. "Likely he's got more bark on him than I expected."

Still, Bill wondered if the mermaid might accidentally drown Myron. He wasn't going to allow that. He reminded himself that Myron couldn't drown as long as he had the pearl in his mouth, but he also wondered if the writer might have dropped it, or if he'd swallowed it. Maybe swallowing it took away some of the magic that made the pearls work.

And there was the fact that Aeliana might have been enjoying "helping" a little more than was necessary. She seemed to be having a high old time keeping the writer's head underwater.

Then Myron stopped flailing and fighting. He relaxed and Aeliana let him take his head out of the water. He shook himself off like a dog and slung water in all directions.

He was grinning from ear to ear. He pushed the pearl out into his hand.

"It works!" he shouted. "Jumping Josephat, I can breathe underwater like a fish!"

"It's pretty amazin'," Bill agreed. "Ain't seen much like it."

Frowning, Myron stepped through the water toward Bill and looked up at him. "Did you hear me? I said I can breathe *underwater*!"

"I did."

"What?"

"I said, I did hear you."

Myron frowned. "*What*?"

"You got water in your ears, you dern fool," Bill said in a louder voice, but he wasn't mad.

He was happy. He had a way of confronting the Sea Hag of the Gulf of Mexico, and that was something.

"So let's all get a good night's sleep tonight," Bill suggested, "an' light out first thing in the mornin'."

†††

Despite how tuckered out he was from riding for three straight days, and all the excitement the evening had brought with discovering mermaids and Sea Hags and magical pearls made by ancient Greeks, Bill still had trouble going to sleep that night, but once he got there, he slept hard.

Nightmares haunted his rest, though. In them, Fockesz had kidnapped Sue and the young'uns. There were *six* of them, three boys and three girls, probably because Sue liked to keep things even, and there was one for each chamber of a Colt pistol Sue told him. Fockesz held them in a brig aboard *The Flying Dutchman.* The young'uns were afraid and weeping something awful, and Sue was beside herself trying to take care of them all.

In the end, Bill had known he was more just unconscious and trapped in bad dreams than he was sleeping. So when he opened his eyes the next morning, he was even tireder than he'd been before laying down.

"You don't look good," Myron said.

The writer appeared weathered and worn. His hair stuck out in all directions. He knelt by the campfire where the coffeepot sat on a platform of rocks above the flames.

"You don't look much like no ray of sunshine yourownself," Bill said. He sat up and reached for his boots. The morning had a chill. "Is there still coffee in that pot?"

"There is."

"Good, because that may be the only thing that keeps me alive."

Bill pulled his boots on, stood and stamped them to get the fit he wanted, and buckled his pistols around his hips. He hadn't worked out how they were going to be of any use against the Sea Hag, but he didn't go anywhere without them.

He looked around and saw the Gulf stretching out wide and brown-green. A few sandpipers strode across the beach on long, stalky legs. But there wasn't a mermaid in sight.

"Where's Aeliana?"

"She said she was going to fetch us breakfast seeing as how we didn't have any. All we've got is a little bit of cornmeal and some bacon fat left over from last night." Myron squinted at the sun barely risen in the eastern skies. "I hope she hurries. On top of everything else we've run out of, this is likely the last pot of coffee we're going to get unless there's somewhere we can get some."

"Not out here," Bill said. "Ain't nothin' out here a man can get that's store-bought. We're on our own, amigo." He shaded his eyes with a hand, looked out into the Gulf, and glanced at the barely risen sun. "Shore didn't mean to sleep so late. Back to home, the cows would have got plumb tired of waitin' an' already milked theirownselves."

"Hey, Bill!"

Tracking Aeliana's voice, Bill spotted the mermaid swimming toward shore. She had several fish on a stringer that trailed behind her. The catch flopped and flipped, but they stayed strung.

He walked down the gently sloped beach to the water's edge to meet her.

"Breakfast," she announced and passed the stringer of fish over to him. "I do the fishing. You and Myron do the cooking."

Bill smiled. "Yes, ma'am. I reckon I can do that."

The Texan knew he'd be doing it alone, though. Myron hadn't proven to be much help when it came to fixing meals.

Aeliana swam onto the sand, rolled over to sit up with her flukes cocked behind her. "Do you have any of that cornmeal left from making cornbread last night?"

"Yes, ma'am. A mite."

"It's been a long time since I had tacos. I don't end up talking with many humans, and fire and I aren't friendly, but I do so dearly love tacos. Corn or flour, it doesn't matter."

"You'll have them corn tacos this mornin'."

"Good. I look forward to them. In the meantime, I'm going to see if I can get hold of a friend."

"A friend?"

"We're going to need transportation to the Sea Hag's Grotto." Aeliana pursed her lips. "She won't be happy to see us, Bill. That undersea cave where she lives is totally under her control and a long way from here. She'll know we're coming before we get there, and she'll be ready to fight. It'll be better to conserve your strength for the fight."

"Yes, ma'am. I reckon you know what's best. But just so's you know, if you can't get hold of your friend mighty soon, I'm goin' on. Don't matter how far away it is."

Bill took the fish back to the fire, filleted them with the Bowie, and set them to cook while he worked up some tortilla dough out of cornmeal, bacon grease, and a pinch of salt. He sent Myron to scour the nearby brush and bring back some fresh wild onions, sage, and garlic.

In only a few minutes, Bill had the tortilla dough rolled up into balls. He mashed one of them out flat as he could and plopped the tortilla onto a smooth rock he'd placed in the fire. The tortillas cooked right quick on the heated rock and he made a nice pile of them on another rock he'd cleaned and washed. He turned the skewered fish and kept on making tortillas.

He also thought about that treasure just sitting out there on some island waiting for him to fetch it up. His young'uns would be set and never know want. That was a nice feeling.

Unless Fockesz took it first.

That thought didn't set so well with Bill and nudged him a little off his feed, but the smell of tortillas coaxed it on back.

At the shoreline, Aeliana sat holding a weird brass tube in the water. She took a breath every now and again and blew into the tube. The deep, throbbing note the device created was barely audible out of the water, but Bill heard it and thought it was one of the saddest things to ever touch his ears.

When the tortillas were ready, he folded cooked fish chunks in them, added wild onions, garlic, and sage, and took a fistful of them down to Aeliana. Myron joined them with tacos of his own.

The writer gestured to the brass tube. "What are you doing?"

Aeliana bit into her first taco with clean, white teeth. "Calling a friend," she said around her bite. She chewed and smiled in satisfaction. "Oh, Bill, these tacos are *so* good. I love tortillas. I just can't usually get them."

"I could do better if I was outfitted with proper supplies, like some peppers an' some salsa," Bill said, "but I think what tastes so good is the fish. You caught a mess of really nice ones." He bit into his own taco and chewed.

"What *friend* are you calling?" Myron asked.

Aeliana took a moment to swallow before speaking. "Herman. That's not his real name. I can't say his name in human talk. You'd never understand it. But Herman's what I call him."

"Who is Herman?"

Out in the Gulf, not far from shore, ripples broke the surface and a monstrous black and white shape rose out of the depths like a small island forming from the sea. The fin on his back stood at least five feet tall and that looked small against the forty-foot long body. The massive creature turned his head and fixed a large eyeball on the three folks seated along the shoreline.

Then he blew a spray of water from a hole at the top of his head and loosed a high, ear-splitting screech that echoed over the water and made Bill's head vibrate.

Aeliana screeched right back at the creature. When she finished, the creature shot into the air and splashed down. The mermaid laughed like she'd never seen anything so funny.

"That...that's a shark," Myron whispered.

Aeliana shook her head. "Herman isn't a shark. He's an orca whale. I can see how you'd be confused, you not knowing the sea any better than you do."

"I've heard orca whales are mankillers," Myron protested.

"No," Aeliana stated patiently. "They're not mankillers. Not by nature, at least, although humans don't always give them a chance to be any other way than mean and spiteful, and maybe a little vengeful after they've been wronged, because humans tend to be stupid and think they know everything. Why, most of the time orcas are just as agreeable as anybody you'd care to meet."

Bill studied the massive creature and wondered how anything so big could be so gentle as Aeliana suggested. Of course, Paul Bunyan's blue ox, Babe, could be as frolicsome as a pup. A mighty huge pup, though.

"Herman is my friend and has been for years," the mermaid continued. "I nicknamed him Herman after that writer who wrote *Moby Dick*. Herman thinks that's just a howl. Herman can be really funny when he's got a mind to. In fact, his greeting to us just now was, 'Good morning. Call me Ishmael.' Like the first line of that novel. Isn't that just a hoot and a half?"

Aeliana laughed and the delicate notes sailed over the Gulf. Herman must have heard them, because he laughed too. His massive body quaking as he chuckled created a series of waves that lapped against the shoreline.

Even though seeing the orca floating out there was a trifle unsettling, Bill grinned and pushed his hat back with a thumb. "Yes, ma'am, it is. Mighty funny."

"Anyway, I told Herman about your troubles with the Sea Hag and *The Flying Dutchman*, and your young'uns coming on, of course, and he's sympathetic to your cause. He's got four young'uns of his own, so he understands trying to look out for them. He's agreed to carry you two out to Cressida's grotto as his gift to your young'uns."

"That's mighty generous," Bill said.

"Herman is generous by nature, like I said. Him carrying you two will be a lot easier than if you had to swim the six miles out to the Sea Hag's Grotto."

Feeling there might be a challenge in there somewhere, Bill said, "I can swim six miles just usin' one arm an' one leg."

"I can't," Myron admitted.

"Be glad that with Herman here you won't have to do that," Aeliana said. "Bill, you might as well ride along with Myron and keep him company during the trip. Save your strength. That way you'll be ready to fight the Sea Hag with all you got when we get there, because you're going to have to do that."

"We're going to be riding a man-killing whale," Myron whispered. He balled his fists up in Bill's coat and looked up at the Texan with fear-widened eyes. "*I'm* going to be riding a man-killing whale. Why it could just upend me into the air and swallow me whole when I fell back down."

Aeliana sighed and spoke quietly to Myron. "You need to be quiet, mister. You keep it up and you'll hurt Herman's feelings."

Myron stared out at the orca. "Can that be done? He's so *big*."

"Yes, he's big, and that's where folks make their first mistake with him. He's the sensitive sort. And if you do hurt his feelings, I'm going to hurt your feelings a lot more." The mermaid narrowed her eyes and looked mean. "I'll probably *bruise* your feelings up a little too. Just so I know I got your attention."

The writer eased away from the mermaid. He looked up at Bill.

"You can stay if you want to," Bill said. "I'm going after what's mine."

†††

Only a short time later, Bill sat astride Herman and rode him on out into the Gulf of Mexico. He had his hat pulled down low and his stampede strap tied up tight under his chin so the Stetson would stay on. The day had warmed up considerable and he rolled up his sleeves.

Myron sat behind him with both arms wrapped tightly around the orca's dorsal fin. He'd gone from being afraid of Herman to clinging to him for dear life.

Aeliana swam alongside the orca and easily matched her friend's speed. She didn't speak to Bill, though she chatted some with Herman in high-pitched squeaks, and concentrated on guiding them to the Sea Hag's underwater hideout. Evidently Herman had never been there.

Bill liked the ride. The orca had a nice gait. The whale crashed through the waves and powered across the sea with confidence and skill. The Texan had to admit, only to himself, that Herman was making better time crossing those six miles to the Sea Hag's Grotto than he would have by swimming. The orca was plenty fast.

The sea spray and the cool wind blowing across Bill was pleasant, and the warm sun took away most of the chill from the wetness.

"Some folks say you created the Gulf of Mexico," Myron said loud enough to be heard over the slap of the ocean against Herman's hide. "I've heard that when there was a drought going on in Texas, you rode out to California, roped a storm cloud, and brought it back to rain all over the land. Only it was too much and that's how the Gulf was made."

Bill shook his head. He knew the story and it was foolishness. At least, most of it was. Folks just couldn't tell a true story without polishing it here and there.

"Nope," he said. "The Gulf was already here. I just helped it along a mite. I underestimated the size of my catch when I threwed my lasso. It happens now an' again. That storm cloud did more damage than I thought it would. Texas used to be a lot bigger, an' I'll always be sad about that, even though we're still the biggest state in the Union. After all that rain, we lost a big chunk of land clear up to Galveston, an' it looked like Houston might have washed away before it was over, but everythin' calmed down. We lost some of the coastline, but the crops an' the cattle was saved."

Myron smiled. "Riding out on the back of an orca to face an evil sea hag has got to be the most audacious thing you've ever done."

"Maybe for right now," Bill said and grinned. "But I'm still alive, an' there's still time for more adventures. Texas is a mighty big place. I'm sure one day I'll top this." He wasn't sure how that would happen, though, but he smiled. "I'm lookin' forward to it. Life would be mighty borin' without all these here adventures. Sue knew that too. That's why she sent me on my way. I'm a mighty lucky man to have that little gal in my life."

Widow-Maker whinnied in agreement.

Bill glanced over his shoulder and saw his faithful mustang riding easily on the orca's hindquarters. Widow-Maker wouldn't stay back at the campsite for love or money. He had been bound and determined to go, so Bill had asked Herman if he was up to the task of carrying Widow-Maker as well. Herman had taken one look at the horse and laughed so hard he blew a small lake from his blowhole.

"That's right, ol' hoss," Bill said and smiled. "Me an' you, we're still full of vinegar."

Widow-Maker nodded happily and reared on his back legs. It was mighty strange seeing the mustang standing there so proudly on the hindquarters of an orca swimming through the Gulf of Mexico.

Yes, sir. This adventure would be hard to top.

Bill laughed. He'd sure be happy to try.

He just had to live through this little set-to.

About fifteen minutes later, Herman coasted to a stop in what appeared to Bill to be the middle of nowhere and lay mostly still in the ocean. Nosy gulls and terns floated on the breeze and circled around to take another gander at the whale and his passengers and the mermaid.

The birds squawked and squeaked something fierce, but Bill couldn't blame them. Humans and a horse riding a whale wasn't something they saw every day. In fact, it might never happen again.

Curious and feeling somewhat tense because he was ready to get to it, Bill studied the waves, but he couldn't find any markers anywhere that would identify the spot as the place where the Sea Hag's Grotto was located. He wasn't sure how the mermaid knew where they were.

Floating in the water below, Aeliana held onto one of Herman's flippers and looked up at the Texan. "Are you ready, Bill?"

"This is it?" Bill asked.

"Yes," she answered.

"How do you know?"

"Do you know where you are when you're riding in Texas?"

"Of course?"

"How?"

Bill pondered the question for a moment and shrugged. "I just know Texas."

"Like I know the Gulf of Mexico." Aeliana smiled. "Besides, I can feel Cressida's evil protection spells from a mile away. It gets stronger the closer I get to it. This is the place. The meanness and rottenness just seep from this spot like infection from a festering wound gone from bad to worse. The grotto is straight down about five hundred feet."

Bill got to his feet and was careful not to cut Herman with his spurs. "Thought it would be deeper. Five hundred feet ain't nothin'." He was sure he'd dived deeper. Somewhere. Maybe.

"The grotto's in an underwater mountain," Aeliana explained. "An old volcano that's settled down and gone dormant. *Mostly* dormant."

"Mostly?" Myron asked. "Mostly's not permanently. Mostly means that volcano could still blow. That's not good."

The mermaid shrugged. "There might be a little fire still in there. I don't know. I've never been in the grotto. Usually folks who go in there don't come out again." She frowned. "I sure am hoping we beat those odds today."

Fear tightened Aeliana's features, but excitement thrummed through Bill. It was like this every time he knew he was about to do something foolish, something big, something that nobody had ever been done before, and, maybe, sometimes shouldn't even have been done in the first place. He lived for those times.

He looked forward to the coming battle so he could get that treasure chart and be on his way to all those gold coins and gems just waiting on him to get there.

And Myron was there to write it all up later. Bill wanted to make sure he got copies of the story for his young'uns. Sue could read it to them by the fireplace of an evening after supper when they were all resting at the end of the day.

Taking a deep breath to clear his head, Bill shucked his pistols and wrapped them tight, then he shoved them into his waterproof possibles bag. The magic Bright Eagle had woven into the bag allowed him to store his Colts in there even though they were bigger than the possibles bag on account of it being bigger on the inside than on the outside.

He hated being away from the Colts, especially if he was going to beard such a dangerous thing as the Sea Hag in her lair, but the separation would only be for a short time. He had to admit that not even he knew how to use a pistol underwater. He only wished he could have put his Henry in there.

That wasn't possible, so he added his boots, cinched the possibles bag up tight so it wouldn't let any water in, and looked over to Widow-Maker. He patted the mustang on the nose affectionately.

"I'm gonna be gone for a little bit, boy. You an' Herman keep a sharp lookout for us while we're gone. Don't want you snatched up by any sharks or pirates."

Widow-Maker whinnied and nodded.

Herman blew a stream of water from his blowhole, and Bill figured that was an agreement of sorts.

Myron didn't look any too happy with how things were developing. He was fretting something fierce.

"You can stay here," Bill said. "I won't think any less of you if you do. I can handle this."

"I'll think less of me if I crawfish." Myron squared his shoulders. "Besides, my editor wants a story about the things I saw, not a story that was told to me by someone else. Not even you. He believes in getting stories from primary sources. No, I have to go and see what happens so I can report it and be the writer I am meant to be."

"All right then," Bill said. "Put that pearl Aeliana gave you in your mouth. We're about to go huntin' us a Sea Hag."

Bill reached into his shirt pocket, took out the black pearl, and tucked

" I'M GONNA BE GONE FOR A LITTLE BIT, BOY. "

it between his cheek and gum so it would nestle in and stay in place. He untied the stampede strap on his Stetson, walked over to Widow-Maker, and tied the headgear to the saddle pommel so a stray breeze wouldn't blow it away.

"Hold my hat," Bill said told the mustang, then he jumped from the orca's side, shouted "Yee-haw!" and arrowed toward the Gulf of Mexico.

He hit the water and went under at once. The pearl worked its magic and he took a deep breath. Aeliana swam past him and headed down into the darker water.

The deeper they went, the more the sunlight faded.

✝✝✝

Aeliana led the way through the greenish-brown sea. She cut through the water easily and her tail flukes powered her along.

Bill trailed a short distance back, watchful of things that might pop out from behind shadows latticed through the depths and deliver an unpleasant surprise. There were plenty of places for ambushes. He didn't know much about the ocean, didn't know much about what-all lived there, but he knew enough to know he was better on dry land, and on top of a horse to boot.

A man could command himself an empire from the back of a horse. Plenty of men had done it. He wondered if Aeliana knew any seahorses big enough to ride. Of course, that would have made Widow-Maker jealous.

He didn't like the closed-in feeling he got from being submerged. On top of that, he had to continually remind himself to breathe because having his head underwater just naturally made him want to hold his breath.

It was confusing, but he was determined to settle up with the Sea Hag and find out if she had the treasure chart Captain de Alfaro had given him. He wasn't going back to Texas without it.

The water got darker and darker the deeper he went. It got colder too, and waves of even colder water washed over him, like there was a river running through the ocean, which was something he didn't expect. It didn't seem likely that water could be running through itself, but that was what it felt like and he was pretty certain that was how the ocean worked.

He glanced over his shoulder to make sure Myron was following and was doing okay. The writer swam with a smooth stroke and only fell a little behind. Aeliana slowed every now and again to allow Myron to catch up.

The writer's pluck continued to surprise Bill.

Schools of fish and a handful of turtles darted out of the way of the three swimmers. Some of those creatures flitted around a little, curious about the invaders, but they didn't come close enough to touch.

All of them fought shy of the stony crest that slowly took shape a short distance in front of Bill only a few moments later. As soon as he saw the underwater mountain, unease threaded through his bones and a voice in the back of his head screamed that he should turn back before it was too late. He had to master that fear like a blacksmith hammering red-hot iron to turn it into determination.

He'd been scared a couple times as a kid, by different things bigger than him, and some things he only heard but never saw. For a while, as a small fry, he'd even been afraid of the night. His coyote family taught him how to get over that, to not be afraid of the dark and what was in it, and to howl at the moon like he owned the night.

When she reached the underwater mountain, Aeliana paused and hesitated for a moment. She bit her lower lip and wrapped her arms around herself. She trembled a little and studied Bill. Her dark red hair billowed around her and rode the ocean currents.

Bill didn't blame her for being skittish, or even downright afraid. She was allowed. She didn't have a dog in the fight with the Sea Hag no matter if she had a friendship with Sue those long-ago days.

She rested one hand on the top of the stony outcrop and looked at Bill expectantly.

Bill treaded water beside her and pointed down decisively.

He intended his message to be clear as a mountain stream in the Colorado Rockies: he was still going.

Aeliana nodded and reached back for the fishing spear she carried. The red coral tip glinted even in the gloomy sea surrounding them. Armed, she flipped over in the water so she was once more headed down, and flicked her flukes. She sailed on down the side of the mountain like a dewdrop sliding down a blade of grass.

Heart banging steadily and ringing in his ears, Bill drew his Bowie knife and followed.

A few minutes later, the cave mouth appeared as a dark shadow on the stone behind a small forest of kelp.

Aeliana pulled a long white coral knife from the net bag at her waist to accompany the fishing spear gripped tightly in her other hand and waited for Bill to join her.

When he was at her side, Bill peered into the cave. A narrow passageway squeezed between slabs of rock that almost fit together like a church deacon's hands frozen while applauding led back into Stygian darkness.

But there was a feeling there that bothered him something fierce.

A whole heap of alabaster and ivory bones littered the cave floor at the bottom of the passage. They laid along the passage like somebody had dropped them there when he—or *she*—had finished gnawing off the meat. Some of the bones looked old, but some of them looked new, fresh even.

Most of them were fish bones, but Bill was pretty sure there were human bones mixed in among them. That disturbed him and raised the hackles on the back of his neck even underwater. Swords of several styles, long and short, straight and curved, and flintlock pistols were mixed in with the bones.

The place looked a lot like the Wendigo's cave Bill had gone into in order to save one of Jim Bowie's descendants.

Aeliana looked at Bill. From her hesitant expression, he was certain she'd never been here. This was all new territory she'd never seen. He thought maybe she hadn't known about the bones.

The darkness bothered Bill enough to make his belly tighten, though. He waited a minute for his eyes to adjust so he could see better, but they never did. The darkness in the passageway stubbornly remained.

Aeliana tapped him on the shoulder and almost startled him. Forcing himself to stay relaxed, he turned around. She tucked the coral knife back into her net bag, fumbled around, and brought out a delicate rectangular scrimshaw box about the size of her palm and a finger-width tall. Intricate designs decorated the box, but the light that leaked through the water was too dim to allow Bill to make out what it was with any certainty.

Hand shaking a little, Aeliana opened the box one-handed and revealed five beautiful red gems that glowed with inner fires. She slung her spear over her shoulder and took out one of the gems. It was about the size of a fingernail and it hung at the end of a small gold chain. Once freed from the scrimshaw box, the gem immediately glowed more brightly and dispelled some of the murk in the water for a few yards in all directions like a lantern would in the night.

Bill blinked and let his eyes adjust to the red-tinted light that changed the way everything around him looked. The light allowed him to see better, but it gave his surroundings an odd appearance because of the red color. He worked hard not to think that the undersea looked like one of the grimmest pits of Hell.

That didn't help. The thought stuck and rolled around in the back of his head like a sharp pebble lodged in a boot.

Aeliana pushed the gem into the cave's darkness and the bauble glowed brighter still, as if encouraged, or maybe challenged, by the blackness that awaited within. The lingering shadows in the passageway fell away and retreated before the gem, but the light made the bones stand out in the red light and they looked like they'd just been dipped in fresh blood.

The mermaid gestured to Bill's left hand. He raised it and she slipped the gold chain over his hand and slid it up to his wrist. She pulled on the chain and locked the gem into place on Bill's wrist. When she released it, the gem dangled at the end of the chain.

Aeliana placed another gem around her own wrist, flipped her hand around and caught the gem in her cupped palm, then mimed pointing it forward into the cave. Light spewed forth from her hand and sliced through the lingering shadows.

Bill nodded and palmed the gem. He pointed the gem into the cave and the ruby light chased away the shadows like a hound chasing after a covey of quail.

Aeliana held up a slender finger and Bill remained stationary.

The mermaid wrapped a third gem around Myron's wrist. The writer grinned like a kid in a candy store, opened his mouth to speak, then grew frustrated when only bubbles and no sound came out.

Bill figured they all looked like giant fireflies gathered outside the Sea Hag's Grotto. The lights drew some of the fish in to inspect the proceedings, and a couple of spiny-legged things that resembled kin of giant spiders sneaked back into hiding along cracks and crevices in the underwater mountainside. Bill realized the lights might have helped with the darkness, but they also marked them for anyone looking for something, or *someone*, that stood out. A cold feeling that was more than the sea washed over him. It was like somebody walking over his grave.

Working in the dark was dangerous, and being lit up so well was equally dangerous, but Bill figured he was more comfortable having the light.

After taking a deep breath to get himself prepared, Bill gripped his Bowie more tightly and swam into the cave. There was no time like the present to get to it. If Aeliana was right, and he had no reason to doubt her, hesitating would only give the Sea Hag more time to prepare for unwanted company.

As he swam, the gem's light pushed back the darkness and always kept it beaten back. He followed the passage and swam a few feet above the cave floor and the bones mixed in with a few plants that grew thinner and thinner until they finally disappeared altogether. Nothing lived there. No fish. No plants.

He was just left among the bones laying on bare rock. He halfway expected them to get up and come after him. That was just his imagination playing with him. Had to be.

The red light from the three gems reflected slightly from the hard walls that surrounded them.

Bill guessed he was about a hundred yards into the cave passage when it widened out. Twenty yards farther on, up and to the left, the passageway widened still more and revealed a huge skull carved out of solid rock.

Glowing orange coral sat back deep in the eye sockets. A ten-foot-long eel thick as a man's thigh slid free of the right sinus cavity, whipped through the water, and streaked at Bill.

Just as the eel reached him, the creature opened its mouth and revealed dozens of needle-sharp teeth that glinted in the red light. Moving more slowly than he would have liked, but still faster than his attacker, Bill batted the eel's head away with his left fist.

He waved his arms and kicked his feet so that he flipped around in the water to see if it would attack again, but it glided on past Aeliana and Myron without offering any threat.

They took a moment to regroup in the chamber in front of the carved skull.

Aeliana pointed to the skull's mouth. She mouthed the word, "Door." Even though Bill couldn't hear her, he read her lips, which were red tinted. Her hair was a mass of fire around her head.

Bill swam toward the skull mouth, used the gem to illuminate it, and searched the surface. He poked at the rock with the Bowie knife and searched for a locking mechanism. Frustrated, he banged one of the huge stone teeth with the knife hilt and a hollow *bong!* came from inside the stone wall.

There was empty space behind the skull and plenty of it.

Then the skull opened its mouth and its jaw dropped wide like a chicken snake unhinging to swallow a hen's egg. Directly after an old woman called out in a creaky, cracking voice.

"Why hello! It's so nice for you to have come by, little mermaid. And you've brought friends. My oh my, do come in. I haven't had any true amusement for a long time. You might say I'm *hungry* for it."

In addition to sounding old, the voice also spoke with an accent that Bill couldn't place.

It bothered him that whoever spoke to him knew they were there, but then there hadn't been much chance of sneaking up on the Sea Hag's lair all lit up in the ruby light. Aeliana had told them sneaking up would be impossible. The Sea Hag had called out just to devil them and break their nerve.

That wasn't going to happen.

Bill gritted his teeth in determination, took a fresh grip on his Bowie knife, and swam through the skull's open mouth. He tried not to imagine what would surely happen if the skull closed its mouth again. The stone teeth weren't sharp enough to cut, but they were solid enough and massive enough to crush whatever got between them.

Then he was through and into another, narrower, passageway. He swam into the channel and it angled up and up. Pale, sickly green light painted the irregular oval at the end of the passageway and hinted at a larger chamber beyond.

The mix of green and red light fell over the walls of the passageway and revealed the friezes that ran the length of the corridor on both sides. The fact that the wall carvings were there meant someone had lived in this place at long time ago.

Bill couldn't help wondering if the Sea Hag had eaten them all.

Images of horrific monsters filled the friezes. Strange ships battled large seafaring creatures the like of which Bill had never seen. One of the images showed tentacles of a giant, unseen thing whipping around several broken ships. The busted vessels and sailors floated down to the bottom of the sea while other, smaller, monsters attacked the sailors who had been thrown overboard.

The friezes reminded him of Indian paintings he'd seen and stories he'd heard when he'd traveled to various places while he was scouting. Tribes moved on or died out, but sometimes they left behind painted images of wars with other tribes, hunters taking buffalo, and strange animals and creatures that might exist where they'd lived.

Folks were always painting or making statues to keep their stories alive for the generations that came after. Out in California, the Chumash had painted cave walls for hundreds of years. The Navajo in the Territory of New Mexico painted with sand. Every manner of folk had stories.

Bill tore his gaze away and swam on. He was in the Sea Hag's lair. There was no time to lollygag about.

The end of the passageway let out into a pool at the bottom of a large chamber.

Bill pushed up out of the pool and realized the underwater cave held an air pocket. The passageway flattened out along the pool and he swam for the edge. In no time, his feet reached the bottom of the pool and he walked forward. He came up dripping wet into the air and the water level dropped around him. The water sluiced from him and his clothing and left stains around him.

"I'm here," Bill said.

"I see you," the woman said.

"I don't see you," Bill said. He played the gem's red light all around him.

Stone walls, many of them covered in more friezes depicting more battles and large ceremonies, surrounded the pool and him.

"You'll see me when I'm good and ready for you to, and I will be the last thing you see."

Behind Bill, Aeliana and Myron came up out of the water. The mermaid looked nervous and distraught. With no legs, she was going to struggle getting around on the stone floor of the huge cave. Bill was sorry about that, but nothing could be done. They hadn't planned on a dry cave.

Bill laid the Bowie on the ground, reached into his possibles bag, and took out his pistols. He wrapped them around his hips, buckled them tight, and tied the holsters down. Confidence spread through him when he had the pistols on. He was more fully dressed. He pulled on his boots, which was a mite difficult with his socks soaked like they were. He stomped them to get the fit as good as he could. His spurs rang and struck sparks from the stone.

Reaching into his possibles bag one last time, he took out Shiver, the ten-foot long rattlesnake he used for a whip. He left Shake, the big rattlesnake he used as lasso, inside the bag.

"You ready to go to work, Shiver?" Bill asked.

The rattler curled around Bill's hand and shook his rattle in anticipation. Shiver loved a good tussle.

Bill hung Slither at his back so the rattler would be ready.

"Are you still watchin', Cressida?" Bill demanded. "Hidin' in them shadows an' talkin' loud?"

He stepped forward with a Colt in one hand and held the gem dangling from his other hand to light the way. The green light was stronger ahead of him, almost so bright it hurt his eyes.

"Ah, you know my name," she said. "I guess you've been talking to one of those accursed mermaids. A bunch of busybodies sticking their noses where they don't belong is what they are. They're just guppies and never do grow up. Always crying and blaming others for their troubles. When they bother me, I turn them into shark morsels. At least, the parts of them I don't eat myself."

"You won't be torturing and eating mermaids anymore, witch," Aeliana snarled. She hauled herself out of the water. "Those days are over as of right now."

Cressida laughed, and the raucous noise chased a chill that rattled up Bill's spine like a line of heavy-footed ants marching double-time. He gripped his pistol a little tighter, watched the surrounding shadows a little closer, and walked on toward the light. The stone floor had a slight incline that led up.

"Is that you, Aeliana?" Cressida asked like she didn't have a care in the world.

"It is."

Cressida chuckled. "Good. I thought I recognized your voice. I've wondered for years if you were as tasty as your mother. Guess I'll find out soon enough. Now she was good eating."

"Shut up!" Aeliana yelled.

The Sea Hag laughed, and it was a soulless, gut-busting effort that echoed and echoed again inside the immense cave.

Bill's heart went out to the mermaid, but he kept his silence. When she'd mentioned her mother's death, Aeliana had kept the nature of her mother's dying to herself.

It was no wonder Aeliana had been so willing to help him get to the Sea Hag, and no mystery about how she knew where the Sea Hag lived.

"I've nearly had you twice before when you came sneaking around," Cressida said. "I've been looking forward to getting my hands on you. I just didn't expect you to make it so easy by coming to me."

"It's not going to be easy," Aeliana said. "In fact, it's going to be downright impossible. Your time is at an end, you heartless cannibal. I brought friends with me. *Good* friends."

"*Human* friends," Cressida said, and she made it sound like that was a bad thing, an insignificant thing. "I can smell them. I never get my fill of those on account of there not being many down this deep. And it's such a pain to go up and fetch them. It's easier to wait for one of you nosy mermaids."

Aeliana scooted herself along with her arms and dragged herself up the incline. Myron walked at her side and glanced around constantly.

"Come on up, guppy," the Sea Hag said. "It's time we met."

Without warning, the darkness hanging stubbornly in front of Bill melted away like a fog parting and revealed the creature seated in the wreckage of some great throne room forty feet in front of him.

Broken and cracked friezes covered the wall behind her. Fungus, mildew, and mold covered most of what had been carved there, but he glimpsed scenes from a prosperous city that had gleamed under the sunlight.

Whoever had lived there before the foul creature before him had lived on top of the water, not below it. Something had changed.

Mostly transparent ghosts of sailors and sea captains flickered and moved about the large cavern aimlessly. They kept glancing around, searching for something. Bill suspected what all of them were looking for was a way out of the cave. Seeing all of them gathered there, trapped, burned within him.

The Sea Hag was small and scrawny, just a hank of bone wrapped in a shiny green dress. She looked like a stiff breeze would have blown her over.

Bill had been expecting some great brute who was grotesque and slovenly. Cressida would never be a fine-looking woman, but she appeared human enough. She had legs instead of flukes.

Her black hair hung in disarray over her shoulders. Bits of bone and gems were woven into her hair. A large, skeletonized black crab ringed her head with its legs in an obscene crown.

Her face was almost devoid of flesh, stripped down to wrinkled skin pulled snug over sharp bones. Her eyes were dark black, dead pits. Her nose was blade thin and defiant, and looked like it could whittle through steel. A hint of a mustache showed on her withered upper lip and whiskered warts covered her chin.

She lazed on a throne carved from a gigantic, multi-faceted emerald and looked bored. One arm rested on the arm of the throne and supported her head.

The other hand plucked a fat shrimp from a cut glass bowl in her lap where a dozen more squirmed over each and flailed their thin legs like chickens trying to flee a henhouse when a fox got in among them.

Idly, she dangled the shrimp above her face and studied the creature for a moment. Then she leaned forward and bit its head off.

The shrimp's body shuddered and it hung from her fingertips. The Sea Hag chewed noisily and fluids ran down her withered cheeks.

"At least," she said and chewed for a moment, "humans are tasty. Cooked or raw. I don't have a preference." She stared at Bill with slack disinterest and frowned. "A cowboy? You brought a cowboy down here?" She pursed her lips like she'd bitten into a sour pickle and shook her head. "I've eaten a couple of those. Can't say that I enjoyed the experience. They're too lean and stringy to suit my tastes, and they're filled with chunks of gristle."

Cressida dropped the remainder of the shrimp into her mouth and chewed.

Spurs ringing with every step and echoing off the walls, Bill walked toward the Sea Hag.

"That's close enough," she warned.

"I ain't stoppin'," Bill said and kept on walking. He wanted to put a bullet between her merciless eyes, but he couldn't bring himself to shoot a woman. Especially not outright cold like that.

Cressida showed him a cruel smile that revealed shrimp legs caught in her crooked teeth. "Well, then you're going to die, cowboy."

When he was twenty feet out from the throne, green and blue speckled things that resembled giant jellyfish, but were definitely not jellyfish, floated slowly down from the roof of the cave. Tendrils almost at least as long as Bill was tall dangled from their concave bodies snapped and cracked like toads' tongues during their descent. All the creatures had multiple eyes like spiders that covered their bells.

"Look out!" Aeliana called. "Those are *Tacet Enim Mori*! The Silent Death! Their venom will paralyze you and leave you helpless!"

Even though he didn't want to, Bill took a slow step back and scowled.

The Sea Hag watched with bright interest. She abandoned her bowl of shrimp and placed it at the foot of her throne. She sat up and pulled at a gold necklace that had a tiny skull pendant.

"You can't escape my *Tacet Enim Mori*," Cressida said. "I've bred them for hundreds of years to be the perfect killing machines. Once you succumb to their venom, you can watch as I eat you alive. I'll start with your toes and work my way up." She raised her voice and glanced back at the mermaid. "You've doomed your little human friends, Aeliana. You see that soon enough, but I promise I'll save you for last so you can watch me devour them. Bite by scrumptious bite."

"Ain't nobody devourin' me," Bill said.

The grotesque jellyfish things puffed their bells and altered their fall to a more direct approach for Bill. They were bigger than what he'd thought, each with a bell at least an ax handle wide and the tendrils had to be ten feet long. Another half-dozen *Tacet Enim Mori* floated after the first wave and more clung to the roof of the cave.

Quick as lightning, Bill dropped the gem to hang from the gold chain and drew his other pistol. Both hands holding shooting irons, he lined up shots in an eyeblink because he only had twelve bullets in his pistols and reloading would take time.

Before the first of the floating *Tacet Enim Mori* reached him, Bill fired his pistols so fast the rounds rolled like summer thunder cracking across a night sky. The .44 loads burst the jellyfish things to pieces and they became the rain that drummed against the stone with meaty splats.

When Bill's pistols were empty, over fifty *Tacet Enim Mori* lay scattered and blown to flinders in front of him. Several pieces had dropped onto the Sea Hag and into her bowl of shrimp. Some of them slapped against the stone floor hard enough to penetrate the ringing in Bill's ears.

More of the creatures drifted down toward Bill, but there were only a little more than a handful. He holstered his pistols and reached for Shiver. The snake coiled around the Texan's wrist the way he always did to provide a better grip.

Shiver's rattle quivered loudly in the enclosed space and revealed the snake's excitement. Bill whipped Shiver again and again and again, and each time the snake's hard-scaled tip exploded one or more of the drifting bell-shaped creatures before a tendril could latch hold of the Texan.

Crack! Crack! Crack!

Shiver flicked out again and again. Bill snapped the rattler about in a wild, whirling dance that ripped the *Tacet Enim Mori* to doll rags and created a rain of bell chunks, tendrils, and flying eyeballs. Bill gave no mercy.

After the area was clear of the floating creatures, the Texan wasn't even breathing hard. His heart danced and he couldn't keep the satisfied smile from his face. He looped Shiver into a nice coil, thanked him, and tucked the snake in at his back once more. Then Bill grinned more broadly at the Sea Hag.

"Welp," Bill said, "looks like you're about all out of them disgustin' varmints, so me an' you are gonna have us a palaver."

Cressida sat with her elbows on the throne arms and steepled her fingers together. "Do you think so?"

Bill took out one of his pistols and reloaded the cylinder quickly. Then he freed the other one and reloaded it.

"I do think so," Bill said. "I've come here chasing *The Flying Dutchman*."

"You came to me?" The Sea Hag put a hand against her chest as though surprised.

"Yep," Bill said. "That ship puts in here to do its business. Ain't no use arguin' that."

The Sea Hag glared at Aeliana. "I suppose Miss Nosy-Britches told you I have dealings with that ship."

Bill ignored that. "Cap'n Fockesz took somethin' of mine, an' I want it back."

Slyness gleamed in the Sea Hag's black eyes. "And if I say I don't have whatever it is you came here looking for?"

"Then I'm gonna tie you up an' take you with me till I find him. I get both of you in the same place, I 'spect I'll get at the truth."

Cressida huffed in displeasure. "That doesn't seem hardly fair."

"You don't deserve fair, you evil witch!" Aeliana yelled.

The mermaid crawled forward. Myron reached down, grabbed her shoulders, and held her back.

"Give Bill a minute," the writer suggested.

Aeliana brushed Myron's hands off her but stayed put. She blew a stray lock of hair from her eyes and crossed her arms. The white coral dagger and the fishing spear stayed in her hands.

"I seen all them bones when I was swimmin' in," Bill stated. "I don't feel none beholden to treat the likes of you fairly. Right now, you got a choice. Get to it."

"Maybe I do have something." The Sea Hag smiled cruelly and tapped her fingers together. "You're talking about the treasure map."

"It's a chart," Myron said in an unsteady voice. He grew quieter but didn't seem able to stop talking. "It's not a map. It's a chart."

"*My* chart," Bill said. He held his loaded Colts in his fists. "*My* treasure. An' I mean to have it back."

The Sea Hag leaned back in her throne. "I'm afraid that's impossible."

"You sayin' you ain't got it?" Bill demanded.

"She has it," Aeliana said. "Fockesz had to give it to her. He has to give her everything that might be worth something so she can pass it on to the Devil as payment for the Dutch sea captain's soul."

Cressida idly drummed the fingers of her right hand on the arm of the throne. "She's right. I do have it. I'm holding the map that for the Devil."

"Chart," Myron said.

"The Devil can't have it neither," Bill said. "It's mine an' I'm not leavin' here without it."

The Sea Hag laughed. "I'm not giving it up. I simply can't. I've got a deal with the Devil and I can't go back on it. He takes a deal-breaking serious.

I'm not going to get on the wrong side of him."

"I'm warnin' you," Bill said, "I make it a point never to put rough hands on a woman—"

The Sea Hag batted her narrow eyes at him in a demure fashion and smiled. "Well, it does my old heart good to meet a man with polite ways. That happens so seldom these days. It used to be men knew how to act with courtly manners and such."

"There's just one problem," Bill said.

The Sea Hag lifted her ropy eyebrows slightly. "And what, pray tell, might that be?"

"You ain't no woman," Bill declared. "You're a foul, bottom-feedin', misbegotten, black-hearted, sinnin', unholy abomination what's got the sulfurous stench of Hell clingin' to you."

The Sea Hag's smile froze, and if it could have fallen off her face, it likely would have shattered right there on the cave's stone floor where the litter of her deadly little pets lay.

"That," Cressida rasped coldly, "was uncalled for and would have been hurtful if I was of a mind to pay any attention to what you have to say. Still, I deserve to be treated with dignity."

"You eat mermaids and human folks!" Aeliana yelled. "You ate my momma!"

"I did do that, and I do like the taste of mermaids and humans. I don't plan on cutting back on meals or changing my diet." The Sea Hag stretched back against the throne like she didn't have a concern in the world. "So what are you going to do, cowboy?"

Bill pointed his pistols at her. "I've had me a bellyful of your sass an' posturin'. Time to give me that chart."

"Go ahead and shoot me," the Sea Hag said. "I promise you, those guns won't—"

On account of the Sea Hag's challenge being like a double-dog dare, and Bill working on his last nerve, he fired one shot aimed at her leg.

The bullet struck Cressida in the shin just below her wrinkled knee. The bullet didn't penetrate, though. It just sat there flattened against her leg.

Eyes narrowed and a frown on her face, the Sea Hag glanced down in irritation and brushed the bullet from her shin with a hand.

"That hurt," she said. "A little. An annoying little sting. That's not going to convince—"

"Welp," Bill said, "let's see how you like a whole swarm of 'em!"

The Texan emptied his pistols rapidly.

Spread out over the Sea Hag's head and chest, the bullets knocked her back in her throne and she grimaced in pain. All the same, after the last gunshot died away, she brushed the flattened bullets from her body.

"That," she declared, "was uncalled for."

Bill holstered one pistol and reloaded the other with fresh cartridges. "Got plenty more where them come from. I'm bettin' you got a soft spot on you somewhere. I got enough cartridges to search for a bit. Probably won't take me all that long to find it. Then I'm gonna fill you full of lead."

"Enough!" the Sea Hag shouted.

The bullets must have hurt more than she let on because she acted madder than a pack of wild dogs on a three-legged cat. Upon closer inspection, Bill noted bruises purpling up under her pale skin. She put on a brave front, but maybe she wasn't as bulletproof as she claimed.

Bill put away the loaded pistol and drew the other to load it as well.

"So," Bill said, "are we done dickerin' over that chart? Or am I gonna have to—"

The Sea Hag screamed something in a language Bill had never before heard. The words spiked through his ears and his brain and sent chills burning up his back and shoulders. Whatever the language was, it was something old, something from before men started remembering things they should write down and tell to their young'uns and their young'uns' young'uns to help keep them safe.

"Oh no!" Aeliana shouted. "Bill! Look out! She's called out to release the—"

The giant stone frieze to one side of the emerald throne shattered inward. Chunks flew across the cave and ricocheted from the walls like buckshot.

From out of another cave that now stood revealed behind the broken wall, a whirling mass of tentacles rode out on a small tide of saltwater. The tentacles whipped around the cave. Then they pressed against the cave floor and the thing's enormous head rose into view.

Bill stared in disbelief at the monster in front of him. The tentacles were at least forty feet long, the color of tar, covered in hooked suckers on the underside, and studded with corded muscle that rippled when they moved.

Atop that, the thing's bulbous head was framed in four triangular fins and held black eyes as big as wagon wheels. Beneath those big eyes was a curved vulture's beak as white as a freshly skinned skull. It looked like a squid, but Bill had never seen a squid with a bird's beak.

" THAT," SHE DECLARED, "WAS UNCALLED FOR."

"What in tarnation is that thing?" Bill asked above the roar of the water cascading throughout the cave.

"It's a kraken," Aeliana answered. "Cressida keeps it as a pet."

"He's more than a pet," the Sea Hag crowed. "He's also my greatest warrior."

Bill searched for places on the kraken to shoot, but nothing about the thing looked too vulnerable. Except the eyes. Everything he'd ever seen had vulnerable eyes.

He raised his pistols.

The Sea Hag screamed those awful words again, or words just as awful, and pointed at Bill.

Immediately, the kraken threw himself forward on his tentacles with greater speed than Bill would have thought possible. The Texan's opening shots missed anything vital, based on how none of the bullets slow the creature down. Before he could fire again, the thing slithered toward him on some tentacles and whipped two others toward Bill.

The Texan dodged to the side and the tentacles struck the stone where he'd been standing. Broken rocks sailed in all directions and some of them thudded against Bill and hurt like blazes.

He fired his pistols at the kraken, but the bullets either bounced off the creature's thick hide or didn't go deeply enough to hurt it.

He bobbed and weaved, but the kraken spun up more tentacles to strike him. Unable to dodge them all, Bill was knocked sprawling and fetched up against a wall near the emerald throne.

"You're not laughing now, are you, cowboy?" the Sea Hag taunted.

Bill holstered his empty pistols because he didn't have time to work out a reload, pushed himself up to his feet, and struggled to realign his vision. He was seeing two of everything, and there were too many tentacles to count.

"Bill!" Myron yelled. "Look out!"

Alerted by the writer's warning, Bill avoided most of a looping roundhouse the kraken threw at him. The tentacle shattered rock from the wall behind him, but Bill caught enough of the blow to get knocked flailing. A moment later, he fell, unable to keep his feet, and skidded on his chin through the inches-deep water rolling over the cave floor for a moment. Hurting everywhere, he recollected himself and got to his feet.

The Sea Hag laughed, full and throaty.

"My kraken's going to tenderize you, cowboy!" Cressida said. "Once he does, I'm going to enjoy eating the meat off your bones even if it is tough and stringy!"

Still reeling from the last blow that had hit him, Bill sleeved blood from his split lips and glared at the kraken.

"It's big," Bill told the Sea Hag, and himself, "but your pet can be broke. I ain't never seen anythin' that can't be."

He ran to the side to avoid the kraken, and the creature propelled himself forward with four of its tentacles while lashing out with the other four. Skidding to a stop, Bill reversed direction and grabbed hold of the desperate plan forming in his mind.

The kraken had to use six tentacles to attempt to shift his mass in a hurry, and the two free tentacles couldn't reach Bill.

Still running, he opened his possibles bag and reached in. "Okay, Shake, it's time for you to do your part in this fracas."

Shake was seventy feet long, the biggest rattlesnake Bill had ever seen. That was one of the reasons he'd had to have him when he saw him. The rattler smiled and flicked his tongue eagerly, and he vibrated like a cat purring in Bill's hands.

The Texan ran behind the shifting, small mountain of muscle that was the kraken, getting around faster than the creature could turn. He dug in with his boots again and turned once more. He ran up one of the thick tentacles the kraken used to shift around.

The tentacle quivered and quaked beneath Bill's drumming boots, but he was surefooted enough to stay on top as it moved. When the kraken rippled the tentacle in an effort to knock Bill off, the Texan leaped at the last second and flew toward the kraken's enormous head.

"Make a big loop," Bill told Shake. He shook out some of Shake's slack.

Fast as a striking, well, fast as a striking *snake*—Shake twisted around and grabbed himself with his mouth. The loop he made was open and generous.

Bill managed to catch a toehold on another tentacle and kept going toward the kraken's bobbing head. He timed his final leap and twirled Snake over his own head. When he thought he had the rhythm and the distance, he let the rope fly.

The loop flew straight and true, Shake was always the best rope Bill had ever had, and settled over the kraken's flared head. Bill pulled Shake tight and the creature fought against being restrained.

Still on the move, swinging from Shake so he pendulumed up the other side of the kraken's head, Bill ducked under a sweeping tentacle and leaped onto the kraken's head.

The Texan landed with both boots. His forward momentum and weight, combined with the awkward angle the kraken was in, tilted the creature over. The kraken's head slammed against the cave's stone floor.

Bill rolled off the creature, grabbed the kraken's head in both arms, and drove the monster against the stone again with as much force as he could muster.

The kraken turned a mite wobbly after that, and Bill figured he'd rung its bell good and proper. The kraken tried to ease his head up; only Bill grabbed hold and rammed it down again. The *splat!* of the kraken's head hitting the stone reminded Bill of a watermelon dropped on flagstones.

Feebly, not steady at all, trembling like an old dog passing hammer handles, the kraken flailed his tentacles at Bill.

Confident and sure now, once more in his element, Bill grabbed the tentacles one by one and used Shake to hogtie all the kraken's tentacles together.

When he finished, he stepped back and admired the knot he and Shake had tangled the kraken's tentacles with.

Weakened, immobile, and beaten near-senseless, the kraken writhed a little and chirped plaintive noises through his curved beak.

"You got him?" Bill asked Shake.

The rattler raised his head, nodded, and hissed with mirth. Shake looked happier than when he'd discovered ostrich eggs. He tightened his coils and the kraken chirped a little louder. Shake hissed laughter.

Bill patted the rattler on the head. "You're the best lasso a feller could ever wish for. Sure am glad we decided to throw in as an outfit."

Shake nodded and hissed again.

"What have you done to him?" the Sea Hag demanded.

"Probably bruised his ego a mite," Bill admitted, "but he'll be fit enough once ol' Shake releases him."

"He's just a baby!" the Sea Hag wailed.

That surprised Bill and he eyeballed the kraken again. For a moment, he got distracted wondering how big a full-grown kraken might get.

Cressida ran across the cave and wrapped her arms comfortingly around the kraken's big head. Those wagon wheel-sized eyes looked up at her and filled with tears. The kraken snuggled his head on her thin shoulder.

"There, there," the Sea Hag said and patted him. "Momma's going to deal with these fools and make them sorry they ever came here. Then you and I will eat all of them we want to. We'll share fifty-fifty."

Bill couldn't believe Cressida wasn't ready to give up the treasure chart. She was standing there holding onto her defeated pet monster and bruises from Bill's bullets were popping out all over her. What was it going to take to make her see she'd been defeated?

She released the kraken and whirled on Bill. "Now for you, cowboy, you're going to die a long and painful death. Then my boy and me are going to eat *all* of you. I'll mount your skulls in front of the Grotto as a warning to others."

She shivered and shook, and her body changed. She grew taller and uglier, and her toenails and fingernails elongated into powerful talons with gleaming razor edges. Large, sharp fangs filled her mouth.

"Bill!" Aeliana shouted. "Run! You can't fight her!"

"She'll kill you!" Myron yelled.

"I ain't gonna run," Bill shouted back. He stared deep into the Sea Hag's black eyes. "I can't do run. It ain't in me."

He'd already backed down to *The Flying Dutchman*. That still nettled him and chafed as rough as porcupine longjohns.

"Run," the Sea Witch said in a deeper voice than before. "Make it last longer. You're doomed."

She laughed and was so loud the cavern shook with it. Stalactites dropped from the cavern roof and smashed to bits against the stone floor. The kraken struggled more, but Shake held him tight. The rattlesnake watched helplessly, already tied up helping Bill.

The Texan was on his own.

Bill left his pistols in their holsters and dug in his possibles bag. "You live in the ocean, right?"

The Sea Hag cocked her head to the side. "You know that I do. I live in this place."

"So you can breathe in the sea and in the air."

The Sea Hag narrowed her eyes. "You're wasting my time with your silly questions. I am not some oracle that you can just question willy-nilly."

Bill smiled. "Welp, I know all that, an' I find myself wonderin'."

"About what?"

"Whether you can breathe in fresh water."

"Stupid human." The Sea Hag took a step forward and dodged when Shake struck at her. One more step and she was out of the rattler's reach. "There's no fresh water in this place."

"I don't think I'm stupid." Bill pulled Sue's watering can out of his possibles bag. The pink petunia stood out bravely against the can's side. "You see, I got somethin' you don't know about."

"A watering can?" The Sea Hag laughed, and the noise echoed in the cave.

More stalactites fell and an avalanche of broken stone tumbled across the stone floor.

"Not just any waterin' can," Bill said and smiled. "This here's my wife Sue's waterin' can. It's mighty special."

"Because of the pink petunia painted on it?"

"No, because of this." Bill reached into the watering can clean up to his elbow, felt around, got a good grip on the slippery mass inside, and yanked that Blue Norther from the can. That dark rain cloud swelled up in his fist in an attempt to bust free, but Bill didn't let it go.

Lightning and tiny thunder shot out of Bill's fist.

The Sea Hag stepped back a smidge and frowned with her fangs showing.

Rain poured down from Bill's hand and drenched the cave floor so fast a small river streaked for the pool where the passageway was. When the downpour gathered in the pool, the water level rose immediately.

The cloud continued to throw lightning and squirm to be free from Bill's grip, and his hand commenced to hurting something fierce from all the electricity and how hard he had to squeeze to keep a grip. He didn't know how much longer he could hold the cloud, and he knew if it got away, he'd play hob trying to get it back before it filled the cave. As he recollected, the cloud had been mighty big.

"Now," Bill said, never giving any sign of his distress and grinning just to be aggravating, "here's what's gonna happen. You're gonna give me my treasure chart or I'm gonna release this here cloud an' let it fill up your little grotto. I ain't gonna let you out of here. I'm willing to bet you an' your big friend will drown in a lake full of clean, sweet Texas water just like any other ocean critter."

A look of shock flitted across the Sea Hag's twisted features. She tried to hide it, but fear gleamed in her eyes. She looked over her shoulder at the kraken still laying hogtied with Shake.

For a moment, Bill thought her massive stubbornness and anger would get the better of her and he'd have to see if there was a way to save Aeliana, Myron, Shake, Shiver, and himself from the coming Texas-sized flood.

Then her shoulders slumped and she shrank down to her original size.

"All right, cowboy," Cressida said in a hoarse, hollow voice. "You win. I'll get you your chart."

Carefully, Bill tried to show no strain and tucked the Blue Norther back in Sue's watering can like he could have held it all day. The cloud didn't go willingly, but it went.

Relief filled the Sea Hag's face.

"There's another thing," Bill said. He waved to the ghosts who had silently been watching the battle. "You got to let them go."

"Then I'll be alone."

"I'm leavin' you your kraken." Bill narrowed his eyes. "It don't have to be that way."

"All right." Cressida waved a hand.

Slowly, one by one, then faster and in groups, the ghosts departed the cave. The grotto instantly seemed a lot less depressing and heavy.

"Okay," Bill said, "an' there's this one last thing."

The Sea Hag glared at him but remained silent.

"You gotta stop eatin' mermaids an' human folks," Bill said. "An' I mean right now. I'm Aeliana's friend, an' she's friends with my wife. I'll be checkin' up on her, an' she'll be checkin' up on you."

Gasping her displeasure, the Sea Hag rolled her eyes in protest. "What do you expect me to eat? A Hag's got needs!"

"Figure it out," Bill told her. "But there ain't gonna be no more eatin' mermaid or human folks. If I hear about it, I'm gonna come right on back down here to the Gulf an' drown you. That's a promise, an' I *never* break a promise."

✝✝✝

Fatigue chafed at Bill on his way up to the surface. His arms and legs weighed heavy as lead. His heart gave a little leap when he spotted Herman's massive shadow above him.

Only a few minutes later, Bill came up beside Aeliana.

Widow-Maker leaned over Herman's side and whinnied a welcome.

"I'm good, ol' hoss," Bill said and smiled up at his old friend.

Herman blasted water through his blowhole and it rained down gently.

Bill laughed because he couldn't get any wetter. Aeliana turned around to face the Texan with happy smile.

"Oh, Bill," the mermaid said. Tears shined in her eyes and she threw her arms around the Texan. "I'm so happy you did everything you did. That worked out so much better than I thought it would."

Surprised and embarrassed by Aeliana's show of affection, Bill didn't know what to do. To his relief, the mermaid pulled away.

"Yes, and I'm glad we're not all dead either. That could have happened so easily down there." Myron treaded water nearby. He gave Aeliana a hard look. "You might have warned us about you and the Sea Hag having some uncomfortable history together."

"If I had told you," the mermaid countered, "would you have come?"

"No," Myron said.

"Yes," Bill answered.

Myron opened his mouth to say something.

"Now, Myron," Bill chided. "It all worked out. Ain't no reason to be hard on her. You got a great story, didn't you? That's what you come out here for, right?"

Myron sighed. "You're right. I did come for a great story, and I got one. I can't wait to get back on dry land and write it up. Our readers are going to be excited." He spread a hand against the sky. "I can see the title now: *Pecos Bill and the Sea Hag of the Gulf of Mexico!*"

"That sounds mighty fine," Bill said. "But we ain't finished yet."

Myron blinked in surprise. "We're not?"

"Welp, I'm not. I still got me a treasure to find."

"Do you have to do that right now?"

"Now's as good a time as any, I'm thinkin'."

"May I see that chart?" Aeliana asked. "I got a glimpse of it when Cressida dug it out of her hidey hole. I think I might know the location of that island that's supposed to have the buried treasure."

Although he was worn from his battle with the Sea Hag and the kraken, and his hand was sore from holding onto that Blue Norther, Bill dug the treasure chart out of his possibles bag.

The mermaid studied the map for a moment, ran a finger along the coastline, pinched out a forefinger and thumb, consulted the chart's legend, and smiled.

"Welp?" Bill asked. "Do you know where it is?"

Aeliana's eyes glittered. "I know where it is. I've been there. We merfolk call it Scupper's Rock. Human sailors have less nice names for it. There's not much to see because it's a phantom island."

"Phantom island?" Myron asked. "Like, with ghosts?"

"No, not with ghosts," the mermaid replied. "Sailors have a name for islands that don't always appear on maps or charts. An island will be on one chart, then not another. Or there's an older chart with no island and a newer chart that shows the landform."

"Islands do get born in the ocean," the writer said.

"This one's an old island. Really old. It's just sometimes it's there and sometimes it's not. That's true even today."

Myron frowned in befuddlement. "So it's a disappearing island? That's even more confusing."

Bill silently agreed that it was a real headscratcher.

"The tide rises and ebbs," Aeliana explained. "Sometimes islands sit so low in the water that the incoming tide covers them up for hours at a time. That's what happens at Scupper's Rock. It got its name because at the wrong time of the day, it's underwater and sea captains don't see it until they've scuppered their ships. Some of those ships have gone down right there. Sailors maintain that ha'ints walk around Scupper's Rock, but I have never seen any when I was there."

"How many feet of water are we talkin' about?" Bill asked.

"It depends. Sometimes it's only a little water. A foot or more. Other times it can be as much as twenty or thirty feet underwater."

"I really don't like the idea of going underwater again," Myron said.

"Water don't matter," Bill said. "We got the pearls Aeliana loaned us. I'm sure we can still have the borry of them for this."

"You definitely can," the mermaid said. "Whenever you like."

"Then let's get started," Bill said.

He took Shake out of his possibles bag, twirled him a mite, and threw him up to drop a loop over his saddle pommel. Once Shake was secure to the saddle, Widow-Maker backed away while Bill held on and climbed on top of the orca.

When Myron was tossed the end of the rattlesnake, the writer wasn't any too excited about taking hold. He grimaced, forced himself to get a grip, and ran up the slick side of the orca while Bill helped reel him in. Myron resumed his seat holding onto the dorsal fin.

"We really ought not go after the treasure, Bill," Myron said.

"I mean to have that treasure," Bill said. "I come a far piece for it already today. I ain't gonna quit on it now."

"I know that. I wasn't saying we shouldn't get it. I was saying right now might not be the optimum time to do that." Myron waved at the westering sun. "We've already lost most of the day."

"I don't like waitin'," Bill said.

"I understand, but we have to look at the logistics. It's going to take time to get to Scupper's Rock."

Bill supposed that was correct. He looked down at Aeliana. "How far is that island?"

"About three hours from here," the mermaid answered.

Bill looked at the sun and knew they'd be awful squeezed for time. "An' how big is Scupper's Rock?"

"It's just the worn-down ridge of a mountaintop," Aeliana said. "It's probably a quarter-mile long and about half that wide. Most of it's flat. There aren't any trees or anything that grows on it because it's underwater most of the day."

"When's it above water?"

"It's above now, but by the time we get there, it'll be under again."

"When will it be above water again?"

"Late this evening. Probably about nighttime."

Bill pondered on that. Baking in the heat of the day and drawed up as he was from being immersed in saltwater, he had himself a powerful thirst. He glanced at the canteens hanging on Widow-Maker's saddle and realized they weren't supplied for a treasure hunt.

As much as he hated it, he knew they had to stop somewhere at least long enough to take on water and grub.

Thinking about his horse standing there in the heat and not knowing what was going on; Bill coiled Shake over his shoulder and walked back to the horse. He took down his Stetson, filled it with water, and held it out for Widow-Maker to drink his fill.

"All right," he said, "we gotta make a stop an' get properly provisioned. Let's get back to shore an' find water an' game."

"Let me tell Herman," Aeliana said.

She squeaked and squealed at the orca and he squealed and shrieked right back at her.

"That's mighty nice, Herman." Aeliana smiled and patted the orca's head. She looked up at Bill. "Herman says he can do you one better than that. He said we weren't far from a small town that's on the edge of the Gulf. It won't take any longer to go there than it would be to return where he picked us up."

Bill drank what was left of the water in his hat and considered. Having a plan felt good and right. He was going to be a daddy. He needed to start planning things instead of blindly charging into them. He sleeved his bruised lips dry and nodded.

"Okay," he said. "Let's do that."

Herman blew a stream through his blowhole, flipped his tail, and they set off north by northeast.

†††

Hours later, seated on Herman as the orca swam south, Bill took out his makin's and rolled a cigarette. He struck a match with his thumbnail and Herman shrilled in surprise. The whale pitched a little bit and Bill had to grab the bushel basket of supplies they'd gotten during their brief stay in Big Blow Cay.

Widow-Maker shoved his head into the bushel basket of hay he was eating and kept it from sliding over the side.

Myron yelped, stopped writing in his journal, and grabbed hold of the dorsal fin.

"What's going on?" Myron demanded.

"Don't rightly know," Bill replied. "Aeliana?"

The mermaid surfaced for a moment and squeaked at the orca. Herman smoothed out to that familiar gait Bill favored so much and kept swimming.

"It's okay," Aeliana said. "Herman saw the match flame and thought for a minute you'd set him on fire."

Bill blew out the match with a puff of smoky breath. "He gonna mind me smokin'?"

"No. I explained to him what it was." Aeliana shook her head. "He still doesn't understand why someone would want to breathe fire."

"Because it's relaxin'," Bill said, "an' it gives me a minute to focus my thoughts."

"You tell Herman that smoking is typical cowboy behavior and Bill doesn't mean anything by it," Myron said. "It's just a juvenile phase he'll grow out of."

Bill wanted to argue that summation, but he didn't see any point in it. He liked the smell of tobacco. Wasn't any more complicated than that. He reached into the basket for another piece of the fried chicken he'd purchased in Big Blow Cay. The diner, and several other buildings, had been undergoing repairs from the latest tropical storm to strike there, and those occurrences gave the town its name, but their cooks turned out mighty fine chicken.

He munched on the chicken, smoked, washed it all down with sweet well water from a canteen, and watched the sun inching on toward the horizon. He hoped he had enough lantern oil because it looked like they were going to need it unless Anne Bonny's treasure was awful easy to find and they got to it before dark.

†††

When they arrived at Scupper's Rock, the island barely stood out above the waterline. Made of murky soil and volcanic rock, the island sat barren in the middle of the Gulf. Streamers of sand that had gotten stranded there when the tide went out shared space with hermit crabs, shells, and part of a broken ship that reminded Bill of the *Swan*.

Thinking about the *Swan* reminded Bill of how Captain Fockesz and *The Flying Dutchman* had gotten the better of him. For a moment, he was pretty steamed, but he reminded himself he was the one that was coming away with the treasure.

That made him the winner.

Water continued to drain from the island in slow, steady streams that slipped on back into the sea. Divots in the island created tidepools that captured crabs, lobsters, and various fish. A large squid flailed in one tidepool and briefly gave Bill unpleasant memories of the Sea Hag's kraken.

He pushed those thoughts out of his mind and concentrated on figuring out which end of the island was what and where Anne Bonny might have buried her treasure.

The orca stopped about twenty yards from the shoreline.

"This is as close as Herman wants to get," Aeliana called up.

"That's close enough," Bill said. "I can swim from here."

"We're going to have to hurry," Myron said. "It's going be dark soon."

"We'll be quick about it."

Bill stepped out of his boots, shoved them into his possibles bag, and picked up one of the shovels he'd bought when they'd stopped for supplies. He hung his hat on Widow-Maker's saddle pommel.

Holding the shovel in one hand with it running alongside the length of his body so it would go into the water smoothly, he dove from Herman's side. When he hit the water, he went under for just a minute and came back up.

Widow-Maker neighed and eased on over to look down at the water lapping against Herman's sides.

"Nope," Bill called out to him and treaded water. "You stay there an' mind my hat. I'll be back in two shakes of a lamb's tail."

The mustang snorted in disgust and pinned his ears back.

"You might as well just be happy about it," Bill said. He turned his attention to swimming.

Myron joined him in the water a moment later, but the writer looked a little fearful. He disappeared underwater, then came up a moment later.

Bill thought about telling Myron he'd forgotten his shovel, but he knew the writer would figure it out in a little while. And he might have forgotten it on purpose.

When he reached Scupper's Rock, Bill walked up the rocky ground, sat down, and pulled his boots on. His sand-coated socks made that a terrible job, but he got it done.

He took out the chart and compared it to what he saw before him. Myron came up and peered over his shoulder. The island looked like what was on the chart, but it also looked—

"Smaller," Myron said. "The island is a lot smaller than is shown on the chart."

"I can see that," Bill said patiently. He had noticed that lack and he was trying to figure out where the X was in relation to what was left of the island. "I got eyes."

"The sea currents are wearing it away," Aeliana said. She heaved herself up out of the water and sat on the shore. "A hundred years from now, this place probably won't exist. All of this will be lost."

Myron surveyed the island. "You ask me, nobody will be losing much." He looked at the shipwreck. "Do you know which ship that is?"

"No," the mermaid said. "Those things drift through the ocean. Unless you find a name on it, a ship's log, or identifiable cargo, chances are it will remain nameless. It will probably leave with the rising tide and never be seen here again."

Bill studied the chart, then the island, then cocked his head to the side and squinted. "Does that look like a fish to you, Myron?"

Myron heaved a disgusted sigh and waved at the various tidepools where creatures were figuring out they were trapped and were getting panicky. "There are a lot of fish here. Which one are you talking about?"

"The one that's on the chart." Bill tapped a finger on the chart where the smidge of what looked like a fish was.

Myron peered at the chart closely. "Are you sure that's a fish?"

"Welp, what else can it be?"

"I don't know." Myron took the chart from Bill and turned it sideways. "A bat?" He turned it sideways again. "A moose head?" Grinning, he tapped the chart. "That's what it is! It's a moose head. See how the antlers flare out?"

"That's a fishtail," Bill said.

"Are you sure? Because it looks like a moose head to me."

"Does it really matter if it's a fish or a moose head?" Aeliana asked. "It's a reference point. If you see it—"

"I see it," Bill stated.

The fish, or moose head, stood revealed in the vanishing sunlight on the slope of a small rut that looked like it might have been a scar left from a ship running aground. A few inches closer, and the offending ship would have erased the mark.

He folded the chart and stuck it back into his possibles bag. He picked up the shovel he'd brought and walked over to the fish or moose head. A quick examination of the mark by dragging a forefinger along the lines to clean out the design proved that it hadn't been rendered by some happy chance. Or by a ship's keel.

Someone had chiseled the mark into the bare stone.

"We were wrong." Myron came to a stop beside Bill and looked down. "That's a frog."

Bill didn't care. He surveyed the ground and the chart, and looked at them again and again. Then, taking his point from the setting sun, he walked south and fetched up just short of running out of island.

Aeliana swam over to that side of the island. Herman remained on the lee side of Scupper's Rock and Widow-Marker watched with sharp interest.

Bill drove the shovel blade into the hill of sea silt that had settled there. An orange starfish lay on top of the spot like it was supposed to be there. With a quick movement of the shovel, Bill picked up the starfish and flipped it into the sea.

"Welp," he said, and tried not to show his excitement, "here goes nothin'."

Four holes later, all of them dug down far enough that Bill had to crawl out because he wasn't going to easily quit on the notion that he was in the right place, the shovel blade finally bit into something that wasn't dirt and rock and shell.

The shovel thumped against wood.

"Did you hear that?" Bill asked. With the treasure probably right underfoot, he didn't mind a little excitement trickling out now.

"I did!" Myron said.

"Go on, Bill," Aeliana encouraged. "Let's see what you found!"

Bill peered at the bottom of the hole, but it was too dark to see. All the pains and aches left over from the fight with the kraken left his body. Rejuvenated, he took a fresh grip on the shovel handle.

"I SEE IT." BILL STATED.

"Myron, let me have my possibles bag."

The writer passed over the bag, which Bill had taken off because, despite the coming night's chill, he'd worked up a good sweat. The Texan dug around in the bag and pulled out the oil lantern he bought in Big Blow Cay. He raised the hurricane glass, struck a match with his thumbnail, and lit the wick. Once the flame was strong, he closed the hurricane glass and handed the lantern back.

The lantern light played over the nearby ground and revealed just how dark it had gotten. Water sloshed up against Scupper's Rock and created an eerie howling.

Down at the bottom of Bill's latest hole, though, there was a wooden chest. It was two foot to a side, and he guessed that it was likely just as deep. He dug a while longer until he was able to free it. When he felt the heft of it, he grinned.

"Folks, this thing is heavy!"

Groaning with effort, Bill heaved the chest out of the hole, and it thumped when it hit the rocky ground and sand. He scrambled up onto level ground right behind it.

"Right there," Myron said and pointed. "Do you see it? That's Anne Bonny's name! This is her treasure. Bill! We found her treasure!"

A rusty padlock and rusty hinges held the chest closed.

"Shine that light over here," Bill said. "Get it on that lock for me."

Myron directed the lantern as he'd been told.

Bill reared the shovel back in both hands and took deliberate aim with the sharp blade.

"Pecos Bill!" a man yelled loudly.

The accent was familiar and Bill was fairly certain he knew who was calling him. He noted his possibles bag laying only a few feet away, but he didn't know how his pistols could help him now. He turned.

The Flying Dutchman sat at anchor thirty yards out from Scupper's Rock. The ghost ship bobbed gently on the black waves under a full moon. Her sails were reefed and the ghost crew watched from the deck with anticipation.

Captain Fockesz stood on the stern deck with his hands on his hips.

"I see you found my treasure," the captain said.

"It ain't your treasure!" Bill roared. "It's mine! It was give to me an' I dug it up!"

"Well," Fockesz said, "now it's going to be mine."

"No, it ain't."

Fockesz patted his lips as though he was yawning. "Please. All that blustering and posturing isn't going to get you anything. At the end of it, you'll just be more tired than you are now, and I'll still have my treasure."

"It ain't your blamed treasure." Bill threw the shovel away and stepped over to his possibles bag. He hauled out his pistols and strapped them on.

"Bill," Myron said in a quiet voice. "What are you doing?"

"I ain't crawfishin'," Bill snarled. "I did that last time. Ain't gonna happen again."

"Might I point out that those ghosts still have cannons?"

Bill looked at the writer and the mermaid. "Likely this is gonna get a mite messy an' you'll want to take cover."

Myron opened his mouth, struggled for words, and finally asked, "*Where*?"

"On the other side of the island," Bill said.

"That's another waste of time," Fockesz shouted from *The Flying Dutchman*. "Do come on and acknowledge your defeat before I have to turn to more severe measures. I am trying to be a gentleman about this."

"Welp, I don't see it. You told me you had to turn this here chart over to the Devil. I find out you give it to the Sea Hag an' I went to some trouble to get it back. Me an' her, we got us an understandin'. I'm sure she didn't send you here lookin' for this treasure, not after the way I left things."

Fockesz smiled. "No, I came here on my own after my Phoenician skull told me you were still pursuing the chart. I knew you were going to be trouble. I did not need the skull to tell me that. I am surprised you survived the kraken. That's a particularly nasty beast. I'm impressed."

"Why would you do come after this here treasure if you don't have to?" Bill asked.

"Because I *like* treasure," Fockesz said. "What ship's captain doesn't?"

"You gonna work that hard for the Devil?"

"Oh, make no mistake. I work *very* hard for the Devil. I have for hundreds of years, and I shall for hundreds more. He won't let me out of our agreement anytime soon. However, I found a loophole in the contract that I have with him."

"What loophole?"

"You see, I already turned that chart over to Cressida, so my part in the matter is effectively over. *She* lost the treasure, not me. Which means she has to recover it."

"She won't," Bill said.

"That's good. It means she won't be coming after me either. That treasure chest, and whatever is in it, is now in play again. It's up for grabs." Fockesz smiled. "So I'm grabbing it."

Bill stood on Scupper's Rock and knew he'd been had. He couldn't fight on account of Aeliana and Myron and Herman and Widow-Maker getting hurt. Fockesz had him caught out with nowhere to turn.

"Maybe this will hurry things along," Fockesz said. He turned and waved.

Several of the pirate crew holding lanterns held them up to display the struggling knot of men that stumbled up onto the stern deck. In the middle of a handful of ghost pirates, a wild mane of red hair clashed with the darkness.

When he saw that hair, so pretty and so familiar, Bill's heart dropped right down into his boots and lay there in the mess of squishy sand that stuck to his socks.

"Sue!" the mermaid yelled.

And when the pirates stepped back so their captive could be seen, that was who stood there: Slue-Foot Sue, Bill's wife and the prettiest woman he'd ever seen.

"Aeliana!" Sue yelled.

"It's me!" Aeliana shouted.

Sue swept the island with her gaze and it landed smack-dab on Bill. Her eyes widened in surprise.

"Bill?" she called.

"It's me, honey!" Bill said.

"Who are these men?"

"They're ghost pirates." That wasn't going to go over well and Bill knew it.

"Ghost pirates?"

"Yes, darlin'. They've come for the treasure." Standing there frozen and helpless, Bill didn't know what to do. He was a man of action, used to doing things without overly thinking about them. It was the first time he'd ever gotten into a fracas when Sue was involved and her life hung in the balance.

There were too many things that could go wrong.

From the time he'd been raised by the coyotes, all he'd wanted was a family and a home. Sue had given him all those things.

And now she was about to be taken away from him. Just the mere notion of that near broke his heart.

"What treasure?" Sue demanded.

"The one Captain de Alfaro give me for gettin' his body home to Spain for a-buryin'. I promised him I would." Bill didn't want Sue to think he was just being greedy, though he didn't really see anything wrong with that. "I was plannin' on fetchin' it for the young'uns. I'm awful sorry, Sue. Didn't figure on gettin' you snared up in this."

"Wait," Sue said. "That's *our* young'uns' treasure chest?"

"It was gonna be."

"These here pirates are planning on taking what belongs to our young'uns, Bill?"

"Yes."

"And you're just going to let them?"

"Ain't got no choice. They got me over a barrel what with them havin' you."

"Bill!" Sue screamed in outrage. "That doesn't sound like the man I married, the man I want raising our young'uns."

Sue's words hurt and shamed Bill. He hated not measuring up to his idea of himself, but he hated even more not measuring up to the man he'd promised Sue he would be.

"Don't you worry your pretty little head," Bill said. "I'm gonna get you outta—"

Sue twisted and grabbed the nearest pirate's belaying pin. He tried to pull it from her, but she yanked the weapon in a cunning way and threw the pirate over the ship's railing. The pirate yelled until he hit the sea and disappeared beneath the waves.

"Sue!" Bill ran toward the shore.

Another pirate stepped up and raised a cutlass in his hand.

In mid-stride, Bill fired a shot that hammered the cutlass out of the pirate's clutches. He'd known his bullets wouldn't work against the ghosts, but he hadn't been sure that the pirates' weapons would be different. Sue had been able to grab the belaying pin and toss the ghost bothering her. Bill didn't know how ha'ints and ghosts and the undead worked, but he held onto that thought about their weapons being vulnerable.

"Avast there, you fools!" Fockesz yelled. "Get those guns trained on that man!"

Several pirates ran for their gun stations. Sue continued fighting against her captors and drove one of her big feet into the nearest man's cudgel and slammed it into his stomach. The ghost screamed in pain and lurched back.

"Bill!" Sue yelled. "You best cowboy up!"

"Yes, ma'am," Bill said.

He holstered his pistols and looked over his shoulder at Widow-Maker standing on Herman floating out beside the island. Bill put his fingers in his mouth and whistled.

Widow-Maker galloped off the orca's broad back and plunged toward the ocean.

Well, there's been lots of stories about how fast Pecos Bill's horse could be. Chasing down tornados, running across the old West nonstop, lots of impossible things if a body was to think about it.

But folks got to remember that Widow-Maker was a one-of-kind horse, and he had a love for Bill like no other horse ever loved his rider. And that there? That's a special kind of magic.

When Widow-Maker's hooves landed on the water, they didn't sink like anybody would have thought. Instead, the mustang landed *on* the water—and he kept on galloping.

Bill was already running flat-out toward *The Flying Dutchman*, and fast as he was, faster than any man had ever been, Widow-Maker overtook him before he got his boots wet.

Widow-Maker whinnied as he drew even with Bill. The Texan reached out, plucked his Stetson from the saddle pommel with his right hand, caught the saddle pommel with his left hand just as slick as snot on a goat's glass eye, and hauled himself aboard that galloping mustang.

Bill took up the reins as Widow-Maker bolted across the water and shot toward *The Flying Dutchman*. The Texan clapped his hat on, tightened the stampede strap, and filled his callused hands with his shooting irons. The whole time Widow-Maker thundered across the waves, Bill kept his eye on Sue.

Sue continued using her feet and her hands and fought those ghost pirates with the fury of a bobcat caught in a forest fire. Still, she was outnumbered and likely not to last much longer.

"Kill that woman!" Fockesz ordered. He pointed his sword at Bill. "And blast that man and his horse off the face of the earth! Fire at will!"

The gun crews hurried to obey their captain and readied the cannons. They fired in staggered blasts, not a concentrated broadside. Flaming cannonballs hummed loudly through the air and rushed at Bill and Widow-Maker.

Senses operating faster than a speeding bullet, and a lot faster than a cast-iron cannonball, Bill studied those cannonballs and saw a daring opening. Even though Widow-Maker ran across the top of the Gulf of Mexico, there was no way the mustang could run up the side of *The Flying Dutchman*.

But just maybe...

"Up, boy!" Bill yelled. "That cannonball yonder! That's where we want to go!"

Even Bill's talking was faster when he was in action!

Understanding exactly what his rider wanted because they'd traveled down so many trails together, Widow-Maker jumped up onto the speeding cannonball, then leap-frogged from one to another, lighting like a flitting flea only to jump toward another cannonball that was closer to the ship in the next instant.

Lickety-split, cannonball by cannonball, Widow-Maker rode right up to *The Flying Dutchman*. Unfortunately, the mustang's path took him right into the sights of a cannon near the stern.

"Bill!" Sue squalled.

A pirate had his fingers knotted up in her pretty red hair, but she'd gotten hold of a baton and was beating every ghost around her within the inch of his—well, life didn't exactly work, but they were hurting.

Widow-Maker whinnied and drew Bill's attention to the cannon aimed at them. The fuse hole was already burning and the flaming cannonball shot out of the wide mouth of the big gun in an explosion of smoke and fire.

The Flying Dutchman carried an assortment of cannons, from eighteen-pounders to twenty-four pounders. This particular cannon was a twenty-four pounder filled with gunpowder and it made a sizeable target for a marksman, and Pecos Bill was the straightest-shooting cowboy to ever come out of the great state of Texas.

Bill fired left-handed, on the fly, so to speak what will all the jumping around. Widow-Maker had made his final leap toward the ship's stern and was fully exposed to *The Flying Dutchman's* cannons. Bill's .44 round smacked into that cannonball when it was not even a foot from the muzzle and the resulting explosion knocked the cannon back into the gun crew and spilled them like tenpins.

A moment later, Widow-Maker landed on the ship's stern deck. The mustang dug his iron-shod hooves into the planks, ripped up ghostly splinters, and spun around.

Bill emptied the remaining ten shots in his pistols and his bullets slapped away cutlasses, flintlock pistols, belaying pins, a pegleg, and an iron hook sported by one crusty-looking ghost.

Since he didn't have time to reload his pistols, Bill reversed them, gripped them by their heated barrels, swung his leg over his saddle pommel, and dropped to the deck. He'd barely gotten settled on his boots before he swung those Colts like clubs, striking swords, pistols, and knives, and strode toward where Sue was fighting. She kicked another pirate, caught his cutlass against his chest, and sent him over the ship's railing.

Pirate ghosts went down before Bill like hay before a scythe. Many of them had knots on their heads bigger than turkey eggs. They commenced to yowling and crying like mange-eaten weasels, and it was an awful clamor.

"Avast there! Avast!"

Bill spun toward Captain Fockesz's commands. The Dutchman stepped through his remaining pirates as they gave way before him.

"This one here is mine, lads, so give us some room." Fockesz gripped his sword and looked fierce.

The pirates backed away and ringed the stern deck. Storm clouds gathered overhead and the night sky drew even darker. Lighting flickered, and rain spilled down.

"You picked a fine night for dying, cowboy," Fockesz promised. "I'll make it quick."

Bill held his pistols in his knotted hands. "Talk's cheap, an' you done messed up when you took Sue an' brought her into the middle of this."

Widow-Maker sidled over to Sue and kicked the last two pirates holding onto her over the side. Sue walked over to the horse and pulled the Henry rifle out of the saddle scabbard. She levered the action and stood ready.

"Bill." Aeliana held onto the ship's railing near the anchor hawser and peered at the conflict nervously. "The captain's a ghost. You can't touch him."

"Welp," Bill said, "I guess we're about to find out."

"Wait!" Dripping wet, Myron clambered aboard *The Flying Dutchman* and reached inside his coat.

Several pirates standing near the writer pulled out their weapons.

Sue took aim at them with the rifle. "You fellers hold it right there."

Myron took his hand out from his coat and revealed what he held. "It's just a journal and a pencil. I'm not a fighter. I'm just going to take notes."

Sue motioned the pirates back with the rifle and they stepped back from the writer.

Aeliana pulled herself over the railing and settled in with her fishing spear in her hands. She struck at the closest deckhand and pierced his foot with the coral tip of the spear. The ghost pirates around her gave her a wide berth.

Bill stared at his friends gathered there and his heart swelled bigger than it had ever been.

"You go on and do what you need to do, Bill," Sue said. "That conniving spook needs his tail kicked up between his shoulders."

Bill faced Fockesz and smiled.

"At least you'll die well," Fockesz said. Unimpressed by Sue's words, he smiled and bowed with his arms spread. "I await your leisure."

Well, you've heard about fights Pecos Bill has had, about the tussle he had with the kraken and the Bear Lake Monster up on the Idaho-Utah border, about how he put an end to Wildcat Tompkins's rustling, beat back an ancient Aztec death cult that came up from Mexico to take a sacred white bull Bill had raised from a calf—

—and this was fiercer than any of them!

Bill and Captain Fockesz went at each other hammer and tong. The Dutchman's sword countered every blow Bill swung with his pistols, and Bill turned away every fast and clever strike and slash with his pistols. Sparks danced from their weapons meeting, and the rasp of Toledo steel against Pittsburgh forged steel given new form and function in the Colt Armory screamed through the air.

All Bill's friends and all the pirates watched, astounded by the display of skill and cunning.

The fight wasn't balanced, though. Bill swung his pistols and hit the captain's sword, and he blocked the sword when it came for him. However, Fockesz drew a dagger and employed that as well. The Dutchman only had to hack and slash at Bill, and he lightly wounded the Texan a dozen times, but every attack Bill launched that was aimed at the ghost only passed through him. Fockesz himself wasn't solid enough to hit.

Bill blocked a sword thrust that would have skewered him. As the keen edge screamed along, caught between the pistol's trigger guard and butt, Bill lashed out with his other pistol and attempted to strike the ghost between his eyes. Fockesz reacted slowly and couldn't counter the second blow.

Instead of striking home, though, the gun butt passed through the ghost's insubstantial form. Thrown off balance by the power of his effort, Bill stumbled forward through the ghost.

The Dutchman laughed, and his pirates laughed with him.

"Give up, Pecos Bill," Fockesz said. "Beg for your life and perhaps I will let you live."

Hotheaded and out of control, Bill came up swinging. Fockesz flicked his sword out in a wily move and swept the Texan's pistol from his right hand. Just as quickly, Fockesz swung again, duplicated the maneuver, and stripped Bill's other pistol.

Ungunned, Bill stepped back.

Fockesz lunged for the Texan with his dagger. The Henry cracked sharply and the dagger leaped out of the Dutchman's hand.

Sue levered the rifle and put a bullet through Fockesz's eyes.

The bullet passed on through, of course, because the Dutchman was a ghost.

Fockesz laughed, and his pirates laughed with him.

"Madame," the Dutchman said in a belittling tone, "you are a surprisingly good shot. I commend you. But, as you have just seen, bullets don't work against me."

"Sue," Bill said, "you need to stay out of this, darlin'. This is betwixt me an' him. *Mano a mano.*"

"Bill, he's no man and—" she said.

"I'm askin' you," Bill interrupted. "Please."

Now Pecos Bill wasn't in the habit of asking for much, and Sue was the only one he ever said please to.

Reluctantly, Sue lowered the Henry.

Fockesz smiled hugely and turned to face Bill once more. "Now where were we?" He made a point of contemplating, like a man checking a busy schedule. "Ah yes, we were at the point where you were going to surrender."

"That's not gonna happen," Bill said.

He reached into his boot and drew his Bowie knife. The weapon looked like a short sword, but it was shorter than the Dutchman's sword.

"You expect to fight me with that?" Fockesz shook his head and tsked. "You Texans. All swagger and no substance."

"Says the ghost who can't be touched," Sue exploded.

The Dutchman took a stance with his free arm behind him. "Very well, Mr. Bill, we'll have it your way. I mean to get that treasure."

"An' I mean to keep it for my young'uns." Bill lifted the Bowie and centered himself.

Before he met his first man and learned to fight them, Bill had learned the military skills of the coyote. He knew how to dance and whirl, to dodge and evade, to look like he was going one way when he was really going another.

At the time he took up the Bowie, he learned how to knife fight from a Creole knife fighter over in New Orleans, a man skilled in *Esgrima Criolla,* Creole fencing. Bill had taken to the way of the knife in the same manner he'd taken to riding and shooting and roping.

There was none finer.

"You mean to best me with that offensive pig sticker?" Fockesz accused.

"I do," Bill said. "This is a Bowie knife, made by James Black for Bowie himself, forged with a secret process that Black took to his grave. There's nothing that holds an edge better or cuts deeper."

Fockesz nodded. "Then do your best and I will see to it you die quickly."

The blades flashed in the moonlight and the driving rain. The weapons met again and again, screamed at the contact. Bill's arm grew tired. Even with all his prowess, he was only a man, flesh and blood, and not a ghost whose own energies looked to be inexhaustible.

Finally, though, the Dutchman made a slight miscalculation on a strike. Bill slipped beneath his opponent's blade and lashed out instinctively. The Bowie sought out Fockesz's throat, but the wily captain pulled his head back despite his ghostly nature.

The Bowie struck only the Dutchman's beard—

—and a fistful of curly hair dropped away.

Stunned, Fockesz watched his beard scatter as the storm winds caught it. The mass of hair disappeared before it hit the ship's deck.

"What have you done?" Fockesz cried.

Looking at the lopped-off beard that would never look good again on account of Fockesz being a ghost and ghost not growing hair nor anything else, Bill crowed, "Told you there weren't nothin' a Bowie knife couldn't cut through, you sidewindin' polecat!"

Reinvigorated by his surprising victory, Bill pressed his attack and drove Fockesz back and back. He slashed through the pirate captain's fine suit and cut slashes in his ghostly form.

The pirates that were behind the Dutchman scattered for the high and uncut.

Well, they would have scattered for the high and uncut, except pirate ships weren't made that way, but if there'd been a nearby woods, they would have run straightaway for it.

They squalled and bawled and cowered while their captain fought for whatever remained of his unlife.

Finally, Fockesz had his back to the wall and Bill pinned him there with the point of the Bowie resting nearly on the Dutchman's nose.

"I never killed no ghost before," Bill admitted, "an' I find myself right anxious to. Only I don't know exactly what will come of it." He narrowed his eyes at his opponent. "Do you?"

"No," Fockesz answered weakly. "I don't, but I'm afraid of what it might be."

"With what-all you been doin', I'd be mighty afeared too if I was you."

Bill held the knife, and he held himself. He just managed to keep himself to keep from plunging the Bowie through the ghost's head, but not doing and giving him a well-deserved sense of satisfaction proved powerful hard to do.

"I'm gonna need you to surrender," Bill said quietly. "It'll be the only chance you get, so think hard about that for a minute."

Fockesz nodded.

"I'm also gonna need your promise as a gentleman, here in front of your crew, that you'll leave that treasure be. There's plenty other treasure waitin' out there in the sea, but this one belongs to my young'uns, so you'll have to find of your own."

Fockesz nodded again.

"I'm also gonna need you to apologize to my wife for abscondin' with her the way you did."

"I surrender," the Dutchman said.

Bill leaned in with the Bowie a little more and made Fockesz lean back a little farther over the ship's railing. The dark sea was clearly outlined behind the pirate and reflections of the lightning overhead danced across the white-combed waves.

Grudgingly, still covered in specks of blood running from cuts that continued to bleed a little, though the rain was already washing them away, Bill stepped back and dropped the Bowie to his side.

With as much pride as he had left to him, Fockesz sheathed his sword and turned his attention to Sue, who still stood holding the Henry at the ready.

"Madame," the captain of *The Flying Dutchman* said, "please accept my most humble apologies for your kidnapping and subsequent rough handling. I have no legitimate excuse. I can only plead my case as a cursed ghost made crazed by an inexcusable lust for riches."

"Hmmppphhh," Sue said. "I'm not going to think good thoughts about you, Captain Fockesz. Not for a very long time."

"I understand," Fockesz said.

"But seeing as how this was the first time you kidnapped me, I'm willing to let it slide."

"Thank you, madame. You are most gracious."

Despite his aches and pains, Bill smiled at his pretty wife's generosity.

Sue always was one to feel charitable to pitiful cases, and the captain of *The Flying Dutchman* looked plenty pitiful apologizing in front of his crew.

†††

Only a short time later, Bill sat on Herman and enjoyed the view as the orca swam back to Texas. He leaned back on the treasure chest he'd dug up. It turned out to be full of gold doubloons, gems, and jewelry just like he'd thought it would.

Myron sat back near the dorsal fin and scribbled in his journal by the light of an oil lantern. Herman wasn't so panicky about it being back there once he found out nobody had set him on fire by accident.

Widow-Maker munched hay out of the bushel basket that still had a little left.

Sue sat on one of Herman's front flippers and gabbed with Aeliana, no doubt catching up with all that had happened since they'd last seen each other.

Bill ate a piece of chicken from the basket of provisions they'd bought, then fell into a slumber. He woke up when Sue came back to join him.

She was slightly damp from the ocean spray that had fallen on her while she'd been talking to the mermaid, but Bill didn't mind. He snuggled her up close and she giggled.

"I sure am proud I married you, Pecos Bill," she said.

"An' I'm right thankful you did," Bill replied, but he knew from experience her statement was leading up to a honey-do list and he was a mite wary.

"You surely found a lot of treasure for us to give to our young'uns."

"Uh-huh."

"It got me to thinking."

Bill knew he was in for it then. "What were you thinkin', honey? You might want to slow down. Sure don't want you to hurt yourself with a lot of big thoughts after the evenin' you've had. And in your condition."

He was wide awake now and the stars above were far and away.

"Our young'uns are going to need cribs to sleep in," Sue said.

"Uh-huh."

"I was thinking I wanted the cribs made out of something special."

"All right."

Sue pushed herself up and looked down at him. "I was wondering if you'd mind riding over to California and fetching back one of those tall redwoods I've heard about. Seems like they would make good wood for cribs."

Sue had never seen the redwood trees that grew in Northern California and towered over three hundred feet tall. One would be more than enough to make cribs, even for four children, but it would be a mighty big adventure bring one back to Texas.

However, it would be an easy ride, no more than stretching his legs a little. He looked forward to it.

"I'll be glad to do that for you, darlin'," Bill said.

"Thank you for being the most wonderful husband ever, Bill."

And there, in the middle of the Gulf of Mexico, with the stars as their witness, and Widow-Maker loudly chewing hay, Slue-Foot Sue kissed Pecos Bill with the red-hot intensity legends were made of.

THE END

Thank the Movies

I saw the first movie theater movie I remember seeing in the summer of 1967. I was nine and a half. I was a backwards kid in a lot of ways, shy, country, and didn't get out much. There were usually places for us to go as kids. Most kids find those places even when parents don't think they exist. I remember one summer when I was eight and I found a culvert big enough to walk through. I got to the other side of the street, something I was NEVER supposed to cross.

I crossed UNDER the street through the culvert, saw my house while standing on the other side of the street, and never told. So I never got in trouble for that. Secrets are necessary things when you're a kid and you're living in a world that's too small.

Anyway, that summer my mom took my brothers and me to the McSwain Theater in Ada, Oklahoma. We were living in Oklahoma City at the time, so getting a trip back to see Grandma was a treat. Aunt Bobbie brought her two kids, and we all got tickets to see *Charlie, the Lonesome Cougar*, a new Disney film.

I don't remember much about Charlie. He was a teenage cougar who got accidently released back into the wild after being raised with humans. At the time, I thought it would be cool to have a pet cougar. Actually, I think I still do think that way.

Charlie got into trouble for going into places he wasn't supposed to go. I could empathize with that. But I have trouble thinking back on what happened during that movie.

However, I remember seeing the Pecos Bill cartoon that opened for the movie quite vividly. Roy Rogers told Bill's story to two kids about my age. I could still picture images of that cartoon even before I found it again on the internet.

The story was exciting and Bill was amazing. I'd discovered comic books by then. Superboy and the Legion of Super-Heroes was one of my favorites because all the Legion members had different heroes.

Even though he didn't have a cape or a costume, Bill seemed every bit as powerful and as adventurous as Superboy and his pals of the 30th century. I watched him rope an old Blue Norther, create the Grand Canyon, and shoot the stars from the sky for Slue-Foot Sue, his best gal.

Slue-Foot Sue was no slouch in the hero department either. She rode a giant catfish across that big movie screen and I wished I had a catfish big enough to ride too.

I came across stories about Pecos Bill as I grew older, but all of them paled in comparison to that Disney concoction. That was the standard I set my Pecos Bill stories by.

Maybe it was just the fact that I grew older. I reckoned that someone from another planet could have superpowers like Superboy and the Legion of Super-Heroes, but I'd learned that the Grand Canyon was made by natural forces, not a wild cowboy. It was a bitter fact that helped push me toward adulthood.

However, that love of tall tales persisted. During my formative years, I devoured Greek mythology. I found the first book on that in Miss Knight's Third Grade class library and almost memorized those stories. Later I found stories about Paul Bunyan, John Henry, and Davy Crockett (he was real, but not all the stories were).

Earlier this year, Air Chief Ron Fortier sent me an email after he'd accepted my latest Bass Reeves story, which features the legendary lawman at a circus arresting a bearded lady and chasing dinosaur bones in Oklahoma. The tale isn't your run-of-the-mill Western adventure and I had fun with it.

Chief Fortier asked me to consider doing a Pecos Bill story for an upcoming volume of *Pulp Mythology*. I thought about it for about five minutes and realized I did want to do it.

However, I wanted to do it as a true "tall tale," something that might have been made into a Disney cartoon. I wanted it to be outlandish and over-the-top and filled with action. I wanted it to be something my nine-year-old self would have enjoyed, yet be sensible enough to pull in any reader who can be young at heart and still believe in tall tale heroes for just a little while.

This was the only way a story about such a legendary figure as Pecos Bill could be done.

I didn't know if I could pull off a story like that, though. I'd never written anything so humorous and so far-fetched, so I guess I was challenging myself with the writing of it as well.

I told Chief Fortier what I wanted to do, and he instantly accepted my notion of a mermaid, a sea hag, a sea monster, buried treasure, and undead pirates sailing the Flying Dutchman up into West Texas where a Spanish ship was sunk in red dirt all bunched up into one rollicking tale.

Since everything was done by email, I didn't know if Chief Fortier was gobsmacked in there for a bit after reading my email reply. Whether he batted an eye. Whether he went back and read the one-sentence description I sent him to make sure he'd read what he read.

It all seems a bit much…but those are all ingredients for what I thought might be a fantastic Pecos Bill story. I don't know where they came from. They were just there when Chief Fortier asked me what tale I could tell.

That story unfolded in my mind as slick as you please. (Well, maybe not so slick. The thing just grew and grew, got taller and taller, you might say.) Not all of my stories are so generous as to come so easily. Creating/ writing is HARD work. When you're a writer and you have a story that literally writes itself, flows through your fingers out of some mystical well of imagination, you go for it and thank your lucky stars.

I had to stop and wonder a few times, though. Will the reader buy this bit? Will the reader suspend disbelief here? Is this too much? Have I jumped the shark? (For those of you who haven't read the story yet, yes, there is a shark too.)

I didn't hold back. I couldn't. This was Pecos Bill! The roughest, toughest cowboy anybody ever saw.

I only hope I did him justice. This is a story that would have kept nine-year-old me in the seat at that movie theater. I hope it keeps you in yours too.

MEL ODOM - grew up in southeastern Oklahoma, where diehard country boys still eat possums and soft-shelled turtles, but now lives in Moore, Oklahoma, a wonderful town that unfortunately attracts Pecos Bill riding a twister on a regular basis. He's lived through hog raising and F-5 tornados, surely two of the most dangerous things in the world.

Over the last twenty-plus years, he's written dozens of novels in many different genres, including some based on television shows like *Buffy the Vampire Slayer* and novelizations of *Blade, Tomb Raider,* and xXx. He's trekked through deadly forests and braved the Sword Coast in the Forgotten Realms, and written adventures of bioroid detectives in Fantasy Flight's Android game.

He teaches in the Professional Writing program at the University of Oklahoma and writes all the time. He can be reached at mel@melodom.net, www.melodom.blogspot.com, @melodom on Twitter, and on Facebook. His current military science fiction trilogy, *The Makaum War,* has been hitting bestseller lists.